thinking 'bout you

CHAPTER ONE

KENZIE

THE LARGE, brightly colored poster hangs on the glass entryway of the library like it's mocking me. Waving at me every time the door opens, or simply smirking at me knowingly when I look up from my desk. Either way, that stupid piece of cardstock knows what it's doing—I am convinced of it.

The fact that the top lefthand corner won't stay in place isn't helping.

I firmly press my thumb against the cardstock, willing it to adhere to the extra sticky tape I just replaced. For the third time this week. Yeah, definitely mocking me.

"So nice that Dustin Wild is coming back for the festival, isn't it?" says Mrs. Chamberlain, longtime math teacher and Hickory Hills native, pulling my attention back to the front desk where she is pushing a stack of books across the counter. "You must be excited to see him. A chance to reconnect."

Glancing at my watch, I wonder what she's doing here in the middle of a school day, but don't dare ask. Instead, I head toward the desk, rounding the corner quickly so I can get her out of here. Taking the stack of books, I scan them one by one, happy for an excuse not to make eye contact.

"You can't tell me you're not excited," she presses.

I don't need to look up to know there is a mischievous look on the older lady's face. I can hear it in her voice. She, along with most of our small Georgia town, is all abuzz about the return of Dustin Wild—or as we all knew him back then, Dustin Wilder—local boy turned country star, for our annual Rhythm and Brews Festival. Of course, her former student being a country star is not the reason that Mrs. Chamberlain is all atwitter in this moment. She's fishing for something—anything—to fuel the gossip mill. And I am not about to give it to her.

"If I even see him," I reply, forcing a smile. "I'll be so busy with everything that I doubt we'll have time for more than a quick hello."

There is a fine line between engaging the enemy and flat-out ignoring, and it's taken years of practice to find the proper balance. To know just how much information to give that will satisfy those curious, while not leaving room for speculation or giving up details you don't want to be made public. It's an art, really. One that only a lifetime in a small town teaches you. In my head, I picture Hickory Hills as the southern version of Stars Hollow. Small town, big charm, and unique personalities. Making Mrs. Chamberlain our equivalent of Miss Patty.

"Oh, I'm sure you will. You know, I always thought you two were going to go the distance. I've seen a lot of couples form over the years, and young love can be so fickle, but I usually have a good feel for who will and won't make it. You and Dustin, I would have put money on that."

And there it is.

Thanks, Mrs. Chamberlain...

I force my smile as big as I can, my cheeks starting to hurt from the pressure. "You're all set, Mrs. C. Just have these back no later than three weeks from Tuesday."

Opening her mouth to comment more, Mrs. Chamberlain snaps it shut just as quickly, realizing she isn't going to get anything else out of me. Continuing with my saccharine expression, I can see the thoughts pinging around her mind —it's fine that I'm being tight-lipped, because she's just going to send in reinforcements later. Too bad for her. I'm not going to be talking to them either.

I have nothing to say.

I have already said too much on the subject of Dustin. And *to* Dustin, nonetheless.

An incident that doesn't need repeating.

Because I, Kenzie Noble, am over Dustin Wilder.

Letting out a long sigh, I try to distract myself, returning to what I was doing before I stopped to deal with that mockingly obnoxious poster—sorting through the books that had been left in the return bin overnight. The summer reading program is in its last days, and if I'm doing my math right, we have a handful of kids who are closing in on their final goal. Success.

An outburst of giggles rings through the library, cutting through the silence. Without bothering to lift my gaze, I already know where it's coming from—I'd watched out of the corner of my eye as the group of tweens had walked in, casually heading for the thriller section, which was conveniently right next to romance. As if any tween girl was going to choose James Patterson over Nora Roberts.

Actually, that isn't fair. I know plenty of young women whose literary interests are firmly rooted in things other than romance, and their fervor for their genre of choice is always so much fun to witness. I also remember being that age, sneaking into the romance section with my two best friends, Willa Hayes and Sylvie Forde, searching out the books for the "good bits," giggling the whole time. Much like the giggles I'm hearing now. Of course, back then, old Mrs. Cassum, the former librarian, wasn't quite as understanding about interest in such subjects as I like to think I am.

No, I *know* I am.

The squeak of the door opening steals my attention, a reminder that I need to apply some WD-40 to the hinge. Add that to the never-ending to-do list. Looking up from the pile of books, I see Willa standing in the entrance, holding the door wide open, letting all the air conditioning escape as she stares at the poster.

"You're letting all the air out," I call out to her a few seconds later, apparently channeling my inner Mrs. Cassum. A sweep of warm August air whooshes toward me, notching up my annoyance.

"I still don't like what they did with the colors," Willa responds, turning to look at me, her nose crinkled in disgust. She pushes at the corner I just fixed, which is already starting to come loose again.

Maybe it's just time to take that damn thing down...

Stepping inside, Willa lets the door gently shut behind her, as she glides across the lobby. A former Miss Georgia, just like her mother, almost everything Willa does is graceful —even when she is cussing you out from both sides of her mouth, which, thanks to six older brothers, she's quite proficient at. Everyone in Hickory Hills knows what a spitfire Willa is—at least until she turns on the pageant queen, and then she becomes the epitome of southern charm.

"Take it up with Mrs. Burch. They're supposed to be veggies."

"Veggies? This is a barbecue festival. No one cares about veggies. She has been on this planet and lived in this town for six hundred years; she should know that."

I shrug, not sure how to counter that. Willa makes a

damn good point. Flicking my eyes back over to the poster and that damned corner, I read the words glaring back at me, even though at this point I can recite them.

Hickory Hills Annual Rhythm and Brews Festival Presented by Southern Brothers Brewing and Hayes Industries With special guest Dustin Wild All proceeds benefit "A Noble Cause" to help fund Ken Noble's medical bills

"Ready for all this?" Willa asks.

"No," I answer tersely, picking up a stack of books and placing them on the return cart. "And not for the reason you think. But because I have five thousand and one things to do before thousands of people descend upon our itty-bitty town in search of barbecue and beer."

"And Dustin Wild."

And fucking Dustin Wild...

"Hey!" Sylvie shouts, walking into the library, hand flying over her mouth as she realizes how loud she is.

"Is this an intervention?" I ask, starting to worry about why they are both at the town library in the middle of the day. I can't remember the last time either of them stepped foot in here, unless expressly meeting me. Much less together.

"Is there a need for an intervention?" Willa asks.

Nope...because I'm not telling you my secret...

"We just wanted to see how you were," Sylvie offers.

The exact opposite to Willa's tall, leggy, and blonde, Sylvie is shorter, curvy, and has auburn hair that shimmers in the sunlight. The thick, black-framed glasses she sometimes wears are currently sliding down the bridge of her nose, making her look every ounce the science teacher she is. In some ways, these two women could not be any more different. But the three of us share a bond that can only come from a lifetime of friendship, and I wouldn't trade either of them for the world.

"Right…so we just took off in the middle of the day from teaching and whatever it is one does as the Director of Corporate Giving for a Fortune 500 company."

"We're on our lunch break," Willa answers, Sylvie nodding in agreement.

I don't believe either one of them and give them a look that lets them know that. For one, I know Sylvie has her hands full teaching physics, chemistry, and freshman physical science this year since they are shorthanded at the high school. Although, as the second teacher I've seen in here in the last twenty minutes, I'm starting to wonder what's going on at that school.

For two, it's Monday, which means Willa has "Munch," a weekly "meeting" where the head of every branch of Hayes Industries—otherwise known as her brothers, plus her and their father—have lunch together to talk about…again, whatever one talks about at that kind of thing. As the biggest employer in the area, tackling industries such as guns and ammo, agriculture, paper, personal safety, a brewery, and the local bait and tackle shop, there is no way the town librarian ends up on Hayes Industries' docket.

Nope. These two have an agenda.

"We just know you have a lot going on," Sylvie adds.

"No more than usual." I shrug, trying to brush it off, keeping my eye trained on the cart. Sure, this is going to be a heavy week, but it's nothing I can't handle.

"No more than usual," Willa scoffs. "Kenz, it's Rhythm and Brews week, which we all know means insanity. With everything you have to do to get ready for this thing, plus then actually execute it, on top of your regular job, that's a lot. Add in your dad having cancer and your sister being no help because she's a hundred and six weeks pregnant—"

"Thirty-six. Moira is only thirty-six weeks pregnant."

"Thirty-six, a hundred and six—whatever. She's no help to you either way."

I heave out a sigh, grateful they care but really wishing they would drop the issue. Releasing the wheel stoppers on the cart, I turn the corner around the front desk and head toward the fiction section. I can feel the two of them hot on my heels, not willing to let this go. Fine, then they can help me reshelve. They might be able to skip out on work, but I can't.

"I'm fine. Is it a lot of work? Yes. But it is every year. Also, I'm *on* the planning committee, I'm not the *whole* committee. And Dad is doing great." I stop, slipping a few books back into place before turning to face them. "Speaking of… Sylvie, I know I've asked before, but are you sure you don't mind that the money isn't going to the school? I still feel bad we hijacked your fundraiser."

"Yes! The town wants to rally around your dad. The robotics team will figure something out. Recycled parts? I don't know. Don't worry about it; it'll be a fun challenge."

I sigh, thankful again that my best friend doesn't care that her funding was pulled out from underneath her. It's not that I don't appreciate the gesture from the town—I do. And yes, we could use the money to pay for Dad's medical bills. But part of me still can't help feeling guilty.

"This is what small towns do," Willa reminds me. "Everyone has a Mr. Noble story. How many times a day does someone come in here and tell you a tale all about something your dad did for them or when he picked them up off the side of the road in his tow truck?"

I nod. She's right. Dad was born and raised here and has

always said Hickory Hills is in his blood. He's also just the kind of person who would do anything for anyone.

"Only about a dozen."

"Exactly."

"And then there's the other part," Sylvie says. "The tall, sandy-haired, megawatt smile, smooth as whiskey voice part."

"Why, thank you, I had forgotten for a brief second not only what he looks like, but what he sounds like."

I stomp off, annoyed at the reminder of my ex, pushing the cart as fast as I can through the stacks. Which isn't very fast. It's not an easy maneuver, but at least it's a distraction from him.

"Kenz."

Facing Dustin's return was inevitable, ever since Mrs. Burch announced at one of the festival planning meetings that she had reached out to him and his people, inviting him to come back for the event. That didn't mean I had to be happy about it.

"He and your dad were always so close, slaving away in that garage," she'd said, her fragile voice and deep southern accent making her sound as sweet as could be. "I figured he'd want to know about your dad's diagnosis and help out if he could. Sure enough, he's agreed."

The rest of the committee had been so excited, I didn't have the heart to speak up. I figured the questions would start soon enough—after all, the rumor mill hadn't stopped churning for years after he took off for Nashville, leaving me behind. When they didn't, well, I wasn't sure if I should be relieved or worried that it was all happening behind my back. Either way, I wasn't going to add any fuel to that fire.

"I know you still don't want to talk about it," Willa says. "But at some point, you have to. Preferably before he shows up."

I stop, whipping around to face them.

"What is there to talk about? My ex—who never actually ended things with me, but instead just left with the promise of returning and never did, and is now a freaking country star—is coming back to town to do a free show to raise money for my father. That's about all there is to it."

"When was the last time you spoke?"

A month ago. When I called him up, totally sober, completely out of the blue, just because I wanted to hear his voice. Because I missed him. *Miss* him.

"It's been a while," I lie. I can't tell them the truth. Not just because I didn't tell them then, but because no part of me wants to own up to what it might mean. That I'm not really over him. Which I am. Promise.

Except I might just be full of shit.

Silence hangs between us, the overhead lights bright enough to leave me feeling exposed, with even my best friends not knowing what else to say. They walked through all this with me as it happened and are here to support me now. I know they have my back no matter what this week throws at us. It's just too soon to tell what that might be.

"Okay, here's what we're gonna do," Willa declares, clapping her hands together. "Girls' night, tonight. Karaoke and dancing at The Giddy Up."

"No."

"Why? You have a hot date? You back with Jake and didn't tell us?"

"No, I am not back with Jake." Although "with" is a bit of an overstatement for the casualness that is my relationship with Jake Wright, manager of the local grocery.

"Then you're free to hang out with us. Blow off a little steam before R and B takes over our lives for the next few days."

Willa makes a damn good point. Again. One that I am having a harder and harder time arguing against.

"C'mon," Sylvie pleads. "It'll be fun. We can karaoke. We haven't done that since…" She trails off, a guilty look taking over. She suddenly remembers exactly the last time we did karaoke.

"The night we realized he wasn't coming back," I say, finishing off her sentence. "Five years ago. Which was two whole years after he left."

Sylvie nods slowly, eyes closed tightly. It's written all over her face that she can't believe she'd forgotten that part. Or that she'd brought it up now. I can't hold it against her. We've moved on. All of us.

"Right, well, I have to go. I'm late for Munch," Willa says, turning to make her exit. Stopping at the door, she sticks her tongue out at the poster, like she was six and it just tugged on her pigtails, before turning back and pointing at me. "I will pick you up at eight. You better have your boots on."

With a snap of her fingers she's gone, leaving Sylvie and me smiling at one another, waiting for the next round of giggles from the romance section.

Looks like I'm going dancing tonight.

CHAPTER TWO

DUSTIN

THE SONG on the radio starts to fade in and out, the signal waning, as I turn into the old town square. It's always been hit or miss whether or not you could get the station out of Macon to come in clearly, a single step in each direction making or breaking the connection. Sure enough, the corner of Broad Street and Depot Road is still a dead spot.

Some things never change.

Driving through downtown, I'm amazed at how much everything looks exactly the same. Hickory Hills has always taken the "small-town southern charm" thing to the next level, priding itself on looking like a feature straight out of *Southern Living*. While a few of the businesses have changed hands and changed names in the years I've been gone—although not many—the town makes sure they still look the same as always.

Something that right now I'm not sure if I should be comforted by or weirded out by.

Comforted. Definitely comforted. It's nice being back home. I haven't been back in…nope, we're not doing that math. Way too long, that's the answer. Something Mama has no problem reminding me of. Life has somehow gotten in the way.

But I'm here now, if only for a little while.

Foot on the gas, I force myself to drive by A Noble Mechanic, the town's local garage and auto body shop, despite Old Blue seeming to know exactly where she is, pulling toward the side of the road, itching to turn into the drive. The garage was our home away from home for so many years and the reason Old Blue is up and running. But I'll stop in there later, when I have time to spend with Ken. That is a reunion I can't rush. Especially now that I know about his diagnosis.

A pang hits me, wishing I'd known sooner. That someone would have told me. That *Kenzie* would have told me. Then again, I guess I can't really blame her for not. It's not like we talk all that much anymore.

Another pang hits me thinking about that—how much I miss her. Her smile, her laugh, the way her overly practical side flirts with the side of her that still loves fairy tales. At least I assume she still loves fairy tales. The sound of her voice had been a salve on a wound I didn't realize I had when she'd called a month ago. One that I need back in my life desperately. One I probably have no chance of getting.

A text chimes on my phone, the little notification flashing over the GPS app.

MAMA

Fresh batch of green tomatoes all sliced,
chicken brined and breaded, just waiting for
your arrival.

My stomach grumbles at the thought of Mama's fried green tomatoes and chicken. No doubt there is a pitcher of sweet tea to go with them too. A southern feast—one I cannot wait to inhale.

I consider texting her back, letting her know I'm five minutes out, but then I reconsider. I'll be there soon enough. Ready and willing to give her the biggest hug possible.

Instead, another text flashes, this one from Eric Valentine, my manager.

ERIC

Let's meet up before you leave. Dinner in 30?

I lean forward, tapping on the message, knowing that I can't ignore this. Or, well, I could, but since Eric was already miffed that I am taking off as long as I am for this trip home, I know I need to appease him at least one more time. I hit the little microphone for voice to text, thrilled when it actually gets all the words correct.

Already gone. All but home. Officially on vacation. Talk next week.

I hit send, turning my full focus back to the goal at hand. Getting home.

Sure enough, in the blink of an eye, I'm pulling into the drive, a sense of calm taking over. Home. The place might be small—about the size of a double-wide, although much sturdier built—but it was all we ever needed. The landscaping all around it looks damn good though, as does the fresh coat of paint and new shutters. My boys are doing a great job helping keep this place up, and there is no way I am paying them enough.

"Well, look what the cat drug in!" Mama exclaims before my truck door is even closed. "Welcome home, baby. It's so good to see you."

"Mama, you were just in Rolling Hills with me," I say, squeezing her just as tightly as she is me.

My townhouse in the little town an hour outside of Nashville is relatively unassuming for someone who has the "star status" I supposedly do, but that's exactly what I like about it. In my mind, I'm still Dustin Wilder, small-town boy who liked T-shirts, my old boots, and slow dancing to old-school country music. Dustin Wild, chart-topping, wild night chasing, country star heartthrob, is someone else entirely.

"This is different, and you know it."

Ushering me in, she leaves the front door open, the warm still-summer sunlight streaming in. Rich, delicious smells waft my way from the kitchen, calling my name as I notice the large plate of sliced tomatoes next to a pan. Damn, it's good to be home.

"Did you stop in at the garage on your way in?" she asks, getting right to work on the tomatoes. "There is sweet tea in the fridge if you want some."

Nailed it...

"I didn't. I figured I'd stop by tomorrow when I had time to talk."

"You had time to talk now. You didn't need to rush home to me."

"I know, but..." I trail off. There are so many ways to finish that sentence, I don't know where to start.

"Yeah, *but...*"

Her tone is understanding, with just enough of that mama-induced guilt laced in. If there is anyone out there who gets what I mean with that one little word, it's her. She was the one I called when I realized just how much I had messed up, without even knowing how it all happened. She was the one with the advice on what to do. Not that I listened.

I meant it when I said that life got in the way. Only, that "life" isn't one that I ever planned on. It's a dream come true —a one in a million chance. But it also snowballed so fast, that by the time I realized how much everything had changed, it was too late. One second I was just another small-town kid, planning his life with the girl he loved, and the next I was at the top of the country music charts, that girl I was singing about still back in our small town. Without me.

"Have you talked to him?"

"A few texts here and there," I say with a shrug. "I tried to offer to cover some of his medical expenses, but he wasn't having it. Said having a real headliner for Rhythm and Brews was more than enough." The statement isn't really fair to all the local bands who play the festival every year, many with their own followings. But I know what he means and am grateful for his faith in me. "It kills me that I can't do more though."

"That's the Ken Noble way. You know that. He's a fantastic giver, but not so great at the receiving."

Much like his daughter...

"I do. He just did so much for me growing up. He was always willing to take me to any of the father-son stuff around town. Sure, he only has Kenzie and Moira of his own, but he's got nephews. He could have taken any one of them. He gifted me Old Blue, helped me get her up and running, taught me everything he knows about cars and was ready to hand over his shop until..."

Until I didn't come back...

I swallow hard, not wanting to say it out loud. The look Mama sends me over her shoulder tells me I don't have to— she knows what I was going to say.

"I think that more than equals a few medical bills," I mutter.

It's not like I can't afford it. I absolutely can. Multiple times over. Being a country star has to be good for something.

"I would agree. In fact, I think most people would. But not Ken Noble," she says. The sizzle from a tomato hitting the hot oil in the pan fills the room, easing my nerves. "There were many a meal on this table after your father left because of Ken and his brother, Rod. Those two take that family name seriously. Pretty sure the boy cousins are continuing that tradition as well."

The boy cousins. That was a term I hadn't heard in a long time—and something only a small town would label people. Well known for their generosity, Ken and Rod Noble had also famously divided the genders of the next generation, each taking one. They liked to joke that they planned it, Ken taking the girls and Rod taking the boys, known locally as the girl cousins and boy cousins respectively. The only thing they hadn't done evenly was numbers of kids, since Ken's wife had passed shortly after Kenzie was born, leaving him with just the two girls.

"Rod needs the extra boys to help him on that ranch," Ken had joked one day when he and I were working late at the garage. "I took the easy way out becoming a mechanic. He decided he wanted to keep up with livestock and the butcher shop, which still sounds like insanity to me. So God knew what he was doing giving him Ezra, Atlas, Landon, and Zachary to help out with all that."

I smile at the memory, missing those nights, wondering how different my life would be if I hadn't left. If I had followed through with the plan to work with Ken after graduating from college, eventually taking over the shop. One thing's for sure in my mind—Kenzie would still be by my side.

Kenzie...

"Do you..." I pause, trying to find the courage to ask the question out loud. The one that I've been wondering ever since Kenzie's dad turned down my help. Mama turns to look at me, still carefully pushing food around in her frying pan. "Do you think he refused because of Kenzie?"

"No, I think he refused because that's who he is. Just like

he tried to refuse that the funds from the festival this year go to him. Tried to insist that the money still go to the robotics program at the high school. I think he knows that whatever went down between you and his daughter is between you two."

Her answer does nothing to soothe the ache inside me, a mixture of guilt and longing that took up residence in my chest long ago. I've gotten good at tamping it down, ignoring it most of the time. No matter how much I tried to prepare, I wasn't ready for it to hit me again the second I crossed over the county line. That said, I also know it's not going anywhere. At least not until I head back to Nashville.

"Mama!" two loud, raucous voices shout in unison, the kitchen door slamming open. The sound of it hitting the cabinet makes me jump, sending my pulse into overdrive.

In a cloud of chaos, my two best friends since childhood, Nash and Noel Keller, pile in, each heading straight to kiss my mother hello. I laugh to myself, shaking my head, loving that they love her as much as I do. Throughout it all, Nash and Noel have stuck with me. Always there to cheer me up when I need it, while also right there to never let me get too big for my boots.

"Hi boys. I should have known. Oil's been hot for five whole minutes, and here's the trouble twins, right on time."

"Like we would pass up your maters?" Noel asks, trying to sneak one from the plate.

"Or your fried chicken?" Nash follows up.

"So, does that just make me yesterday's leftovers?" I ask, pushing up from the table.

Nash turns to look at me, his eyes raking up and down my body, as if he were assessing livestock at the county fair.

"Unless you learned to cook on that fancy-ass tour bus of yours, you absolutely come second to this goodness," Nash comments, hitching a thumb over his shoulder toward the stove.

I bark out a laugh. I can't compete with that. Not even going to try.

A second later, Nash has his thick landscaper's arms wrapped around me in a bear hug, Noel hot on his heels. Fraternal twins who might as well be identical to those who don't know them, I have no problem telling the tall, brawny, light brown-haired guys apart. Ignoring the fact that Noel's face is longer compared to Nash's slightly rounder, both have sharp jaws that could easily land them on the cover of any magazine. Add in Nash constantly looking like he is up to something—although let's not lie, he probably is—and Noel's permanent brooding, their personalities shine through the rest of them that look exactly alike.

"Wait, did you learn to cook on that fancy-ass tour bus?" Nash follows up, pulling back from the hug.

"I did not."

"Then you are solidly in third place."

"Third?"

"Food, Mama W, then you," Noel counts out.

"That's fair."

"You better eat up; we have a wild night ahead of us," Nash says.

"No, no. I don't do wild nights."

A scoff comes from the other side of the kitchen, all three of us turning to look at my mother.

"Dustin, I love you, but I also follow you on social media. And was there for the grand opening of Fire Lights, that honky-tonk with your name on it. I am fully aware that you do, indeed, do wild nights."

"Busted…" Nash sings under his breath.

"Not in Hickory Hills, I don't."

"Dude, you got a long week ahead of you being the town

starlet. Not to mention, coming face-to-face with Kenzie. One night out to loosen you up won't hurt."

The sound of Kenzie's name sends a zing through me. Not all that long ago one of these guys saying her name would have barely registered. We were a pack—Willa, Sylvie, the twins, Kenzie, and me. Then I followed my dream.

"Front yard looks great," I say, changing the subject as fast as possible. "You did a great job with it. Which tells me I'm not paying you enough."

"One—we were not done talking about the first subject, so nice try," Nash says. "But two, you paid for the materials; that's all we need. We told you when you left that we had Mama W taken care of, and we meant it."

"Not to mention," Noel adds, "you provided the money for us to start Keller Landscaping, so consider it a return on investment."

"That's not why I did it. Starting a landscaping arm from your parents' nursery was your dream. It was the least I could do."

"Right, so back to the first subject," Nash segues, obviously uncomfortable with all the talk about money. "One MacKenzie Rose Noble."

I sigh, giving in. Because I do want to talk about her. So, so fucking badly. I just don't want to admit that I want that. These two see straight through me though.

"How is she?"

"Library is open ten thirty to eight, every day except Sunday, if you want to go ask her yourself," Noel offers. "Although she is hit or miss after about six."

"I need to think before I go see her. Before I talk to her."

"Right, because those seven years since you left town haven't given you much time to *think*. Or the how many years since you haven't talked to her? Five?"

"It hasn't been years since I talked to her. Only weeks."

The words are out of my mouth before I can stop them. I didn't mean to say that.

"Weeks? Boy, you got some 'splaining to do," Nash says, in his mock gossipy tone.

I guess I do.

CHAPTER THREE

KENZIE

THERE ARE JUST some places that manage to hold on to memories, no matter how many new ones you might make. In Knox County, Georgia, The Giddy Up is such a place.

Walking into the old honky-tonk, nestled right on the county line, I inhale deeply, trying to stay calm. The unique scent of the place takes over my senses, making all sorts of memories flood back—all age events in high school, trying out our fake IDs in college, sharing our first drink as a group the night Sylvie, the baby of us, turned twenty-one. There is no arguing that this place is a part of me.

"Are we down to karaoke tonight, or no?" Willa asks, pausing at the bottom of the spiral metal staircase that leads upstairs to the karaoke room.

"No. The moratorium on karaoke still stands," I reply. "Never to be lifted."

"Fair enough."

Fair enough. Glad she thinks so, since it seems like everyone else thinks I'm being ridiculous. Karaoke had been our thing, the six of us spending hours and hours singing along to the highlighted words on the monitor. Some of us were better than others—Nash famously unable to carry a tune in a bucket—but that didn't stop us from belting our hearts out. But karaoke had also been the catalyst for my heartbreak, twice over, and no part of me feels the need to try and relive it.

Spotting an open table off to the side of the bar and not too far from the dance floor, Willa scoots over to it, claiming it as ours. Every eye in the room is on her, in her painted-on jeans, black T-shirt that's scrunched along her sternum, pulling the hem up to show off her flat stomach, and high-heeled cowboy boots, clearing a path like the Red Sea parting for her to pass. Thankfully, that path stays open long enough for Sylvie and me to join her, the murmur of conversation barely audible over the music playing.

"Will you stop tugging at your skirt?" Willa scolds, batting Sylvie's hand away from her thighs.

"It's too short. I feel like my ass is on display to everyone in here," she replies, tugging it down again.

"Your ass is not on display. And would it be so bad if it was? Might land you a date."

"Why did you wear it if you're not comfortable?" I ask.

"This one dressed me," she answers, nodding at Willa. The flowy black skirt comes to her midthigh and looks cute paired with the burgundy top Sylvie's wearing, making her auburn hair pop. The outfit is a little trendier than Sylvie would normally wear, but is by no means outrageous. "She forgets that not all of us are seven feet tall and can wear whatever we want."

"You need more confidence, Sylvie."

"Willa's right."

"Easy for you to say—neither of you are built like a female Danny DeVito," Sylvie mutters, glaring at both of us.

"You are not!" Willa and I shout in unison.

Sylvie rolls her eyes, her mind unchanged.

"You look hot," Willa continues. "Although, you know who you don't need to dress up to look hot for?"

"If you say Camden Tyler, so help me…"

I sputter out a laugh, loving where this conversation is going. This is the beauty of female friendships—knowing each other so well that you know exactly what is about to come out of each other's mouth. Granted, Willa has been teasing Sylvie about the same thing for years. Partially because we know it will get her worked up, and partially because we both wish she would see what is right in front of her in the town vet.

Flagging down a waitress, we order our drinks. The rumble of the bass in the music thrums through me, letting me get lost in the moment. I need this. I need time out with my girls. A distraction from everything that is my life right now.

From the one thing I can't stop thinking about. Dustin Wilder.

There's a list as long as my arm of things I need to be worrying about. None of which are him. No, I take that back. He's here because of the festival, and making sure that goes off without a hitch is on the list. The forty-seventh annual Rhythm and Brews Festival is not going to fall down on my watch.

Dad's health, my sister's pregnancy, my nephew, my job —all these things outrank him. Still, my mind keeps wandering to the sound of his voice. How surprised he sounded when he answered the phone, quickly morphing into the low, raspy sound that sent tingles up my spine. Like taking a hit of a drug that I had weaned myself from, those few quick minutes were all I needed to fall back down the rabbit hole.

One that I'm afraid I'm never going to be able to climb back out of.

"Earth to Kenzie," Willa says, snapping her fingers in front of my face.

"Yeah?"

"We lost you there for a second."

"Sorry, my brain just has so much going on."

"Jake is over at the bar with the boy cousins. I'm sure he'd be up for clearing your mind for a bit." Willa winks, her meaning perfectly clear.

"I'm sure he would," I reply, not bothering to turn and look. Both Sylvie and Willa's gazes are locked on something behind me—no doubt the *behinds* of one of my cousins. I just can't bring myself to flirt though. "And if y'all wanna stop staring at my relatives, that would be great."

Sylvie averts her gaze, blushing. Objectively, I know that Ezra, Atlas, Landon, and Zachary are good-looking, and I can understand the appeal. But they are still my cousins.

"I'm not done looking," Willa says, keeping her eyes trained on them. "Besides, it's not like I'm staring at…oh…"

"Oh, what?" I ask, my pulse skipping a beat. I freeze in place, not daring to look. I can tell by Willa's expression that I don't want to know.

"Yeah, what?" Sylvie asks, pushing up on her tiptoes to get a better look. "It's just the…oh…"

That's two "ohs." Which means that it's not good. Really not good.

My heart starts to race, my mind already jumping to conclusions. There's not a whole lot in this world, much less in Hickory Hills, that warrants two "ohs." Right now, I can only think of one thing.

As nonchalantly as I can, I twist to face the door. Almost instantly, I find exactly what I already know is there. My heart leaps into my throat, our eyes making contact.

Dustin Wilder.

Dusty…

There's a day's worth of scruff on his cheeks, an old ball cap resting low on his head, trying to obscure his face. But I would know those ice-blue eyes anywhere. Those eyes that I once thought could see into my soul, turning me to mush. Hell, they probably still can.

He doesn't take his gaze off me, my heart calling out to him, trying to draw him closer. My head says no; it knows better. That part of me wants to turn and run in the other direction, put distance between us. The rest of me seems to have a mind of its own though, aching to close the distance. To run to him until his arms are wrapped around me, holding me as close as possible. But we can't. That's not who we are anymore. Or who we will ever be again.

Sucking in a breath, I try to calm my raging pulse, beating in time with the dance remix the DJ put on. It suddenly feels like it's a million degrees in this place, the walls closing in on me. I need to do something. To move, but I can't. My feet are like cinderblocks, heavy and useless.

"Fucking Nash."

Willa's outburst knocks me out of my trance. What he did to deserve it, I don't know, but my head is back in the game now, in just enough time to see the Keller twins headed our way, Dustin between them as if they were his bodyguards.

"Kenz, we can leave if you want," Sylvie says. "We can hit up the Whippy Cone, eat our feelings."

"No, no." I shake my head. I got this. I'm a big girl. I can deal with my ex showing back up in town. Even if he is a country star. Who I haven't spoken to in…oh fuck. Doesn't matter. I'm over him. "We don't have to leave. We were here first. It's no big deal. This was going to have to happen eventually, so at least we have alcohol to help us deal." I hold up my beer, taking a long swig. "Big girl panties on—I can handle this."

"You can wear panties in those pants?" Willa quips, trying

to lighten the mood before the boys arrive. "Where's the fun in that?"

"Where's the fun in what?" Nash asks.

"Go away, Nash," Willa says. "No one invited you."

Willa glares at him, laser beams all but coming out of her eyes. Nash responds the only way he seems to know how, grabbing Willa around the waist and picking her up. The shriek she lets out would be enough to make anyone's eardrums bleed, if not for the DJ. I've never seen anyone more annoyed by another human being than Willa is by Nash—something that has been going on since we were teens. Nash eats it up though, loving to poke and prod, his ire for her just as strong.

"One day they'll move past this, right?" Noel asks, leaning into Sylvie.

"We've been saying that for years," she replies with a shrug.

"Miss Kenzie," Nash says, tapping his cap in my direction.

I smile, my heart softening to the twins. For as upset as I am that they just walked into my hangout—no, our hangout—with the man they know turned my life upside down, I could never really be mad at them. They've been by my side too long. Which also makes me wonder why on earth they're here. Because they do know. They were right upstairs in the bar with me the moment I fully realized that Dustin and I were done. They walked through that with me. Held my hand, passed me tissues, and made so many trips to the Whippy Cone on my behalf that I'd lost count.

"Ladies," Dustin says. My heart stops at the sound of his voice, my throat going dry. He's here. He's really here. "Kenzie."

"Hi Dustin." I manage to get the words out sounding like a normal person, a swell of pride coursing through me.

"Dustin Randall Wilder, do not just stand there. Get over here and give me a hug!" Willa demands.

Doing as she says, Dustin steps around me, trading places with Nash, giving Willa a hug before turning to Sylvie and doing the same. A rush of relief and regret swirls around me as he moves. I want this to be as normal as possible. The gang is back together. There is no reason that we can't pretend like nothing ever changed. That we're still the same six kids, still living in our small Georgia town, not a care in the world.

Except we're not.

Those kids had their whole lives ahead of them. Anything and everything was possible. The six of us now are a different story. Looking at each of my friends, it occurs to me that maybe I'm the only one whose dream didn't come true. Willa was Miss Georgia. Sylvie is instilling the love of science into kids, helping them see that the magic of knowing how the world works is all around us. The twins have taken their parents' nursery business a step further, creating Keller Landscaping. Dustin is off making music—a dream that he'd kept secret for so long, thinking that it was never possible. Me, I'm just the town librarian, my early education degree going to waste.

"We didn't expect you in town so early," Sylvie says, trying to keep the conversation going.

"I actually cleared two weeks so I could come back," Dustin says. "It worked out in my schedule and I haven't had time off in a while, so I thought it would be nice. Come home, see Mama, hang with the guys, maybe spend time at the garage."

My skin heats up at the mention of the garage, my mind flashing back to a teenage Dustin, covered in oil, bent over that old Chevy truck. The one he told me he still drives. I can still feel the sizzle in the air and see the dim automotive bay lit by nothing but the portable lamp, the rest of the garage dark, Dustin tinkering with the engine, me sitting on a stool watching him.

"So you don't have to rush back after R and B?"

"Nope. My next commitment isn't until the following weekend. Luke Bryan and I are doing an appearance at the UGA/Tennessee game, representin' the Dawgs." The twins fist-bump him, thankfully keeping the barking to themselves. I love my alma mater as much as the next girl, and I will go down fighting anyone who wants to say there is a better SEC team out there, but there is a time and a place for barking. The Giddy Up isn't it. "Kenzie, did Moira ever find him on her hunt? I should have asked when you called."

A record screeches inside my head, the whole world slamming to a halt. *I should have asked when you called.* Oh shit.

All eyes are on me, two sets of which look like they are about to pop out of their owner's faces. Sylvie stares at me, slack-jawed, and Willa blinks rapidly. The twins, however, do not look surprised. Which means only one thing. Dustin told them I called.

Great, just great.

"Ummmmm, I don't think so. At least she never said," I answer, my voice trembling.

"When was this?" Willa asks, her face returning to normal. At least, mostly normal. I can still see the questions ripping through her mind, and I know I'm in for it later.

"Last month, when she and Stacey Conrad went up to Nashville on that girls' trip with KatieRae Gates."

"Ran into Moira at a Circle K, of all places."

"And you two talked about it after…" Willa gestures between Dustin and me. "Like, on the phone?"

Nash snickers, not bothering to hide his amusement. Glad this is funny to someone. Because right now, if the earth could just open up and swallow me whole, I think I might prefer that. Anything would be better than standing here like this. Dustin seems to have caught on that I hadn't shared that call with anyone but him, his ears turning pink, same way they always had when he was embarrassed. Well, that makes two of us, sir.

"Hey Kenzie," Jake Wright says, squeezing in between Sylvie and Noel.

Noel gives him a dirty look, as if to ask Jake who invited him to the party, but Sylvie just slides out of the way to make room. My heart jumps, the rest of me unsure whether he is the most unwelcome interloper ever or just what I need to rescue me from this insanely awkward situation.

Jake flashes me his smile, one that makes most of the women in Hickory Hills swoon, but that I can't help but compare to another—that happens to be standing all of six feet from Jake, a bashful look on his face.

"Care to dance?" He winks, nodding toward the dance floor.

It's a two-step, the most basic of all country dances, one that I know I can do in my sleep. It also is the chance to give me some breathing room from Dustin. From the admission that I not only called him, but that I didn't tell my girls.

Yes. Yes, yes, yes. Dancing sounds great.

"Sure. Lead the way, cowboy."

CHAPTER FOUR

DUSTIN

LEAD THE WAY, cowboy...

Kenzie's words ring through my ears, like a gong being struck to announce dinner. Four little words that make my heart race and jaw tic. Annoyance flashes over me as she saunters away with Jake, ever the fucking quarterback. All these years later he still looks the same, with dark wavy hair, matching eyes, and that damn smile that made all the girls swoon. Everyone except my girl.

Until now apparently.

The sharp reminder that Kenzie isn't my girl anymore hits me square across the face, just as Jake slips an arm around her waist, leading her onto the dance floor, her perfect curves fitting into those jeans so well it makes my dick ache. I hate how comfortable she looks in his arms, her chestnut hair cascading around her shoulders, soulful brown eyes locked on him. Like she used to with me.

"So, Kenzie and Jake Wright, huh?" I say, turning back to the group, unable to help myself. I know damn well that none of my friends are going to want to talk about this, trying to avoid drama, but I don't care. I need to know.

"Nash, I need another drink," Willa says, not bothering to look up from her phone, furiously tapping away on it with one hand, holding up her still half-full martini with the other.

Nash quirks an eyebrow at her, a scowl tugging at his lips. "Go get it yourself, and who the fuck are you texting?"

"None of your damn business."

Nash tries looking over her shoulder, but Willa simply shoves her glass toward him again. I don't have to look to know that she's texting Kenzie, in shouty caps, wondering why the hell she had to learn about that phone call from me.

Nice job, Dustin...

"Tell me who you're texting and I'll consider getting you a refill."

"Not how this works. You ruined my night, so you can go get the drinks."

"And just how did I ruin your night?"

"Your presence is more than enough."

Nash groans, chugging the rest of his beer and slamming the bottle down on the table. Muttering something under his breath, he heads toward the bar, shaking his head the whole way. It's a dynamic I've oddly missed, although I still get an earful from my buddy any chance he gets about what a pain in the ass Willa is. I've been watching these two dance around each other like this for so long, and I still don't know if what they need is a boxing ring or to fuck it out. I lean toward the latter.

"Y'all are just going to ignore my question, aren't you?" I say to no one in particular. At this point, I'm not even sure they are listening.

"It's been seven years since you left town, Dustin," Willa starts.

"Five since you didn't bother telling her you moved on," Sylvie finishes.

It's like they've rehearsed this. A coordinated attack to hit right where it hurts the most. They're succeeding too. My gut churns, the knowledge of what I did, or better yet, what I *didn't* do, eating away at me once again. If ever an apology is owed, this is it. Problem is, I don't know how to do it without dragging up all the hurt I know is already there. That we've moved past. Or that I think we've moved past.

Judging by the smile on Kenzie's face as she stares into Jake's eyes, I'm right. But why does that hurt so fucking much?

"I'm just asking, as a friend," I defend, holding my hands up in surrender. It's a lie, and I can tell that neither of the girls believe me. They know me too well. Country star or not, these two give zero shits. Same as the twins. Just means I'll have to plead my case a little more to get what I'm after. That, and say a little prayer that they cave. "Same way I would ask about Noel here, if I thought that maybe he'd stopped grunting long enough to actually speak to a woman."

"When I meet a girl who cranks my tractor, I'll let y'all know," he says out of the corner of his mouth, taking a slow swig of his drink.

A more Noel response I have never heard.

A very full martini glass slides across the table, sloshing over the rim, landing right in front of Willa. The unamused look on her face as Nash slips back in between her and his brother almost makes me want to laugh.

"There's only one olive in here. I like two. You know this."

"Whoops," Nash replies with a shrug. "You tell him about Kenzie and Jake yet?"

"No."

"And we're not going to," Sylvie adds.

"Why not?"

"Yeah, why not?" I repeat.

"Because I believe in the age-old adage of 'chicks before dicks,' thank-you-very-much," Willa snarks.

"You don't choose anything over dick," Nash returns.

"Oh, fuck off!"

"Okay, children!" Sylvie exclaims, throwing her hands out. "Don't make me separate you two. I swear to God, I have teenagers better behaved than you." Turning to face me, Sylvie puts her hands on my shoulders, head craned back to look me in the eye. I'd forgotten just how much shorter she is than I am. "Dustin, it's not that we don't love you; we do."

"You just love her more. Got it."

For the first time tonight, I'm feeling out of place. As much as this place looks the same, even feels the same, it's clear that Hickory Hills isn't stuck in a time vacuum. That it moved on without me. I guess there's a reason that guy said you can't go home again.

"Dustin—"

"Willa, don't worry about it. I know how bad I fucked up. It eats away at me every day. There may or may not even be a song about that now," I admit, swallowing hard. I've never told anyone what the inspiration behind that song was, despite all the times I've been asked.

"Chasing Falling Stars," Sylvie says. It's not so much a question as it is a confirmation that they already knew that.

I nod. *Just like every other song I sing...they're all about her...*

"I love that after all these years you are still her pit bull, trying to protect her. I just want to know she's happy."

Willa sighs, lips pursed, a look of surrender taking over. "I can't believe I'm telling you this. But yes, she and Jake see each other sometimes."

"See each other?"

"It's casual. Zachary Noble set them up on a blind date a couple of years ago because he thought she needed to get out of the house."

"They go out from time to time," Sylvie adds. "But she's said that she can't really see a future with him."

Can't see a future with him...

I can't help but wonder if that's a Jake specific thing, or if that's because she can't see a future with anyone. My Kenzie had all sorts of dreams of settling down, raising babies, growing old while sitting in a porch swing. What had happened to those? Thinking that I ruined those dreams is another stab to the gut. One more thing that I wish I could make right. Because if she would consider forgiving me, I'd build her all the porch swings she wanted.

The song overhead fades into something slower. Something that is ill-suited for a two-step. Glancing back out to the floor, I watch as couples switch gears, transitioning to a waltz. My mind instantly flashes back to Sunday afternoons as teenagers, during "family day" at The Giddy Up, learning each one of these dances. All the hovers, spins, and counting had confused the hell of Kenzie, leaving the tops of my feet bruised for weeks thanks to the boots she'd been wearing. What I can't remember is how I'd gotten her to relax enough to give up on counting, trusting me enough to lead. She had though.

My heart swells at the memory, my arms aching to hold her. To spin her around the dance floor again. To feel that trust.

Without a word, I step away from the table, heading toward the floor. My head is screaming that this is a bad idea, but my body doesn't listen. It's too lost in the music and the memories to care about the damage this could do.

"Dustin!" Willa says, grabbing my arm. I spin around and look at her, unable to speak. Whatever I would say would be wrong anyway. She lets out a long, resigned sigh, letting go of me. "Just know that if you hurt her again, no one will ever find your body. That is a promise."

I nod. Message received.

Next thing I know, I'm on the floor, sidling up to Jake and Kenzie, who are too busy trying not to trip over each other to notice me at first. Kenzie is counting too fast, all caught up in trying to take the right step. Just like when we were younger.

"Mind if I cut in?"

"Dustin!" Jake greets, stepping to the side of the floor, letting others continue by. "Heard you were coming back."

"Here I am."

There's an awkward silence between us, Kenny Chesney's "You Save Me" filling the space it leaves. My mouth goes dry, my mind blank. Fuck, did I really forget how to speak in the twenty steps it took to get over here? Apparently, I did. Jake and Kenzie seem to be suffering from the same ailment, only serving to make this worse.

"So, how 'bout a dance?" I ask, holding my hand out.

"We were in the middle of—"

"It's cool," Jake says, excusing himself. "I'll go grab us drinks. See you back at the table."

I don't wait for him to disappear. Wrapping my arms around Kenzie, I pull her in close, starting the count off in my head.

"Dusty…" she whispers.

The sound of my name on her lips is music to my ears, sending shivers down my spine. My whole body is alert now, responding to the feel of her in my arms. Her soft curves meld into my hands as her body relaxes, recognizing my touch. Those eyes sparkle back at me, melting me down to my core. I've missed this. So much. More than I want to admit. Nothing has ever felt as good as holding her, and I know that nothing ever will. It's better than every memory I have combined.

"You never could count for shit," I tease.

She lets out a soft laugh, her head dipping forward. "I can two-step."

"I'd be very worried about the young minds you are molding if you couldn't."

"Because librarians need to be able to two-step? I don't seem to remember that being a requirement. Mrs. Cassum certainly would have never gotten the job."

A loud, deep roar of laughter escapes me, my insides lighting up like the Fourth of July. Fuck, have I missed this. The easy companionship we shared, laughing and joking our way through everything. Nothing was off-limits. No amount of sass or sarcasm too great. We understood each other. Knowing that we can pick that up again gives me hope. Friendship might not be off the table.

"So, you and Jake, huh?"

Wariness flashes in her eyes. Instantly, I can tell I pushed too far. Apparently we did not pick up where we left off.

Shit, why did I lead with that question...

"I don't see how that is any of your business."

"I'm just making conversation."

"Just making conversation," she hisses, spinning in time with the music. "No, making conversation would be talking about the weather. If I know whether or not pigs or cows are stronger this year from the boy cousins. It's not asking about my relationship."

Spinning back to face me, she glowers at me. It's not anger I see, though, it's hurt. The pain is front and center, no matter how much she tries to disguise it.

I did that...

"So, it's a relationship," I push. I have no idea why I'm saying this. I don't really want to know.

Except, I do. I want her to tell me it's not. That it's harmless and that he means nothing. But I can't ask that of her.

That would be a dick move. I've already pulled more than my fair share of those.

"No…yes…it doesn't matter." Kenzie stops, stepping off to the side again. "What do you care, Dustin? You left. Did you really just expect me to become a nun? To sit at home, waiting, hoping that someday you might walk back into my life? Because that is not how this works."

"No, Kenz, that's not it at all."

Shit. This is not going how I wanted it to go. This is not me showing her how much I care. I need to fix this. Now.

I open my mouth to continue, to defend myself and my actions. To tell her that I still care and want her to be happy, but the DJ cuts me off. With my own song.

"Chasing Falling Stars," my first number one, the song that changed everything, blares through the speakers. A song I had written about Kenzie.

Ice surrounds us, the temperature of The Giddy Up dropping rapidly as the song continues. Tears well up in Kenzie's eyes. Fuck. Fuck, fuck, fuck.

"I have to go."

Pushing past me, she doesn't bother looking back, leaving me in the middle of the dance floor. I look over at our table, trying to catch Willa or Sylvie's attention, but the second I do, someone recognizes me, screaming my name. In an instant, I'm surrounded by fans, cell phones up, all trying to get a selfie. So much for lying low.

And so much for not hurting Kenzie again.

CHAPTER FIVE

KENZIE

WILLA

PHONE CALL?! PHONE CALL?! WTF
PHONE CALL IS HE TALKING ABOUT?

DID YOU CALL HIM AND NOT TELL US?

KENZIE, HOW THE HELL HAVE YOU BEEN
KEEPING THIS SECRET?

WHEN YOU GET OFF THAT DANCE FLOOR,
YOU HAVE A LOT OF FUCKING
EXPLAINING!

SYLVIE

Breathing is a good idea W, you should
try it…

WILLA

Not until I hear about this phone call, and
why we had to find out about it from effing
Nash…

I SCROLL THROUGH MY TEXTS, eyes skimming over the barrage of messages I received while on the dance floor, my head propped up against my headboard, the pillow crammed behind my neck not doing much in way of support. Willa's voice couldn't be louder or clearer if she'd left voice messages rather than texts. Her dismay about being kept in the dark only barely overshadows how she found out.

Which is totally fair. I shouldn't have kept it from her or Sylvie. In my defense though, no part of me ever thought that it would come up in conversation. At least not a conversation with witnesses. I can't be mad at her for being upset. If there is anyone to be mad at, it's Dustin.

For a number of reasons. Not the least of which is him cutting in on the dance floor.

> Pretty sure you actually heard it from Dustin,
> not Nash…

SYLVIE

Where are you? Are you ok? You ran out of
here pretty fast.

> I'm fine.

I pause, fingers hovering over the keyboard on the screen, trying to figure out how to finish that text. There are so many emotions swirling around me, I'm starting to feel like I could drown in them.

> Just needed to be alone with my thoughts,
> that's all. Didn't want to ruin your night.

WILLA

You're not ruining anything. Whippy Cone?

> I'm already home

WILLA

Soft serve travels

I laugh, loving her persistence. I know exactly how well a Whippy Cone travels, and just how long it takes to get from there to here. At this point, I'm pretty sure they'd deliver if I called and asked.

No, it's ok. Dad's asleep and I don't want to risk waking him. It was a treatment day and they tend to kick his ass

WILLA

Acceptable

I close my eyes, trying to force my racing heart to settle. It hasn't slowed down even a slight bit since Dustin walked into The Giddy Up, slaying me with that smile. Forget panty-melting—that smile lit them on fire, incinerating them. Just like it always did. Always would.

Then he put his arms around me, pulling me in close for that waltz. If I had thought that there was any resolve in me, it was gone. In an instant, I was back to being the teenage girl who couldn't get enough of him. It was a good thing he'd said what he did, or I might have stayed there in that dance hold all night.

SYLVIE

So…about this phone call…???

Ugh. Sitting up, I look around my childhood bedroom, now filled with my "adult" furniture, working up the nerve to tell my best friends the very embarrassing truth about what I did. When I moved back in here to help take care of Dad, I wondered if it would feel awkward, being an adult, living in the room I grew up in. Up until now, it hasn't been.

Resting on the desk, staring back at me, is a picture of the three of us as girls. I don't remember which one of the boys took it, but I remember the moment as if it were yesterday. Fried to a crisp after a day hanging out at Rocky Pond, our cheeks and shoulders glowed red in the light of the bonfire, smiles stretching from ear to ear. Before life got complicated.

Sylvie and Willa were by my side then. Just as they are now. There is no use keeping them in the dark.

I called Dustin

SYLVIE

Yes, we caught that part

WILLA

Were you drunk?

Perfectly sober

SYLVIE

Why?

Well, that's the million-dollar question, now isn't it?

I missed him. I wanted to hear his voice.

Moira had just gotten back from that
Nashville trip and told me about how she
saw him, and how great he looked. And then
"Chasing Falling Stars" came on the radio
and I just…

SYLVIE

oh, Kenz…

I miss him

I miss him. Present tense. A tear slips down my cheek, my

heart ripping in two. I want to be stronger than this, but I'm not. At least not in this moment.

WILLA

New plan! Starting tomorrow, it's Operation:
Avoid Dustin

> And just how is that going to work? Hickory
> Hills isn't that big, and he's playing at the
> festival we're on the planning committee for.

WILLA

IDK, walk the other way if we see him?

SYLVIE

That's a grand plan

WILLA

I'll work on the details later. But we can make
this work

SYLVIE

Noel and Nash will help

WILLA

Noel will. Nash…well, fuck Nash

> While we're on the topic, could you do just
> that? Save us all from having to listen to you
> bicker

I hold my breath, waiting for Willa's response. The three dancing dots under her name appear and disappear half a dozen times, her answer clearly being thought about. God only knows what sass-tastical response she's going to have for this. Willa can dish it out with the best of them, and thankfully she takes it just as well.

SYLVIE

I'll even provide the condoms! 😏

WILLA

Save them for Dr. Camden Tyler, S. I have my
own and won't be wasting them on the likes
of Nash Keller

I laugh, reaching for the cord and plugging my phone in. It's time for sleep. Tomorrow is going to be a long, long day. I need a clear head and a patched together heart if I'm going to face this. Leaning back on the pillow, I close my eyes, searching out whatever is going to get me to dreamland fastest—counting sheep, singing the ABCs, I don't care. Only problem is, the only thing running through my mind is a familiar melody and lyrics that I feel in my soul.

Because all I want...is to be back chasing falling stars, with you...

CHAPTER SIX

DUSTIN

A FAMILIAR MELODY greets me as I walk through the open bay door of A Noble Mechanic. Mark Knopfler's distinct voice fills the garage, a warm, gentle welcome home. I'd have been worried had it been anything else. Ken Noble was a mood listener. Which always made it really easy to tell what was going on in his mind—or at least what he was feeling, as specifics were rarely shared.

If he was anxious—Guns 'n Roses. When he was sad or upset The Cure. Pissed off? Yes, that was Pearl Jam. But when all was right with the world, and he was his laid-back self, then it was Dire Straits all the way. Which means I still know every song by heart—both backward and forward, and potentially even inside out.

The smell of used motor oil surrounds me, another welcome, easing my own anxiety. It feels good to be back here in this space. Even if I know it's not the same, that time has marched on without me, the old familiar feeling deep within me lets me know not all is lost. I also know that it's not quite found either.

That, and I have no idea what "it" is.

A loud clang, the distinct sound of a wrench hitting the concrete floor, rings out, drawing my attention to the back bay. Ken's hunched over an old, short bed truck that reminds me of Old Blue. Running my eyes along the bumper and the headlights, I'd guess she's a few years older, the faded pale yellow paint in desperate need of a touch-up.

"Let me get that, old man," I say, rushing over to pick up the wrench.

"Who you callin' old?" he quips, not even bothering to look up from under the hood. "Ever consider that maybe you're just not old enough?"

I laugh, his response exactly as I had expected. It was the same exchange we'd shared a hundred times, and every time was as comforting as the last. I'm pretty sure I'm the only person who could ever get away with calling him old, outside his family. One more thing to love about him.

"You just going to stand there?" he asks, hands held out behind him waiting on the wrench. "Or are you going to make yourself useful? This oil filter isn't going to change itself."

I make quick work of rounding the truck, grabbing a rag off the work bench, and getting to it. My phone buzzes in my back pocket, but I ignore it. There isn't anyone I need to talk to right now except the man on the other side of this truck.

"This looks like Ezra's old truck from high school," I comment, memories flooding back to me of the oldest boy cousin. In Nashville, almost every car looks the same—mostly shiny and new, completely anonymous. Even the guys I do see all the time have rides that might be recognizable up close, if I'm in a parking lot and expecting to see them, but nothing like this truck here, where you'd know it from across town.

"That's because it is Ezra's truck."

"It's still running?"

"Isn't Old Blue?"

Touché...

"How's it feel to be back?"

"Weird," I answer, the truth popping out of me faster than I can think better of it. "Some moments it's like nothing ever changed and then…"

"It's like everything changed?"

"That about sums it up."

"Hmmph."

It's a sound of understanding, completely free of judgment. A reaction that I didn't realize until now that I needed. Knowing that someone else out there understood this completely surreal feeling that has taken over since I crossed into town yesterday is freeing. It leaves me to wonder—had I stopped in yesterday and experienced such a moment before heading to The Giddy Up, would I have been just as stupid as I was last night?

Yeah, probably. Let's not lie here—open mouth, insert foot is a set of directions I only had to be given once and have followed perfectly fine on my own ever since.

"Cancer diagnosis has much the same effect," Ken says softly, in between guitar riffs. "Different set of emotions, I imagine, but same concept."

I stop what I'm doing, leaning against the frame of the truck, my eyes settling on Ken. He continues to work, as if all he said was that it was supposed to rain this afternoon, rather than voiced the stark reminder of why I'm here.

"How are you feeling?" I ask, turning the conversation onto him, something Ken hates.

He lets out a long sigh, looking up at me. His brown eyes are the same as Kenzie's, full of love and a wisdom I can only hope to achieve. "Good days, bad days, all of that."

My phone buzzes again in my back pocket, interrupting the moment. I pull it out, glancing down at the screen to see the face of my manager, Eric. I roll my eyes, knowing that he isn't happy I'm here, then hit the decline button and toss the device over onto the work bench. I'm on vacation. Work can wait.

"Treatment is going well?"

"Doctors say so. But you know how it is with this kind of thing. They want you to think they know more than they do, because frankly, they don't know much. And that's not a knock against them, at least not totally. But there are too many factors, and everyone is too different for them to say with any kind of certainty that something will work, or how the disease will progress. So, we wait and see."

"I really wish you'd let me pay for your treatment. It's the least I could do." I don't bother holding back. I can't, not with him. He's too important to me. Ken Noble is a major reason I am the man that I am. The man I hope to be.

"I can't take your money, son."

Son...

"Is...is it because of Kenzie? Because of..." I trail off, not sure how to finish that sentence.

Ken shakes his head, leaning back over the engine. "You two will sort yourselves out. I have no doubt."

That makes one of us...

My phone goes off again, rattling against the table, the noise grating. For fuck's sake. I have no doubt it's Eric, clearly thinking he's more important than anything I could have going on back here in Hickory Hills. Reaching behind me, I hold down the power button, cursing it under my breath. I chuck it back on the bench, letting it skitter across the top, banging into an old coffee can full of miscellaneous nuts and bolts, the contents shifting.

"That the price of money for nothing?"

Something like that. Only it's not for nothing. The long days and weird schedule take their toll. The chicks though?

Yeah, those are free. Mark Knopfler got that part right. I just wouldn't know anything about that part.

"Something like that."

"But you love it, don't you?"

I pause. "Yeah, I do. It's…my life looks nothing like I thought it would." Pushing back from the truck, I lean against the work bench. "I thought I had it all figured out. The perfect life planned. Finish up school, come back here, work with you until you were ready to retire. Then I'd take over, be the next Noble Mechanic. Build Kenzie that cute little cottage she's always dreamed about up there on Hideaway Hill and spend the rest of my days watching her teach kids their ABCs."

"Hideaway Hill?"

"Yeah, that's what we named that big hill on the back half of your place, the one that overlooks the creek before you get to the start of the cow pastures," I explain. Ken nods, knowing exactly where on his hundred acres I'm talking about. He and his brother had grown up on a cattle farm, the one Rod and his sons still run, splitting the land when they inherited it. Ken took the land upwind from the livestock so he wouldn't have to smell them, building the house he still lives in today. The one where Kenzie grew up. "We used to drive out there in Old Blue and watch the stars."

Among other things, but Ken doesn't need to know that part. He'd given me the safe sex talk as a teenager, making sure I understood how it "really works, and not just whatever bullshit they teach in school these days." Past that, the subject never came up. In the back of my mind, I always assumed he knew what Kenzie and I were up to, and that's why he'd given me the talk. Didn't stop us from trying to hide it though, sneaking around like thieves in the night, Kenzie convinced that getting caught would be the worst thing in the world. So I'd climb up the live oak tree outside her bedroom, crawling through the window, praying to God I didn't fall just to hold her while she slept. Worth every second of risking my life.

"But being Dustin Wild?" I continue. "It's unreal. It's that rush that I got when Mrs. Burch agreed to let Nash, Noel, and me perform senior year at the school dance and the crowd loved us. But all the time. Being up on stage is…indescribable. Getting to pour my heart into everything I create, knowing I've put something out into the world that brings people joy and they can relate to, is amazing. Having someone stop me at a store and tell me that "One Touch, One Kiss" was played at their wedding or that "Ray of Light" made them feel less alone after losing a parent…I feel like I've contributed to the world somehow. And the thought that maybe, out there somewhere, in some other small town, there is a garage with some teenage kid listening to me, inspired to follow his dreams, well…that's pretty fucking cool, isn't it?"

I let out a rush of breath that I hadn't realized I'd been holding as I word vomit all over the place. I didn't mean to. I did mean every word of what I said though. My life is incredible, and I love what I do, even if being back here makes me miss so much of what my life used to be. I've been given a one in a million chance to follow my pipe dream; not taking it would have been stupid.

Which is exactly what Kenzie had said to me.

"You have to go," came her sweet, gentle voice full of emotion. Sitting on a stool, her gorgeous legs on display in her short shorts, one crossed over the other, a foot bobbing along to the music on the radio. She was a teenage dream, brown hair knotted on top of her head, hand fiddling with a screwdriver as she watched me work late one evening. "You can't let me or this town hold you back. This is an opportunity of a lifetime."

"I'm not even sure it's a real offer and not some scam. Real record reps don't just walk up to guys singing karaoke and offer to make them a deal. In fact, I'm pretty sure that's how so many young women end up in porn—some dude approached them and said, 'I'm gonna turn you into a star.' What kind of name is Eric Valentine anyway?"

Kenzie giggled. "Just keep your pants on and it won't be a problem." I rolled my eyes at her. "Seriously, though—go. What do you have to lose? Call him, hear what he has to say. Spend the summer figuring out if you really have a chance, and if it doesn't work out, then okay. We'll finish up senior year and then get on with our lives. At least you'll know you took the chance. And we can spend the rest of our life talking about how you were almost the next Luke Bryan."

I'd agreed. As always, my beautiful, smart girl made an excellent point. It was just a few months. Next thing I knew, I was leaving for Nashville, the day after Moira's wedding. Convinced I would be back for our senior year, I kissed Kenzie goodbye that morning as if I was only running to the grocery store. In the blink of an eye, that all changed. By the end of the summer, Eric had me signed to his label and was scheduling me studio time, which meant I wasn't going back to school. Six months after that, my first single hit the air.

And the rest, as they say, is history.

"It is pretty cool."

"Huh?"

Ken's words knock me out of my headspace. I take a second to stare at the corner where Kenzie's stool used to sit, not realizing I had wandered off. I'd been so lost in thought, my feet had taken on a mind of their own.

"Hearing you on the radio. It's pretty cool to be able to say I knew you when."

"You know me now. I'm here, aren't I?"

"You are." He laughs. "Just know, son, that just because

you're Dustin Wild to everyone else doesn't mean that you aren't still Dustin Wilder to those who love you. And that all that stuff you said before, about the way you thought life would look, you can still have that. You just have to decide if it's worth the effort."

"Pretty sure I can't tour *and* run a mechanic's shop," I quip. I pick at a spot of rust over the wheel well of the truck with my thumb. Ken clears his throat, jutting his chin in the direction of the stuff needed to fix it, as if to once again tell me to make myself useful. I do as I'm told.

"Lord knows I wish you could. Because as good as the boy cousins might be at livestock and butchering, they are shit with an engine. Hence this oil change. But everything else…"

"Whatever happened to all those times you drilled it into my head that you have to make sacrifices in life, because you can't have it all?"

It was one of many life lessons he'd taught me while we'd worked on cars together throughout my junior high and high school years. Life's not always fair, you can't have it all, and honesty is always the best policy. Those were his three big ones. Hard work was a given, but he never missed a chance to throw that one in there either. As someone who'd grown up without a man in the house, I appreciated every second and every word Ken had for me.

"You can't," he states, matter-of-factly. "And we just determined the garage is out, so ipso facto, that's not *it all*."

"So, you're saying there's a chance?" I ask, in the same nervous tone I had when we'd stood in here when I was fourteen, asking him if I could take Kenzie to the movies—on a date. He'd known that there was a girl I liked—*like that*, as I had put it—and looking back, he probably had always known it was her. But saying it out loud that day had made my stomach ache, afraid of what his answer would be.

"I have no opinion on that," he lies. I know he does; it's

written all over his face. He wouldn't be entertaining this conversation if he didn't. But I also respect that he values the relationship he and I have enough to not make it about me and his daughter. "Just that if you want something bad enough, you'll find a way to make it happen."

We continue to work in silence, falling back into old rhythms with ease. Muscle memory is a fascinating thing sometimes. At one point Ken flips to the local country station, turning it up when my song comes on. I shake my head as he sings along, the lyrics about not wanting to be like the man who abandoned my mother and me hitting extra hard as they come from the mouth of the man who did his best to step in. The man I wanted to be just like. Still want to be like.

What he said earlier thrums through me though. About wanting something bad enough to make it work. It's not the first time I've thought about it. Every time, however, it comes down to more than want. All the want in the world isn't going to make it possible. Because if it was possible, it wouldn't have fallen apart in the first place. Or so I tell myself every time I go down this road.

Footsteps faintly register over the music, but I don't look up. I'm too in the zone, focused on the parts in my hands, thoughts far away. Until I hear her voice.

"What are you doing here?"

CHAPTER SEVEN

KENZIE

I INHALE DEEPLY, letting the change in the air settle inside me. It's subtle, but it's there. Fall is coming.

It's still plenty warm, and the weather won't change for a couple of weeks, but I can tell—there is a tinge in the air that hints that something has changed. With perfectly clear skies and lower than normal humidity today, I have zero complaints. Especially if it stays like this for Rhythm and Brews this weekend.

Flipping the sign on the front of the library so everyone will know I'll be back soon, I quickly make my way toward A Noble Mechanic. Dad snuck out before I was up this morning, leaving both his lunch and his meds in the fridge. I'm not sure if that was an honest mistake on his part or a calculated move so he has an excuse to go play ladies' man down at Dolly's, the town's greasy spoon, but either way, it's me to the rescue.

Radio turned up loud, Carrie Underwood's iconic voice greets me as I walk in, expecting to find my father, up to his elbows in grease, working away. The sight that greets me is something else entirely.

My breath hitches, my whole body freezing, sure that I must be seeing things. That this is a figment of my imagination. I'm only seeing what I want to see. What my heart has been holding out for—despite the impossibility—for the last seven years.

Dustin Wilder, a tool in each hand, a rag hanging from his back pocket, working on my cousin's truck.

"What are you doing here?"

The words are out of my mouth before I can stop them. Instantly, I wish I could shove them back inside, keeping the question to myself. But it's too late. They're out there. And he heard me.

So much for Operation: Avoid Dustin.

Everything moves in slow motion as Dustin looks up from the spot of rust he's working on, pushing up to his full height. His hands are greasy, his brow slightly shiny with sweat, all of him looking good enough to eat. Everything inside me wants to run to him, leap into his arms, wrap my legs around his waist, and kiss him. What about him that got exponentially sexier all of a sudden, I have no clue. But it wasn't an easy feat, because Dustin is effortlessly sexy. Always has been.

I blink hard, trying to remind my lady bits that he's off-limits. Hard pass. We are not going down this road. Even if seeing him standing here like this is my fantasy come to life. The dream I thought I had missed out on.

Here and now, covered in grease. Fuck me.

I am in so much trouble...

"Hey kiddo!" my dad greets, oblivious to my internal screaming.

"Dad."

"Kenzie," Dustin's deep, smooth voice says, sending shivers up my spine.

This is even worse than last night. I would have bet

money that being in his arms again was the worst thing that could happen. Feeling him close, his hands knowing just where to hold me, how tight to grip me, our bodies melding together, perfectly fitted for each other. Our hearts beating together in time with the music. But I was wrong. So, so wrong. Because seeing him like this, standing here with my dad, two old friends just tinkering away on a truck, does something to me.

My insides are shattered. Like a piece of glass that is cracked, a million different spiderwebs of fractures going in every direction but still held together by tension, ready at any moment to collapse, the shards scattering everywhere—that's me. I'm afraid to move, knowing that I will never be the same after this. It doesn't matter how long I've lied to myself, to my family, friends, this whole fucking town. It doesn't matter that I even started to believe my own lies. Because that's all it is—pure deception.

I'm still in love with Dustin Wilder.

Which is every reason this has to stop. Why I can't see him anymore. Forget talking to him—that is absolutely out of the question. I will do whatever I need to do for the festival to go well, and that's it. Which does not include interacting with Dustin. Nope. There are plenty of other people on the committee who can take care of that. Like Mrs. Burch. It was her idea to contact him and bring him here, so she can be the one who deals with it. I'm out.

"Dad, you forgot your lunch and your meds," I offer, holding up the bag. "I'll go put it in the fridge."

I march past him toward the very small kitchenette in the back of the garage, not bothering to acknowledge Dustin. Is it rude of me? Sure is. But it's the only way I can stop myself from doing something I'll regret. Like falling into his arms and telling him I love him. Because I can't separate the love from the hurt. And there is still *so much hurt*.

"And here I was hoping to get to Dolly's," I hear my father mutter. Called it.

"I think we can still make Dolly's work," Dustin replies. "I'll buy you lunch."

I can hear the wink in his voice and it makes my blood boil. How fucking dare he. Back in town for two days, acting like nothing has changed. That is not how this works. He is not a part of this anymore. Not Hickory Hills, not A Noble Mechanic, not my family. Most certainly not me.

Spinning around on my heels, I slam the fridge door shut. "You will not!"

"Pardon?"

"No Dolly's. He has a diet he has to stick to."

"I'm sure we can find something at Dolly's that will work."

"No."

"Is this about Dolly's or is this about me?" he asks, stepping in closer. He squints just a bit, his mouth turning upward in a smirk, as if he already knows that answer. Which I'm sure he does.

You...it's always been you...

"Not everything is about you, Dusty," I snap, instantly regretting using my old nickname for him. Showing no weakness and keeping him at arm's length means not leaning on the familiar. If only my subconscious would catch up to the rest of my brain and understand the situation a little better.

Dustin's full-on smiling now at the use of the old moniker. That big, toothy grin could light up a whole stadium, chipping away at the walls I'm trying to maintain. I somehow manage to keep my composure, even though behind the scenes my stomach is doing cartwheels. Oh, how I have missed that smile. It's one thing seeing it on an album cover or on social media, it's another thing entirely when it's directed right at you. That smile borderline ruined a lot of panties when we were younger, and fuck, it's coming close to doing the same thing all over again.

Kenzie, get it together...

"Kenz, I'm here to help, that's all," he says, taking a few steps toward me. He reaches forward, quickly drawing his arms back again, like he was going to pull me in then thought better of it. It doesn't matter though, I can feel his hands on my hips, fingers toying with the belt loops on my pants, making me crave his touch even more. "Please let me help."

I suck in a deep breath, slowly letting it out in an even stream, trying to settle myself. The war brewing within me —fighting between wanting to kiss, wanting to scream at him, and wanting to break down and cry—is taking up too much of my energy. Either way, I don't want to do any of this here. Not with my father watching. He's always loved Dustin. I don't want to change that. I want Dad to still be able to be friends with the kid he viewed as the son he never had.

One heart broken over Dustin Wilder was enough for the Noble family.

"You've done more than enough by agreeing to play at Rhythm and Brews. It would be unfair of us to ask more of you."

There...nice diplomatic answer.

"He's offering. Take him up on it," Dad says.

Thanks, Dad, don't need your help here...

"He's right; I'm offering. Let me help."

"It wouldn't be—"

"Kenz," Dustin cuts me off. His eyes are serious but full of something else I can't name. It looks a lot like love, compassion, but I know that can't be right. Dustin doesn't love me anymore. He's made that clear. "I know what goes into running Rhythm and Brews. Mama was on that damn committee for years, remember? What can I do to help? Use me."

Both my mind and body go wild with his suggestion to *use* him, going places that no one should ever be thinking about with a parent present. Is it hot in here, or is it just me?

"Yeah, use him," Dad chimes in. Not what I needed. "There must be something the committee could use him for."

"Really, I promise, it's under control. Plus, given your star status, I'm sure you showing up anywhere would only cause more chaos than anything else. As soon as word gets out that you're in town early," I add with a shudder, thinking about all the groupies that will be showing up, just for a photo op.

"What you should do is harness that," Dad suggests.

"What?"

"Host a special event where people get the chance to meet him. Twenty bucks for a selvsies or whatever."

"Selfie, Dad. They're called selfies."

"Yeah, that."

That's actually not a bad idea. It'd be easy enough to coordinate. I could use the library, clearing out the reading nook to make enough space. Willa could spread the word via social media. I'm sure it wouldn't take long for the news of a private meet and greet with country star Dustin Wild to spread like wildfire. Plus, it would give us a chance to raise money for the robotics team, so they wouldn't be without their funding this year.

I look back at Dustin, trying to gauge whether or not he'd be willing to put himself out there like that. It might be too much to ask.

"Would you be okay with something like that?"

"If that's what you want."

"That's not what I asked. Would you be comfortable with us putting this together? We'd have to do it tomorrow, since Thursday and Friday are filled with festival setup and sound check and all that. But we could use the library, and Willa is a social media wizard. So, if you're okay with it…"

"Kenzie, I mean it. Use me. However you need. I will sign autographs and take selfies all day if that's what's going to make you happy. Whatever brings in the most money for your family."

I swoon as he mentions my being happy—pretending for a brief second that my happiness is what he really wants. But then I snap back to reality. Where I need to stay.

"Oh no, whatever we raise tomorrow will go to the robotics team. That way Sylvie still has something to work with this year. I already feel guilty enough that we've hijacked the festival; we can't hijack this too."

"Good idea, kiddo."

"I like it."

Good. Great. We have a plan. A plan that brings Dustin into my home away from home, the library. I am hardcore failing at this avoidance thing.

"I'll get with Willa then. She'll let you know the details," I say with a nod, making my way to the door. I need to get out of here. My outing was supposed to be quick—a simple lunch drop-off. Instead, I've managed to embarrass myself and add an extra event to my already jam-packed calendar. Enough. Time to go. "Dad, make sure to eat your lunch that is in the fridge. Please."

I don't say anything else, afraid of what might escape. I'm halfway down the sidewalk, almost to the intersection so I can turn and head back to the library when Dustin calls out my name. I pretend not to hear him, the sound of his feet pounding against the concrete growing louder and louder.

"Kenz," he says, grabbing my arm. My skin sizzles from his touch, aching for more. His breathing is heavy, chest moving with each inhale. "Got a sec?"

"No."

"It's just that…I'm sorry."

The whole world slams to a halt, my heart right along with it. He's…sorry?

"I….er…what?"

"I'm sorry," he repeats.

"For?"

"Everything, Kenz, absolutely fucking everything."

Closing the gap between us, his hands find my hips, just as I had wished for earlier. The familiar feel of them has me reeling. Or maybe it's his apology. Either way, I'm happy he's holding me steady. Because without that, I'd be on the ground, nothing but a pile of skin and bones.

"There is so much I could say—*should* say—but I don't know that you want to hear any of it. And I can't blame you. I did you so wrong, Kenzie, and I hate myself for it. Things spun faster than I ever could have imagined and by the time I looked up…I…" He trails off, shaking his head. "I didn't do what I should have, and by the time it was too late and I owed you an apology…I didn't do that either. The last thing I have ever wanted to do—would ever want to do—is cause you pain. And yet, that's pretty much all I've done. So, I'm sorry. Just please don't hate me, because I don't think I could live with that."

I open my mouth to respond, but I can't. My throat feels like I tried to dry swallow a pill, closing in on itself. Tears sting my eyes, threatening to fall. But I can't let myself cry. Not here.

His apology is everything. In a way that is pure Dusty, he knew exactly what to say. Exactly what I have been waiting to hear for so long. My heart hurts it was so perfect. There is no way to be mad at him, even if this speech is years too late. Because he acknowledged that too.

"I don't hate you," I manage to whisper. "I could never hate you."

"You have no idea how happy I am to hear that."

Tightening his grip, he lets out a long, stuttered breath. He's so close I feel it dance across my skin, still tingling from his earlier touch.

"Dusty…"

"I know. You have to get back to the library. I should get back to your dad. But, friends again?"

"Always."

"Good."

Gently pressing his lips to my forehead, he hovers there for a moment. The softness of them, paired with the tenderness of the gesture, makes my knees wobble. I hear my own breath hitch as he pulls away, missing the connection.

I am in so much fucking trouble.

CHAPTER EIGHT

DUSTIN

WHEN KENZIE SAID that Willa was a wizard with social media, she wasn't kidding. It shouldn't surprise me, yet I'm still in awe of her magic.

We still have more than an hour until the meet and greet is supposed to start, and there is already a line outside the library. And I don't mean that there are a few people who showed up early and are milling around. I mean a line. One that starts right up at the library entrance and goes all the way down the sidewalk, past Hickory Hills Baptist, starting to wrap around the corner. Which is seriously baffling.

"Hometown boy turned star? Of course people were going to line up for this," Willa quipped when we noticed how many people had already shown up.

A "star"—whatever that means. That's not how I see myself, or a title that I'll ever get used to. A couple of number one songs and some sold-out shows doesn't make me Bon Jovi. Certainly doesn't make me someone that people line up to meet an hour before an event. Much less *hours*.

Yet, a small group was huddled around the door when we arrived, some looking like they had slept there in their camp chairs. In Willa's tizzy last night, she demanded the twins and I be at the library no later than seven thirty to help with setup. Noel grumbled about it, while Nash outright told her she was "out of her damn mind," but she'd won them over with the promise of Dolly's breakfast. Which she had indeed delivered on.

"I can't believe all these people are here just to take a picture with your ugly mug," Nash comments, peering out the window of the library, neck craned at an odd angle to see how far the line stretches.

"Or that they're willing to pay for it," Noel adds, taking a big bite of his breakfast biscuit.

"Just what did Willa do to make them all appear? You only decided to do this yesterday afternoon."

Good question...

"Just social media, I think," I answer, not at all sure of how this all went down. One minute I was standing on the side-walk, reveling in the feel of Kenzie's curves in my hands, the soft warmth of her skin against my lips. The next, Willa was blowing up my phone, asking for my manager's number, tossing out ideas for this event.

I hope he overnighted her enough photos for all these people. And that he didn't give Willa too much of a hard time over all this. He'd made his opinion perfectly clear before I left—I shouldn't be taking this time off and doing a free show. That's part of why I've ignored all his calls and texts since arriving. I can deal with the fallout and his grumpy ass when I get back to Nashville.

My eyes flick to the corner where I caught up with Kenzie yesterday morning, her words ringing in my ears. *I could never hate you.*

Those five words are a salve to the raw spot on my soul that I was convinced would never heal. I don't deserve her forgiveness. The fact that she hadn't hesitated in giving it to me though, that only makes the ache in me stronger. If I'm not careful, sweet, friendly forehead kisses will turn into something more. As desperately as I want that, I can't. I broke our hearts once. I can't do it all over again.

I'm not sure I will survive.

"All this from social media?" Nash questions, pulling me back to the moment.

I shrug, slumping down a little in the folding chair I found so we could sit and eat. Sitting here with my two best friends busting my balls should be helping me to keep my head on straight. Instead, all it's doing is making me think about everything I walked away from.

And everything I want back.

"I guess."

"Yes, it is," Willa snaps, appearing out of nowhere. "You should know better than to doubt me. And hurry up and get done. We need to finish setting up."

"What else could there possibly be left to do?" Nash asks, his tone incredulous. "We already rearranged the lobby, put up the pipe and drape in the meeting room, and created the exit pattern out through the back door."

"Which just leaves the children's room shelves that need adjusting. Right, Kenz?" Willa asks.

Kenzie stops in her tracks, looking like a deer in head-lights as her gaze locks with mine. I watch the muscles in her throat contract as she swallows hard. "Err, whatever Willa says."

Turning on her heel, she scurries away, not giving us a second glance as Willa smirks victoriously.

"I'm starting to think Willa's to-do list isn't just about this event," Nash mutters.

"Wishing you were on said to-do list?" Noel teases.

I force a smile, only half listening as the brothers rib each other, my gaze and thoughts still trained on Kenzie as she fiddles with something behind the checkout desk. Her beautiful chestnut hair is pulled up in a French braid, little wisps of it falling out, perfectly framing her face. She looks so natural and at home as she stands there, a perfectly cut sundress hugging her in all the right places, the emerald-green color making her brown eyes pop. The desire to walk over there, slide up behind her, wrap my arms around her waist, and tug her against me is flowing through me like a river. But I know I can't. Doing that would be an epically bad idea for many reasons.

Not the least of which—she doesn't seem to be speaking to me at present.

We've been here for two hours and the most she's said since I walked through the door was "thanks," after I took a box from her. Thanks—just the one word, a small smile attached to it.

I thought we were on the same page. That everything was good between us. Or, at least it had been when we parted yesterday. Sure, I'd taken Ken to Dolly's for lunch even after I implied I wouldn't, but I think we all knew that was going to happen. She couldn't really be upset about that.

The only other thing that could have done it was my text last night.

It wasn't anything earth-shattering—a quick note about how I was looking forward to today. I wasn't expecting a novel in return, but a "me too" or even a smiley face would have sufficed. Instead, the only person who sent me anything at all was Willa, who was out of control, taking the planning of this event way too seriously considering it was supposed to be low-key and impromptu. Then again, that was Willa. No one had ever been able to control her, especially once she got going. I thought about sending a text about that too, but Kenzie's lack of response to my first one had me second-guessing everything. And I do mean everything.

Did I misinterpret something somewhere? I'm pretty sure I didn't. So why didn't I get a response?

She said we were friends. Always. Which means we're okay. Or at least it should. She wouldn't have called me last month if we weren't. That call wasn't a drunk dial. She was perfectly sober, if not a bit wistful. Although, that was before all this. Or at least before I showed back up in Hickory Hills. I had already agreed to the festival when she called. Maybe she didn't know it at the time though.

Nope, not possible. I agreed months ago, and Kenzie is on the committee. There is no way she didn't know I was coming, even if it wasn't mentioned.

The only thing that had changed was what I said. Fuck.

"I think I did something stupid," I declare, turning to face the guys.

"No, dude, we know you did," Noel responds, eyes still turned toward the line outside. He waits a beat, turning back around, eyes flicking between me and Kenzie. "You should have broken up with her properly."

Ouch. How long has he been waiting to say that?

Five years. That's how long. Seven if you count the two I left Kenzie in limbo after I left town. These two are my best friends, and have been since we were kids. They'd kept their opinions to themselves about how it all went down with Kenzie, never once prying or pushing me in any way. But they were her friends too, and no doubt had to help pick up the pieces of the mess I'd made. Without ever saying a word.

"I deserve that."

"And more," Nash adds.

I nod. He's right.

"That's not what I mean though."

They both quirk an eyebrow, the subconscious yet fully synchronized move catching me off guard, derailing my thoughts for a split second.

"Then what?" Nash asks.

"I apologized."

"To Kenzie?"

I nod.

"Five fucking years too late," Noel grumbles.

"I'm sorry, did you suddenly become Dr. Phil? Or is there something between you and my girl I should know about?" I snap, whisper shouting so the rest of the group can't hear us, my hackles up. I know that I have no right to be defensive—I walked away. I'm the one who fucked up and broke her heart. I certainly have no right to call her my girl. But it slipped out and there is no taking it back. Not that any part of me wants to.

"She's not your girl anymore, dude," Noel reminds me.

Fuck. I know.

"First off, let's breathe," Nash says, motioning for us to calm down. "Because we are dangerously close to a situation where I'm going to be the voice of reason, so that should tell us all we're in deep shit."

I scoff out a laugh.

"We know that you know that you were a jackass. So none of that needs to be rehashed. And we built in the cost of all those Whippy Cone trips—plus interest—into the material for Mom's landscaping. So that's covered too."

"Thanks."

"Why do you think apologizing was stupid?" Noel asks, stepping away from the window.

"Because now she's not talking to me."

Their eyebrows quirk again, just as in sync as before. Their skepticism is written all over their faces, the both of them equally amused and unsure about my sudden insecurities.

Which is a damn good question.

"She hasn't said much to anyone this morning," Nash

comments. "So, I don't think it's you. But maybe if you stopped acting like a twelve-year-old girl, you could go ask her."

Fuck, I *am* acting like a twelve-year-old girl, aren't I? Slumping against a bookcase, I try to get it together. This isn't me—either version. I could pretend like I don't know why I'm all up in my head, but it would be a lie. I know damn well.

"The apology was needed," Noel states, his tone softer than it had been a minute ago. "But if she wasn't mad at you before it—and we know she wasn't because she called you recently just to say hi—then she's certainly not mad now. Also, this is Kenzie—she doesn't exactly do mad."

"Nash! Are you done yet? I need this stuff moved," Willa barks from across the room, interrupting our conversation.

"For fuck's sake," he mutters under his breath. "If that girl lives to see this event it will be a miracle, y'all." He ambles away, his twin snickering.

I turn to follow. I need to know what is going through Kenzie's mind. I won't be able to concentrate on this event if I don't, and the last thing I want right now is for this to be unsuccessful. Noel's words hit me again though. Always the defender, it isn't a surprise that his reaction was protecting her feelings and calling me out for what I did. More surprising is how long it took. So I can't help but wonder why now.

"Is…was…there something between—"

"Absolutely not," Noel replies, cutting me off, knowing exactly where my head was at. "Not now, not ever. She's your girl. Sometimes things just need to be said."

Touché…

I quickly make my way across the room, slipping behind the counter. Kenzie doesn't look up as I come up next to her and lean back against the counter so that I can see her face.

"What's the matter?" I ask, keeping my voice to a whisper.

"Why would you think anything is the matter?"

"Because I know you. It's written all over you."

Kenzie forces a smile, glancing up at me, her eyes soft but full of worry. Nailed it. I say a silent prayer that I'm not whatever is wrong, giving her the time she needs to open up.

"Sylvie won't take the money."

"From today?"

Kenzie nods. Internally I sigh, thankful that is all that's wrong. "Is that really so bad?"

"Yes, Dusty! You have no idea the guilt I feel that the festival money is being taken away from the robotics program. Their funding is so limited. And now she won't take this."

"Kenz." Reaching over, I place a hand on her hip, pulling her into me, the front of our bodies all but flush with one another. My dick twitches with the feel of her soft curves against me, the rightness of being like this taking over momentarily. "We all just want to help."

"I know, and I'm grateful. I am." Relaxing into me, her hands land on my waist, grabbing hold of my shirt. "But we're fine. Dad has a plan; we don't need all this."

"If she wants to do this for you, let her—"

"But the robotics team!"

"I will make sure that they get their funding, okay? And before you object, because I can already see it forming in your brain, don't. Let me do this." She nods, her smile brightening. That's my girl. Cupping her face in my hands, I hold her still, staring into her deep brown eyes, hoping that she can feel what I am feeling. That the bond between us is still there, even if our relationship looks different than it used to. "How 'bout this, beautiful, you let me take you to dinner tonight after all this, and you can tell me all about this plan of yours."

"Dusty, I don't—"

"Well there he is!"

Fuck...

If cockblocking had a voice, it would be the slightly nasal southern accent of Moira Noble Schneider. It was the sound that killed many a boner in high school, and apparently is still doing its job all these years later.

"Aunt Kenzie!" a little voice screams, a toddler running toward us.

"Hi, little man!" Kenzie greets, stepping away from me and rounding the corner to pick up who I assume is her nephew.

"Good to see you again, Dustin," Moira continues, her big, pregnant belly leading the way.

"You too, Moira. You've grown since Nashville."

"Four weeks left!"

"Who dat?" the little boy asks, pointing to me.

"That's your Uncle Dustin. Can you say hi, Matty?" Kenzie asks.

Matty waves his hand frantically, his whole face lighting up. "Hi, Uncle Duttin!"

Uncle Dustin. I'm officially done for.

CHAPTER NINE

KENZIE

SIX HOURS.

That's how long we've been here. And the line is still going. If I'm doing my math right, based on how many people we've pushed through here today, we have at least another hour to go. So much for this thing lasting from eleven to one.

Dustin's a trooper though. His smile hasn't slipped once, treating each new person who comes through the line as if they are his new best friend. The gaggle of teenage girls who were waiting at the door when we arrived this morning had even driven down from Atlanta—a solid three-hour trip depending on where in the city you were—just for the chance to say hi.

Willa had a system in place, moving people through the library with ease, allowing for me to still hold our weekly story time in the children's section—something I think all the moms in line were thrilled about. Nash even took over at one point, holding a large group of kids captive with each new crazy voice he busted out.

My feet hurt, my whole body is tired, but my heart…my

heart is so full I'm not sure how it still fits in my chest. Logically, I know that all these people are here for Dustin. The sheer amount of women, all with their hair and makeup done, outfits meticulously chosen, made it obvious that the philanthropic part of this event was not their main focus. Which was fine. Whatever got them through the door and the money raised.

Or so I keep telling myself.

Too bad I don't believe myself.

Because reality is, the green-eyed monster is alive and well inside me. Watching one pretty girl after the next flirt with him makes my stomach churn. I try to remind myself that it doesn't matter. Dustin isn't mine anymore. We're just old friends. He can flirt with whomever he wants. But then I remember how good his hands felt on my hips yesterday or cupping my jaw this morning. How my body reacted to his touch—like metal being drawn into a magnet—as if his arms are where I belong.

Stop it. Stop it, stop it, stop it. You are over him...

A low, whistling sound to my left pulls my attention away from the show in front of me. Willa's there, jaw clenched, the sound coming from her like a cat hissing at someone getting too close.

"What is your issue?" I ask. Willa's claws rarely come out, but when they do, we all know to stand back.

"Pussy Galore over there, all up in his business."

I look back over to Dustin just in time to see Kitty Cataway, former head cheerleader and Willa's former pageant rival, hug Dustin for a couple of beats too long.

"Don't call her that; it's beneath you," Sylvie scolds from my other side.

While I agree with Sylvie that name calling would normally be beneath Willa and her very graceful and diplomatic public appearance, I can't help but agree with Willa on this one. Kitty is all up in Dustin's business, no doubt trying to find a way to ride his coattails. Also, name calling was Willa's go-to snark when she knew no one else was listening.

"Why? She's the freaking town bike. Everyone in Hickory Hills has taken a ride on her. Name one guy who hasn't."

"Dustin…" I whisper.

"Well, she's trying real hard to rectify that right now."

Indeed she is. Dustin isn't having it though. It's the first time all day his smile has slipped. It's brief, and I doubt anyone else even sees it, but I do. And it makes my heart sing. As does watching him hand the little slip of paper Kitty shoved in his pocket—no doubt with her number on it—to Noel the second she walks away. The face Noel makes is one of confusion and borderline disgust, making me giggle as he crumples the paper and tosses it in the trash.

"So, not trying to make anything of it, but…" Sylvie whispers as we watch the line finally start to dwindle. "Did I hear you say 'Uncle Dustin' earlier?"

"Yes," I answer, my defenses rising. "Just like Nash and Noel are uncle and you two are aunt."

"Really? Syl, has Matty ever referred to you as aunt?" Willa asks, leaning around me. I don't have to look at her to know the skepticism on her face.

"Nope!"

Busted.

"I should go make sure that Nash put the children's section back in order. He'd pulled out like half of the Geronimo Stilton books, and I'm sure they were not put away correctly." Slipping away quickly, I ignore the comments from my best friends as I make my escape. It isn't pretty, and I know I'll hear about it later, but right now, it feels like the best option.

Because I don't have a good answer. "Uncle Dustin" slipped out faster than I could think. I don't know if I was just caught up in the moment, my head and my heart overwhelmed by how seamlessly he slipped back into my life. I need to be stronger, to not let this go any further, but the second he's near me, all my resolve goes out the window, right along with Operation: Avoid Dustin. There will be no avoiding him. I just need to fortify those walls I put up.

So that's what I do. I lose myself in the tidying and reshelving of the little room off the atrium, taking a detour from the task at hand every now and then to get lost in the pages of a story I haven't read in ages. The small room looks much the same as it did when I was a kid, the same skylight brightening the room, allowing the sunshine to stream in and highlight the books. Tales of adventure, friendship, love, honesty, loyalty, and so much more. I love that this room is a safe haven for so many. A place where no matter what might be going on in the outside world, in here the Boxcar Children will always be solving mysteries, while Annie and Jack Smith are off discovering new things in their Magic Treehouse, and the Baby-Sitters Club will still be holed up in Claudia's bedroom ready to book a gig.

"Hey you."

The smooth, deep voice sends lightning through my veins, my heart skipping faster. There are very few sounds in the world that are both calming and exhilarating, but Dustin's voice is one of them.

"All done?" I ask, peering over my shoulder from my perch on the stepladder. Dustin's bright smile greets me, my heart fluttering all over again. I seriously need to have a talk with that stupid organ about how much it's betrayed me these last few days.

"Yup. Willa locked the front door too. I know the library is supposed to be open for a couple more hours, but she figured that there had been enough traffic in and out of here for one day."

He holds out a hand, helping me step down. I take it, even though I don't need it—I do take this step every day—getting lost in the chivalry of the moment. The library might have been my happy place as a child, but it was never Dustin's. His had always been my dad's garage. But that never stopped him from sitting with me for hours in here, watching as I wandered the stacks. The same look is in his ice-blue eyes now, making me feel just as special as it did back then.

"I think an exception can be made for one day. Pretty sure the whole of Knox County was here today. I saw some people I don't think I have ever seen set foot in here."

"Good. Then I did something right."

"You do a lot of things right, Dusty."

"Maybe. But I also do a lot wrong. Especially where you're concerned."

"You've already apologized; you don't need to again," I say, my voice a lot breathier than intended.

Dustin steps in closer, shrinking the already small gap between us. My breath hitches. It's suddenly very, very warm in here, the shelves around us closing in, until there is nothing left but him and me. He's close enough to touch, but I don't dare. That would be tearing down walls, not putting them up.

"I disagree. But let's discuss it over dinner, just you and me."

My heart screams yes, my head fighting back, screaming no at the same time. *Walls, Kenz...walls...*

"I don't think it's a good idea to fall back into old habits," I reply, my answer only half making sense, even to myself.

"It's not a date," he says, seeming to understand exactly what I meant, even with my poor communication. "Just two friends catching up. Like we did when you called."

"I shouldn't have done that."

"What? Called?"

I nod.

"Again, I disagree." Closing the gap even more, his hand lands on my hip, once again like it's made to fit right there. After all this time, I'm starting to believe that it is. Metal, magnet—simple as that. "Another topic for dinner. Add in that plan you were telling me about earlier, and well, we have a whole meal's worth of conversation."

I choke out a laugh, unable to resist his charm. My heart gave in long before my head, so it isn't taking much persuading. Why can't I say no to him? "Your choices for dinner are Kountry Kitchen or Little Slice of Heaven, unless you want to drive all the way down to Tifton, or up to Macon. And no, the Kountry Kitchen has not improved since you left town."

"Pizza at the Slice sounds perfect then."

"HOLY HELL, they still have this tacky wallpaper?" Dustin mutters as we walk into Little Slice of Heaven.

Tracing his finger along the outside of the cartoon slice of pizza on the dingy wallpaper, his mouth agape in a mix of amusement and horror, he looks at me as if I'm going to tell him it's all a dream.

"Of course. It's part of what makes this place so…"

"Gaudy?"

"I was going to say kitschy," I giggle. "Commit it to memory now though. I'm not sure how much longer the Slice is going to be here."

Sliding into a booth in the back corner, the one that was always our favorite in high school, I take a second to soak in the memories. Lots of big and little moments have taken place surrounded by the offbeat wallpaper and faded pleather booths.

"What happened to the Francos?"

"Nothing. They are just looking to retire, and their kids aren't interested in taking over the place. Katie is down in Orlando working for the mouse, and John is up in Ohio with some bank. Mrs. Franco told me last week that if they don't find a buyer for it by the end of the year, they're just going to close. I told Willa that Milo needs to get on it and somehow combine it with Southern Brothers, because beer and pizza, but she doesn't think he's all that interested in the idea."

"That reminds me that I need to call him, see if they would be interested in sponsoring my next tour. There's talk about getting National Beverage to do it, but I'd rather support Milo."

"I'm sure he would. His little brewing hobby has really grown over the last few years. They're the official beer of the Atlanta Rising and have some deal with a bar up in Atlanta that is associated with the team. Oh, and Willa said something about some honky-tonk in Nashville that recently opened."

"Fire Lights," he says, trying to hide a smile. "Yeah, that's mine."

"You have a bar?" I question. Willa certainly left out that detail.

"Sort of? My name is attached to it, but it's not like I do anything with it. It's really just a tourist thing, but it brings in decent money. When the whole thing came to be, I made sure that the official beer was a good one."

"Wow." I don't know what else to say, fidgeting with my fingernail trying to think of something to avoid an awkward silence.

"All the rest of Willa's brothers still doing the same stuff?"

I nod, thankful for the segue. "Yup. Milo's got Southern Brothers, and they've opened a little taproom bar that they aptly named Pour Decisions, Gus is currently over guns and ammo, Ewan is running the Booby Trap, which is what he renamed Knox County Bait and Tackle when he took it over, Huxley does paper, Jace does all the personal safety protection, and then Anton has the three Ps."

"Peaches, peanuts, and pecans," he says with me. "You're gonna have to write that down for me. I never remember who does what, and I've been asked about their guns a bunch."

"I'll text it to you."

"Or you could just call again."

My cheeks flush instantly. Shit, why did he have to go there? Twisting in the booth, I look for a waitress, Mr. or Mrs. Franco, someone who could come and distract us right now. Anything so I don't have to talk about that call.

"Why are you so embarrassed about that call?" he asks.

"It…because…" I stammer.

Sucking in a deep breath, I try to find the words. An excuse that would be believable. The only thing I can think of is the truth though. Dustin is looking at me, his eyes sincere, melting my insides. I need to be honest with him.

"Because I miss you. I heard your song on the radio, and I wanted to hear your voice. Your real voice. And I know how silly that sounds—"

"It doesn't. Because I miss you too."

Forget melting, my insides are now just one giant puddle of goo. He misses me?

Time for a change of subject. I cannot—will not—get lost in the idea that Dustin Wilder misses me.

"How hungry are you? After standing all day, I'm sure you're starving," I ramble. "Let me find the Francos."

Sliding out of the booth, I stand quickly, every inch of me an anxious mess. I need an escape. Except there isn't one. Because right in the space where I need to step for said escape is Jake Wright.

Oh, fuck.

"Whoa, Kenzie, slow down."

"Jake, hi!"

The extreme pitch to my voice could probably break glass, earning me a funny look from Jake. Thankfully, that only lasts a second before he turns to Dustin.

"Sorry to interrupt your date," he says. I open my mouth to correct him, but nothing comes out, leaving him to continue. "I meant to get over to the thing you were doing today, but the grocery was slammed and I couldn't get away. But I have two nieces who recently moved from here to Tifton and will be bummed if they find out they missed a chance to get your autograph."

OMG, this is not happening...

Dustin smiles. "No problem. I don't have anything on me, but I can get something to Kenz to get to you. Or, if they'll be here for the festival, we can get them backstage or something."

"I'll double-check with my sister, but I'm pretty sure she's planning to bring them, so that'd be great. Thanks, man. I'll leave you two to your dinner. Have you ordered yet? Or should I have Mrs. Franco send over the usual?"

"Yeah…errr…sure, thanks," I manage, lowering myself back into the booth. Jake nods, heading back to the counter without another word.

I bite down on my lip, wishing I could disappear. Nothing like being the hot mess express while out to dinner with your insanely sexy, literally a superstar, ex-boyfriend.

"You want to just die right now, don't you?" he asks, holding back his laughter. I can see it in his eyes though. He's always been able to read me better than anyone else.

"Yup, sure do," I admit.

"Because your boyfriend thinks we're on a date or because something else?"

"Jake isn't my boyfriend." We're on the honesty train,

right? Might as well go full speed ahead. "We've gone out a bunch, but it's always been super casual. Mostly if one of us is just looking for something to do."

"So you do each other?"

"Dustin Randall Wilder!"

We both burst into laughter, my whole body heating up with embarrassment. I can't believe he just said that. By the smirk on his face, he can't believe it either. My heart feels light though, laughing with him like this. Just like we used to. Maybe I did need this.

"Sorry, that was crass. And not any of my business."

It isn't his business. Still, I want to let him in, confide in him all the things I feel, or rather *don't feel*, where Jake Wright is concerned. How none of it has been the same as it was with him. Except that is not a conversation to be had over pizza. Or at all.

"For real though, I want to know about what's going on here. About everything you're doing with the library. About why it's so hard for you to accept that this town wants to help you."

"I told you; we have a plan. There are other things here that need the money more."

"Kenz, your dad has given more to Hickory Hills than anyone I know. Let Hickory Hills take care of you for once."

Defiance rises in me. "No. The robotics team needs it more than we do. Dad is going to sell part of the farm. The boy cousins have been looking at expanding, so if he sells that back portion to them, that money should cover his treatments."

Dustin's eyes widen. I can see his brain working it all out, realization hitting him.

Hideaway Hill. Our spot.

We sit in silence for a long stretch, emotions getting in the way of everything we want to say. Dustin slides a hand over mine, gently squeezing it. It's a comforting gesture, filling all the spaces and cracks that words can't quite reach. For as awkward and tense as this silence is, the rest of the restaurant buzzing around us, there's a comfort to it. An understanding that could only happen between Dustin and me. One that my heart soaks in, having missed this more than I want to admit.

Once the pizza shows up, our conversation starts back up again, this time flowing easy, as if I hadn't dropped the bomb. I catch him up on all the town gossip, share stories from the library, and talk about all the things I know the twins conveniently leave out when they talk to him. He tells me about life on the road, the new songs he's working on, and all the work that goes into recording an album. Things I never would have thought about. We laugh until we're in tears, falling into an old rhythm, like we're simply Dustin and Kenzie again. Two kids hanging out, eating pizza.

"Here's what I've always wanted to know. How do you wash your clothes?"

"In a washing machine. Same as everyone else," he replies.

"Ha-ha, I mean on the road."

"A washing machine. There's this service, Rockstar Laundry, that will come collect it while we're at a venue and then someone runs to the laundromat for you. We use that sometimes, but when possible I prefer to do it myself."

"Are you that picky about how your clothes get washed?"

"No,"—he shakes his head with a laugh—"I just get kinda weirded out about who's touching my skivvies."

I bark out a loud laugh that bounces off the walls, unable to control myself. Dustin laughs right along with me, making me feel less alone at finding this so funny.

"I see that some things never change," Mr. Franco says, ambling over. "You two are still closing the place down."

"We're what?" I twist in my seat, looking around. Sure

enough, Dustin and I are the only two people here. When did that happen?

Scrambling up from the booth, Dustin slips his hand in mine, leading me to the front door. I know I should object, but my bucket is too full right now to do anything but enjoy it.

"You don't have to go home, but you can't stay here," Mr. Franco says with a wink, locking up behind us.

"I can't believe we sat there all night," I say, swinging our conjoined hands.

"Oh, I can," Dustin replies. "Old habits die hard."

I sigh, tightening my grip on his, our fingers interlocking. The cool air surrounds us as we make the short walk back to the library from A Little Slice of Heaven, making me wish we had farther to go. I don't want this to end. Dustin is right; old habits do die hard, which is why I had told him I didn't want to slip back into them.

That's tomorrow's problem though. Making sure there isn't a repeat of all this can wait until then. Right here, right now, I'm going to revel in just how good this feels.

"Are you okay to drive home?" he asks, stopping at my car door.

"I am."

"I was kinda hoping the answer would be no, so I had to drive you."

"How would I get to work tomorrow if my car were still here?"

"Guess I'd just have to pick you up for breakfast too then."

I swoon, Dustin's perfect answer locked and loaded. Of course it is.

"I had a great time tonight, Kenz," he whispers.

"Me too."

We stand there for a moment, anticipation hanging in the air. It's like we're teenagers again, neither of us wanting to make the first move, desperately waiting for the other to do something. Only difference is, we know how much trouble that will cause. Just how much my heart will hurt when he leaves again.

"Night," I say, breaking the silence. Unlocking my car, I barely get the driver door open when Dustin spins me around.

His ice-blue eyes darken, his lips upturned into a smirk. Carefully tucking a wisp of hair behind my ear, he cups my jaw, running his thumb along my cheek, butterflies taking flight inside me. My whole body is on fire, desperate for him to act. To do what I don't have the courage to.

I don't have to wait long though. Half a breath later, his lips lightly graze mine in a soft, gentle, chaste kiss.

Pulling back just as swiftly as he'd leaned in, Dustin steps back, hands dropping to his sides. My pulse doesn't know whether to speed up or slow down, my lips tingling from the brief contact. I can barely think—the only thing rushing through my brain is how I want more.

"Dusty..."

"Shhhh," he says, pressing his forehead to mine. "I'm going to do that for real, promise. Just not tonight. But, Kenz, when I do, I promise, it's going to be the best fucking kiss of your entire life."

Another chaste press of his lips to my forehead, and he turns to go, leaving me pressed up against my open car door, head still dazed.

Because what Dustin Wilder doesn't know is *that* right there might have been the best kiss of my life, and it hadn't lasted but two seconds.

Forget walls. I'm going to need to dig a moat.

CHAPTER TEN

KENZIE

DUSTIN WILDER IS A COUNTRY STAR. I need to remember that.

It doesn't matter how much fun I had last night. That we felt like Dustin and Kenzie again, like nothing had ever changed. Like Eric Valentine never walked into our lives, turning my world upside down with a single flick of his wrist.

Eric Valentine had walked into our lives though. And that stupid wrist flick, complete with a three-inch piece of cardstock, had been the proverbial butterfly flapping its wings and causing a tidal wave.

A tidal wave that turned him from Dustin Wilder, easygoing, small-town boy, to Dustin Wild, country crooner with a megawatt smile and a voice as smooth as whiskey. Topping the charts song after song after song.

A fucking star.

No more kisses...

That's easy enough to say. I've been repeating it to myself all day as if it's my new mantra. No more kisses. Too bad my mind and my body aren't on the same page about this. Because my body aches to feel those strong hands on me again—holding me tight, pressed up against his hard body—in a way that only Dustin can. My body responding in a way that it only does with him.

My heart, however, is a lost cause. That stupid organ never stood a chance.

My lips still tingle from the gentle caress of his. The teasing touch followed by a promise so zealous there was no escaping it. No forgetting it. I can't let it happen though.

Right? Right. I can't. If I ever want to recover from this, hope to have a chance at moving on, then there can be no more. The only thing I have to offer Dustin is friendship.

And friendship doesn't involve kissing.

Dustin Wilder kissed me...O.M.F.G...

My heart starts to race, all of it hitting me once again. Dustin. The date. The kiss. Oh, that kiss. Seriously, how was something that was over so quick so damn powerful? I need to sit down. I need something to distract me. Anything that will take my mind away from what happened.

Nonfiction. That will do. There is without a doubt something in the nonfiction section that will take me away from the only thing I have managed to think about all day. Yes, even through story time, because—as would be my luck—today we got to the chapter in *The Princess Bride* where Westley and Buttercup profess their love for one another. Which only led to Dustin's promise from last night replaying in my mind again.

I don't know whose bright idea it was to have the library's summer theme be favorite movies that were books first, but they should be fired.

Oh wait, that was me. It was *my* bright idea.

"Kenz?" Sylvie's voice calls out. I jump, caught off guard by the sound, so stuck in my own head that I didn't hear the door open.

"Yeah?"

"You ready…" her voice trails off as I come into view, rounding the corner of the tall shelf I was hidden behind. "*Guns, Germs, and Steel*? Isn't that the book Dustin gave your dad that one year for Christmas?"

I look at the book in my hand, the memory registering. Shit. It absolutely is. Damn it, I can't even pick out a distraction without somehow subconsciously involving him. I need to find my paddles and get the hell out of shit creek, or else.

"Just reshelving," I answer as nonchalantly as I can.

Sylvie nods. "You ready?"

"Ready? For what?"

"To head to Rocky Pond. For the bonfire. Noel sent a text this morning."

I shake my head, no idea what she's talking about. Then again, my phone is turned off, in my purse, locked away in my desk drawer, all so I could spend the day avoiding texts. From Dustin. From Sylvie and Willa. From anyone who might have seen us at Little Slice of Heaven last night and wants to know about my date with Dustin. That wasn't a date. Just two friends catching up. Those were the words he'd used.

Before he kissed me. And promised to do it again.

Shit, I am such a mess…

Scrambling behind the counter, I mutter something about not having checked my phone all day, quickly switching it on. The trills and beeps start almost immediately.

NOEL

Bonfire tonight. Usual spot. Boys will grab
the beers if the girls bring the s'mores. Deal?

NASH

Dustin will bring the guitar

DUSTIN

Maybe

SYLVIE

Change some of those beers to seltzers and
I'll upgrade the Hershey's to Andes mints

NOEL

SOLD!

WILLA

I have a late client call, but will be there as
soon as I can

NASH

Reschedule it. We're more important 😊

WILLA

Only in your mind, Nash...

Right below the group text thread was one from Dustin, sent only to me.

DUSTIN:

Morning beautiful. I had a great time last
night, hope you did too.

Looking forward to seeing you tonight.

My insides melt, eyes glued to his words, pulse kicking up a notch. Stupid ex-boyfriend making it damn near impossible to be rational. The only thing still keeping my feet on the ground is the memory of just how much it hurt when I realized he wasn't coming back. That it was over between us, without so much as a goodbye.

There's something for you to write a song about, Dusty...

"So, bonfire," I say, finally looking up.

"I already hit up Wright's. Graham crackers, marshmallows, Hershey's, Andes mints, and skewers all procured."

"Peanut butter cups?"

"Peanut butter cups?" she repeats, confused.

"Dustin likes his s'mores with peanut butter cups."

"How do I not remember that?"

I shrug, not sure why I remember it. Guess it's one of those things you never forget about a person. No matter how much I wish I could.

"I have some," I answer, opening the very bottom drawer of my desk, pulling out the emergency stash I keep on hand. Because you never know when a situation is going to call for chocolate. It's a small package, with only two pieces in there, but it's better than nothing.

Tossing it in my purse, I sling it over my shoulder, lock my computer, and follow Sylvie out the door. Ten minutes later we're climbing out of her small sedan, parked right in line with Noel's truck and Old Blue, the shoulder barely wide enough to accommodate the vehicles. I inhale deeply, letting the calmness of the trees surround me. So many happy memories are housed in these woods, in the small clearing just before the pond that the twins had picked as our spot when we were in junior high. All these years later it is still our spot, even if we don't make it out here as much as we used to.

The sound of gravel under tires fills the air, Willa pulling up right behind us. Slipping out of her SUV, she looks wrinkled, like she's thrown on whatever she happened to find in a pile on her bedroom floor.

"You okay?" I ask.

"Why wouldn't I be?"

"Because you look like you rolled out of bed," Sylvie answers, stealing the words right out of my mouth.

"I ran home and grabbed something quick so I didn't come out here in my heels and skirt, that's all."

I don't believe her, but now is not the time to bring that up. Willa has a secret. She's entitled to that, I suppose. It's not like I share everything. But whatever this is, it's big. I can feel it. Or maybe I just really, really want it to be, to take the focus off me.

"Truth time, Kenzie," Willa says. So much for taking the focus off me. "Operation: Avoid Dustin, still a go? Or has it been nixed?"

"Considering we are a three-minute walk from a bonfire with him, isn't it a little late to be asking this?" Sylvie remarks.

"We could ditch. Or, we can adjust and make it Operation: Minimal Contact. We're in a group, so we can run interference. Depends how that date went last night." Willa waggles her eyebrows, a sly smile taking over. So that's what she was really after.

"It wasn't a date. We went to the Slice."

"Isn't that where your first date was?" Sylvie asks.

It was. One more thing I spent the day trying not to think about.

"Bonfire." My voice is firm as I point to the opening in the trees that leads to our spot. I am not talking about this.

Only, I want to talk about it. I want to tell them everything. I need to.

Willa and Sylvie crash into me as I stop dead in the middle of the trail. Sucking in a deep breath, I spin around, letting the words tumble out.

"Dustin kissed me. Last night. Up against my car. It was quick. Sweet. Perfect. Then he promised to do it again. For real. And make it perfect. Which would be hard, since that one was already…perfect…"

They both just stare at me, their surprise clear even in the dwindling daylight around us.

"And before you ask, no, I don't know how I feel about it. Because I know that it would be a colossally stupid idea to do it, or even entertain it. Because he broke my heart once, and he's a fucking rockstar, who we know is leaving again soon but—"

"But you want to," Willa says, finishing my sentence.

I nod slowly.

"So, what do you need from us?" Sylvie asks.

"Don't let me kiss him. Or maybe do. I dunno."

Taking my hands, Sylvie squeezes them, the simple sign of support more comforting than she can know. I feel so all over the place, and her touch grounds me, stopping me from flying off to God knows where.

"Want to know what I think?" she asks, not bothering to pause for an answer. "Kiss him. Let it all play out. Have some fun, enjoy whatever happens, knowing he's going to leave. So much was left up in the air before, but maybe this is your chance for a goodbye fling. Get him out of your system once and for all."

"Who are you and what did you do with Sylvie?" Willa asks.

"You disagree?"

"No, not at all. But you're the cautious one. And here you are stealing all my lines about throwing said caution to the wind. Now I have nothing else to contribute to this conversation."

I sputter out a laugh. These two. The universe knew what it was doing bringing them into my life.

Let it all play out. I could do that. Just because he said he was going to kiss me again doesn't mean he's going to. For all I know he was just as caught up in the moment as I was. Now, a whole day later, he's had the chance to clear his head and realize that it was a mistake. I'm probably worrying over nothing.

"You're right."

"We know," Willa replies.

"Ladies!" Nash's voice booms, his heavy footsteps preceding him up the trail. "Sorority meeting almost over, 'cause we got a bonfire to get to."

"You're just getting here?" I ask. Running through the lineup of cars parked at the trailhead, it occurs to me his truck wasn't there, just Noel's and Dustin's. I'd just assumed that Nash was with them. That was odd.

"I had something I had to *do*."

"Something or someone?" Willa snarks.

"Jealous?"

Willa rolls her eyes, pushing past me.

"Fly's down," Sylvie says, gesturing to Nash's groin.

Having the good sense to act embarrassed, Nash fixes himself. Once he's put back together, he throws one arm over my shoulder, the other over Sylvie's, leading us the rest of the way. A small but crackling fire greets us, the familiar, comforting smell filling my nostrils. My insides relax immediately, the warm embrace of beloved memories rushing over me.

Surveying the scene, it's hard not to let myself slip into thinking that everything is as it should be. Because it is. The six of us together, nestled back in the woods, along the shore of Rocky Pond, a night full of laughter and fun ahead. It's the kind of reunion that dreams are made of. Dreams that I'd long let go of, resigning myself to the fact that this would never be again. And not just this, but any future versions of this, where spouses and children were dragged along with us, the party growing bigger as our lives evolved, the same core group of us never wavering.

"Anyone think about dinner? Do we have real food?" Willa asks, scrounging through one of the Wright's bags.

"S'mores are dinner," Nash answers, his tone incredulous.

Without looking up, Willa flips him the bird, continuing on her search. Dustin snickers from over my shoulder, the sound making the warm fuzzy feeling inside me grow. Funny how something so simple can be so comforting.

"There's some popcorn in the same bag as the beer," Noel tells her. He's already settled into his usual spot, close to the fire with his back to the pond, directly across from where the trail leads in. Always the defender, he'd claimed the spot the first bonfire we had in high school and had never moved, always saying he wanted to be the first to know if we had intruders. It's valiant of him, but it's been almost fifteen years and I'm still not sure what kind of "intruders" he's expecting.

Following Noel's lead, I park myself on the large fallen oak tree to Noel's left. One of the guys tossed a blanket over it, making it a lot more comfortable than sitting directly on the rough bark.

"My spot still open?" Dustin asks, pointing to the portion of unoccupied blanket next to me.

"Of course," I tell him, unable to hold back my smile. "Some things never change, as you can see."

I nod toward the rest of the group. Willa and Sylvie have taken the two other camp chairs across from us, Nash still on his feet with his back to the woods. Never one to really sit, he might crouch down for a bit, but he'll spend most of the night pacing, working off whatever energy he somehow manages to have left from the day. Patting the open spot, I signal for Dustin to sit. Despite my mixed feelings about last night, I want him there. I want to feel the heat of his body, only a few inches from me if I need anything. More than that, I want to feel the rush again of wondering when—if—he'll reach over and take my hand in his or wrap an arm around me. There's a giddiness in me I can't describe, and I'm loving every second of it.

I don't have to wait long though. Dustin takes his seat, grabbing my hand almost instantly. It does not disappoint. The warmth of his skin touching mine sets fire to the rest of me—my insides feeling like it's July instead of September. The smile he gives me makes my heart skip a beat, as if we're sharing a silent secret while the rest of the world disappears.

"I should have gotten you a drink before I sat," he whispers, eyes locked on mine. "That wasn't very gentlemanly of me."

"It's fine." A giggle bubbles up, escaping from me like I'm still in junior high. "I can grab my own."

"Nonsense. Besides, I should mind my manners now, in hopes you'll forgive me later when I throw them out the window and get all kinds of ungentlemanly." Dustin winks, squeezing my hand as he pushes up, heading over to the cooler.

My entire body lights up brighter than the strip in Vegas. Damn it, I'm going to need that drink, if for no other reason than to cool down, my mind running wild with all the things he could mean by "ungentlemanly." And just how bad I want to experience them. All of them.

Returning with drinks and supplies for s'mores, Dustin settles back into his spot. I get to work on preparing the graham cracker while he roasts the marshmallows, excitement flowing through me to surprise him with the candy. A few minutes later he turns to me, two perfectly seared, gooey delights ready for assembly. Smashing them between the prepared crackers, I giggle again, enjoying how good this all feels.

"Is this…" Dustin exclaims, biting into the s'more I hand him. "A peanut butter cup! You remembered?"

"Of course! Not the kind of thing a girl forgets."

"Damn, I haven't had one of these like this in…well, probably since the last time we did this. I could kiss you for remembering."

My cheeks flush with the mention of kissing, a coy look taking over my face. I can't hide either. Dustin sees it too quickly, winking again.

"I meant what I said last night, Kenz," he whispers, hand landing on my thigh and squeezing gently.

Sucking in a deep breath, I open my mouth to respond, but am cut off by Nash.

"Okay, standard rules apply! Truth or dare…none of that double dare or promise to repeat crap. If you don't want to answer your truth, then you have to do your dare. If you don't want to do your dare, you have to answer your truth. Nice and simple," Nash explains.

"I haven't had enough to drink yet to do any of that. This is still number one," Willa snarks, holding up her can.

"Then drink up, princess! And hope the coin lands in your favor."

"I thought we could chug if we didn't want to do either," Sylvie says, her tone somewhere between a statement and a question.

"Only if you give me your keys," Noel replies. Without hesitation, Sylvie reaches into her pocket, tossing her keys at him.

"She still a chicken?" Dustin asks, quiet enough for only me to hear.

"More so than the rest of us, but she's opened up a lot over the last few years. At this point I think it's more about advertising that she has the out so Willa doesn't try and purposefully back her into a corner about answering something."

"Heads is alphabetical and tails is birthday, from there it's your choice who's next. Any objections?" Nash asks.

"Better fucking be heads," Willa mutters, taking a long drink.

Nash flips the coin into the air, all of us holding our breath to see how it lands. We've played the same way for forever, the two options being the only fair way we could decide who got stuck going first. Dustin came first alphabetically, while Willa was the oldest.

"Heads it is! You got lucky, princess." Willa snarls, making the rest of us laugh. "So, Dustin...truth or dare?"

"Truth."

CHAPTER ELEVEN

DUSTIN

WELL, that was a stupid answer.

I should have said dare. Started this game off with a bang. Instead, I'm now stuck answering whatever off-the-wall, asinine, designed to embarrass the fuck out of me question that Nash pulls out of his ass. And I know that's exactly where he's pulling it from. Guy's been my best friend for more than twenty years; he already knows everything about me. Anything that matters at least.

Which is why whatever is about to come out of his mouth is going to be dangerous. Seriously fucking dangerous.

I feel Kenzie shift next to me, the heat from her body waning for a few seconds, returning as she leans back into me. My hand is still resting on her thigh, closer to her knee than I would really like, but one thing at a time. And by that I mean that's how I'm figuring this whole thing out too—one thing at a time, flying by the seat of my pants.

Because right now, the only thing I know for sure is that I've never needed anything more than I needed to kiss her last night. And it was fucking perfect.

"What was the last thing you looked up on your phone?"

Nash asks, a sly look on his face. Like he's about to catch me out in something. "Incognito mode counts!"

The last thing I looked up on my phone? That's what he wants to know? Fucking Nash.

Still, a wave of relief washes over me. No thanks to the stupid question, but to the fact that I didn't need a search bar for what I went looking for last night. The picture I'd secretly grabbed of Kenzie yesterday while she was reading was already saved to my favorites folder. Perfectly framed by the tall shelves of the young adult section, wisps of her chestnut hair falling out of her braid, her eyes trained on the page as she got lost in a story I'm sure she knows by heart. The faint smile pulling at the corner of her lips was more than enough to make my dick react, much less the way her dress clung to her breasts, making me want to get reacquainted with them. She was beyond beautiful in that moment, my heart aching as I committed it to memory. It was a scene I never wanted to forget.

Truth be told though, I didn't need the photo for what I was about to get up to. The sound of her giggle over pizza, the feel of her soft curves against me in the parking lot, and the brief press of her lips against mine were more than enough to fuel my fantasies. Talk about just like old times—lying in my childhood bedroom, cock in hand, stroking furiously, Kenzie filling my mind.

"What do you put on peaches so they don't brown," I answer, a smug confidence filling me. None of them are expecting that answer.

"What?"

"What do you put on peaches so they don't brown," I repeat.

"You did not!" Nash exclaims.

"Lemon juice," Sylvie says. "The ascorbic acid stops them from oxidizing. Basic science."

"That is not what you last searched!" Nash says.

"It is." I laugh, pulling out my phone. "Mama was cutting up peaches this morning for something she's making and didn't want them to brown before whatever she's doing with them. So she asked if I knew, and I didn't, so I looked it up."

"Bullshit."

Kenzie leans over, her shoulder resting against mine as she takes my phone from me. Seemingly without thinking she inputs my passcode, the screen unlocking with a soft click. I like that she didn't hesitate or question if the number was still the same. A number that I hope still means as much to her as it does me. "It's not. I'm looking right at it. That's the last thing he searched."

Vindicated.

"At least it wasn't himself," Noel mutters.

"No, that was the second to last thing he searched," Kenzie replies, ratting me out. She holds up my phone, turning it so he can see the screen.

Noel lets out a loud guffaw, the sound cutting through the night air. I grab my phone back from her, sticking out my tongue, resorting to playground tactics to express my displeasure. Not that I'm all that upset about it. It's exactly what I would expect out of Kenzie, or any of my friends. Her playing along and giving me a hard time means we really are on solid ground. But more than that, she's still touching me. What started with just our shoulder when she grabbed my phone has turned into a lean, her upper body angling toward mine, my hand still firmly resting on her thigh. No complaints here.

It might just be time for some payback though.

"Kenzie, truth or dare?"

She pretends to think for a bit, but I know my girl. She's going for truth. And I know exactly what I'm going to ask.

"Dare."

Didn't see that coming...

"I dare you…" I trail off, trying to buy some time. I was not prepared for this. If it was one of the twins, I could easily think of a dozen stupid things to make them do. But with her, I have to make it something good. "Send a dirty text to the last person who texted you."

"Seriously?" Her eyes go wide and I can see her cheeks start to flush even in the dim light of the fire. It's the cutest thing I think I've ever seen.

"Only caveat is if your last text was your dad. Then you can move down to your second to last text."

"Fine."

Narrowing her eyes at me as she accepts the challenge, she whips out her phone, her fingers flying over the screen so fast I can't make out what she's typing. She hits send, and before I can lean over to make sure she fulfilled her end of the bargain, my phone chimes.

The whole group stops, realization hitting everyone at the same time. Kenzie's eyes darken, still glued to mine. My dick twitches, mind running wild with possibilities. All of them make my blood heat up, lust fueling my next move.

KENZIE

I miss the feel of you inside me

Oh, fuuuuuck...

"Well?" Willa asks expectantly.

"It's sufficiently dirty."

"That's all you're going to say?"

I nod once. There is no way in hell I'm sharing that. With anyone, ever. Although, on second thought, I might need to discuss it more with Kenzie later. In detail.

"Noel, truth or dare?" Kenzie asks, not missing a beat.

"Truth."

"Last time you lied."

"This morning. I told Mrs. Phillips that I got an overship-ment of topsoil so I could take care of her flowerbeds at no charge."

"You lied to Mrs. Phillips?"

"You didn't say it has to be a malicious lie," he points out.

"I don't care about the intent, I'm just amazed you had the balls to lie to Mrs. Phillips."

"Dude," Nash chimes in. "She's gonna have your nuts if she finds out. She hates you not letting her pay. And I don't care that she's ninety-five years old, that woman is scary. She also can't tell the difference between us, so now I'm worried about my own balls."

The whole group laughs, Noel simply shrugging, zero shits given that the town matriarch—and mother to the current fire chief—would indeed castrate him for such special treatment. She is a no-nonsense woman, even in her advanced age, and takes no prisoners when it comes to handing out a piece of her mind. I'm almost sad that I'm going to miss her making such a discovery.

The game continues, Noel tossing it to Willa, who chooses a truth. Her answer turns into background noise though as Kenzie leans into me more, her hand falling to the inside of my knee. The contact sends a rush through me, making me wonder just how cozy we can get. Based on that text, her mind isn't far from mine, but I still don't want to make any assumptions. It was a dare after all, so it's possible she didn't really mean it.

"Do you want another s'more?" I ask her quietly, not wanting to disrupt the game.

Twisting, she looks up at me, those perfectly brown eyes filled with something I can't name. "If you do. There is one more peanut butter cup with your name on it."

"I love that you remembered that."

"I won't lie; it was a last-minute thing. I didn't even see

Noel's text about the bonfire until Sylvie showed up at the library asking if I was ready to go. These were from my secret stash."

"Hold on. You dug into the secret stash so that I could have my favorite s'mores?" I verify, pulling out the skewer with the marshmallow on it. Kenzie nods, the one corner of her mouth coyly tilting upward. Putting the sandwich together, she hands me mine, taking a big bite of her own. "Well, now I feel special."

"Is that all you feel?" she asks, mouth full of gooey goodness.

A small piece of melted confection is stuck to her lip, my entire body fighting back the urge to kiss it off of her. If I thought my dick was ready to go after her text, sitting here as she takes another big bite of her s'more is only upping the ante. Fuck, is she sexy.

"Where you're concerned, Kenz, it's only the start. You have no idea all the things you're making me feel right this minute."

"Yeah? What else?"

"For starters…" Leaning in, I lightly brush my lips against hers, even softer than last night. I nip at her bottom lip, the sugar left there exploding on my tongue. That marshmallow has nothing on Kenzie though, her own sweet taste taking over quickly, minimum contact or not. "You had some marshmallow stuck to your lip."

"Thanks."

"Any time."

I run my thumb across my bottom lip, my calloused fingertips a sharp contrast to the softness of Kenzie's skin. Her kiss is everything I didn't realize I needed until this moment, a spark igniting something in me that had been extinguished along the way. Same as last night, it was short and sweet, but so fucking powerful. I need to kiss her for real. Make good on the promise I made as I said goodnight.

This still wasn't the place though. For more reasons than just my personal knowledge that I won't be able to stop with one kiss. No, I'm going to kiss Kenzie until we can't breathe anymore.

Wrapping my arm around her, I tug her in, wanting to revel in the closeness. Our friends are deep into conversation about something—Willa's hand animatedly flailing about, Nash rolling his eyes in response—all of it still background noise to the sweet song that is surrounding us. A melody only we can hear, made just for us, accented by the beat of our hearts.

At least until the trill of Kenzie's phone interrupts us.

Kenzie bolts out of my arms, popping up off the log. As she frantically taps away at her phone, her face morphs into worry.

"What's the matter?" Noel asks, turning his attention to us.

"It's the library alarm," she says, voice laced with panic. "We locked up, right, Sylvie? We must have. Or else the alarm wouldn't be going off. Oh my God, this has never happened."

"Don't panic," I tell her. It's an empty statement, since she's already doing just that, but I try to calm her regardless. "We can go check."

"I...I didn't drive..."

"You can take my car," Sylvie says.

Noel reaches into his pocket for the keys, but I hold up my hand, stopping him. He nods, knowing exactly what I'm saying.

"I'll go with you," I tell her.

"No, you should stay. Enjoy the night."

Fear and worry are radiating off her, even as she tries to play it cool. Her concern about me enjoying my time here is appreciated, but there is no way I'm going to enjoy anything if I'm worried about her running off. Hell, let's not lie—what I'm enjoying most about all this is *her*. I fight the urge to haul her into me in an effort to comfort her, reminding myself that is not going to help.

"You're not going alone, Kenz," Noel says.

"Absolutely not," Nash adds.

"One of the twins can come," she insists. "Tomorrow is sound check; you have a big day, Dusty. You should relax tonight."

Neither Nash nor Noel budge, both of them knowing that I won't back down on this. They wouldn't dream of trying to step in either.

"I can do sound check in my sleep. I'm going with you."

Taking her hand, I squeeze gently in an attempt to soothe her worry and let her know my escorting her isn't optional. She swallows hard, her eyes still full of panic, tightening her grip on mine, her own silent acknowledgment. I throw a goodbye over my shoulder, not wasting any more time, and lead her to my truck. The cool night air settles around us now that we're away from the fire, and Kenzie shivers a bit.

"There's a sweatshirt under the seat if you want it," I tell her as she's climbing into Old Blue.

"I'm…I'm fine. Just worried. What if something is really the matter, Dusty?"

"I'm sure it's nothing. But we'll be there in five minutes for you to make sure."

"We're ten minutes outside of town."

"Five minutes, beautiful. Promise."

CHAPTER TWELVE

KENZIE

Five minutes.

That's two and a half times as long as it took Secretariat to run the Kentucky Derby, but still only half the time it normally takes to get to the center of town from Rocky Pond. And just like he promised, all the time Dustin needed to get us there.

My heart is pounding at the same speed I imagine Secretariat's was after his race as Old Blue turns into the parking lot on two wheels. My heart has been in my throat since my phone went off, my mind wild with all the things that could possibly go wrong. And let me tell you, it's a really long list.

Thankfully, the building is still standing, and from first glance, it is in one piece. There's no damage that I can see. That does little to settle my nerves, however. If there'd been any major external damage, the fire department across the street would have seen or heard something. Instead, whatever tripped our sorry excuse for an alarm system must be internal.

I throw open the truck door, hurling myself from the

vehicle before Dustin even has it in park. I can hear his voice calling after me as I run toward the door, quickly drowned out by the high-pitched beeping of the alarm. That horrible noise is all I can think about, wanting—needing—to make it stop. My hands are shaky as I try to punch in the code to unarm the building, but I'm trembling too much, causing me to mispunch the number.

The beeping continues, seeming to pick up pace and rise in pitch as I mispunch again, and then a third time. No, no, no, this isn't happening. The walls of the already small atrium close in on me, all my senses on high alert. The ground beneath me feels uneven and unstable, what I imagine quicksand would feel like. Or maybe that's just me and my own unsteadiness as the world seemingly crashes down around me.

"Oh five one oh?" Dustin's smooth, silky voice asks from behind me, his steady hand covering mine. A rush of relief rolls throughout me, Dustin's closeness making me feel safe. My legs still feel like they could collapse right out from under me, but I'm confident he'd catch me if they did.

"Oh five two five."

"Two five?"

I nod. He punches in the number, but instead of the three quick beeps that should follow the last number, the alarm continues at its current pace. Fuck, now what?

"You…you don't think we were hacked, do you?" I ask, my voice trembling. The idea sounds crazy in my head—and even more so out loud—but it's the only reason I can imagine that the code wouldn't work. The same code that I used to lock up.

Glancing back at the alarm, his face twisted in discomfort from the sound, Dustin squints at it. "This thing looks old," he shouts. "What services does it connect to?"

"None."

"None of the locals?"

"No, none at all."

Dustin glares at me, the "you've got to be fucking kidding me" look on his face unmistakable, even in this dim light. Stepping around me and letting out a groan, he turns back to the alarm, smashing it with his hand.

"Dusty!"

Pulling back, he repeats the motion, the heel of his hand landing squarely on the discolored, off-white box, the blaring finally ceasing. My ears are thankful, but my heart is now worried about his hand. He has sound check tomorrow, and then has to play the festival on Saturday. Now is not the time to be busting up required appendages.

His anger and frustration isn't fully resolved though. Wrapping his fingers around the hard plastic, he flexes his wrists, yanking back on the box. The unit separates from the wall with a lot more ease than I was expecting, dangling from nothing more than a few wires.

"Well, that answers my question as to why Landon's truck is still across the way at the fire house and why the sheriff didn't beat us to the scene," Dustin mutters. "How old is this thing?"

"Old."

"Right. We're getting you a new one. One that actually connects to the Internet so that it alerts first responders."

"This one connected to the Internet!" I defend. Sure, I don't know exactly how it all works, but I do know I had to have Wi-Fi installed, since Mrs. Cassum didn't trust the Internet, just so I could get alerts from this system. A system that had been installed long before I was in charge here. Now that I think about it, I don't have any idea when it was installed. "That's how I got the text."

"You need a better one."

"That's not in the town's budget."

"It's in mine," he retorts, typing away on his cell phone. "And before you object, it's too late. My manager is already working on it."

I sigh. My pulse is still racing, all of me on edge but thankful for the brief moment of distraction. Not to mention over the moon thankful that he's with me. I should probably be more upset with him for swooping in to save the day with his money, having his people handle it all for him. But the guy did just punch an alarm system for me. And the swoon factor from that outranks everything else right now.

"I just want you to be safe, Kenzie."

Next level of swoon factor achieved.

"So you think it was just a faulty alarm system?"

"I do," he answers, stepping into me. "But we can go look around if it'll make you feel better."

I nod, unsure if I really feel the need to check the library, or if I just don't want this moment to end. The heat of his hand on my lower back is soothing, my tense muscles relaxing from his touch.

"One question first."

"What?"

"Oh five two five?" His brows knit in confusion, clearly trying way too hard to figure out why the library code is different than his phone code. Biting down on my bottom lip, I look away, holding in a giggle.

The answer is simple—he might have taken me on our first date on May tenth, but he didn't work up the nerve to kiss me until two weeks later, the evening of the Memorial Day parade on May twenty-fifth.

"You'll remember," I answer, my tone a lot coyer than I'm actually feeling. Yup, I don't want this moment to end.

Darkness greets us as we step into the main part of the library, the large open space that held more visitors than I had ever seen yesterday. I can still hear the voices and conversations of the group, everyone cheerful and excited. I loved seeing the place so busy, but my inner—or not so inner—librarian had to remind herself multiple times not to ask everyone to quiet down. Silence was not golden then.

It isn't now either, taunting us through the dimness. The only light to be found is the bright green from the exit signs, which do little more than create a glow around them. I make a mental note to add security lights to the budget request for next year, but much like a new alarm, already knowing that if I really want them, they are going to have to be privately funded, a.k.a come out of my own pocket.

Pulling out his phone, Dustin turns on the flashlight, a finger pressed to his lips, silently shushing me. I have to bite back a laugh. Who's the librarian now? He must sense my reaction, his own chiseled features melting into amusement.

"I can turn on the lights, you know," I whisper.

"Where's the fun in that?"

I might have been frightened out of my mind a few minutes ago, but my heart is happy that he's the one here with me. That we are getting this moment. Part of me still feels guilty that I stole him away from the bonfire, from his chance to relax and hang with our friends before the craziness of the festival kicks in. But a bigger part me loves that he insisted, without hesitating, just jumping in his truck and leading the way.

The Keller twins are great—some of the best friends a girl could ask for. But they aren't Dustin.

Slowly we make our way up and down the rows of bookshelves, tiptoeing as if we might disturb whatever we are going to happen upon. Like we are the intruders. Each new aisle is the same as the last—empty. Nothing but the books on the shelves, exactly where they should be, standing proud and unbothered.

"I feel a little bit like Ray and Egon in Ghostbusters," Dustin says, rounding a corner.

"Shhhhhh," I mockingly correct him. "This is a library; keep your voice down."

"Are you afraid we're going to disturb an elderly female apparition dressed in Victorian-era clothing in the reference section?"

"If that's what we discover, you're on your own."

"Not interested in directing her to some better reading material?" he teases.

I shrug, allowing myself to fully relax for the first time since we got here, the adrenaline high starting to subside. "I don't get involved in other people's reading choices unless asked for my opinion outright or someone wants a recommendation. Not every book is for every reader. That's the beauty of them. A story that is everything to one person, might be 'meh' to another."

"Same with music."

"Difference is, thousands of people like your songs."

Dustin turns to face me, stepping in close so our bodies are all but touching. My heart skips, wanting to close that gap, feel him against me. But I don't, too chicken to do anything but stare into his eyes.

"I don't think that people choosing not to change the station when I come on is any different or better than you helping someone discover a book that takes them on whatever journey they are looking for. Both offer people a way to escape for a brief time, to feel things, to help them deal with whatever life threw at them. All it is, is a different medium."

"Dustin Wilder, the philosopher."

His fingers dig into my hips, setting off sparks in me. I hadn't even realized that he was holding me, too transfixed by his words. The air sizzles around us, the cool air from the AC unit no match for the heat that is radiating through me.

Dustin is so close, yet so far away, that stupid quarter inch of space still separating us. I'm screaming internally for him to kiss me. To follow up on that promise.

"Not even close. Just a guy who can play the guitar."

"I seem to remember you being able to do a few other things."

The coy, flirty words are out of my mouth before I can stop them. Not something I meant to say out loud.

"Oh yeah?"

His grip tightens even more, that quarter inch shrinking but still falling short of the contact I crave.

"If I remember correctly, you were also semi-decent with a wrench."

"Semi-decent, huh?"

I smirk, nodding slowly. Dustin murmurs something I don't quite understand, my brain turning to mush as his hips meet mine, something hard pressing against me. Something that is most certainly not his phone.

His hands are on my ass a split second later, holding on firmly as he leans into me. The whisper of his breath against my skin sets loose a swarm of butterflies I haven't felt since the first time he held me like this. Dustin paused then too, more out of fear of doing the wrong thing rather than trying to drive me wild, but it had also made me more sure of what I wanted.

Him.

It's always been him.

Unlike that moment, this time he knows what he's doing. His mouth meets mine, his strong lips gentle at first, testing the waters. I gasp into the kiss, my mind going completely blank. It's impossible to think as Dustin grips me tighter. A whole new surge of adrenaline appears, this time accompanied by lust. I tug on his T-shirt, trying to deepen the kiss, my insides on fire. There is a whole raging inferno in me, fueling my every move.

Dustin doesn't take the bait though, keeping his movements slow and steady. He has nowhere to be. Nothing to do but stand here and kiss me, his only mission to rock my world. Which he is absolutely doing. His lips are the perfect combination of softness and strength as they work against mine. This could be a frenzied mash of hands and tongues and other body parts flailing about. But it's not. It's calm, controlled, making me melt with each new movement.

No, not melt. That is the opposite of what I'm doing. This is making me come alive. All of me is tingling, my nipples tightening, wetness growing between my legs. I am so turned on I could probably power the whole of Hickory Hills. All from one kiss.

I promise it's going to be the best fucking kiss of your entire life. He was not kidding.

"Dusty…"

His name is the only thing I can think to say. Scratch that. It's the only thing I can think of. Hard stop. His kiss fried my brain.

"I've wanted to do that since I got back into town. It took a strength I didn't know I had to stop myself last night."

"You should do it again."

Dustin groans, spinning us just enough to push me back against the shelves, our mouths fused together. Everything is right with the world as his tongue finds mine. His movements remain unhurried, both of us savoring the moment. The feel of each other. It's new and different—unexplored territory just waiting to be discovered—while also being a return to something familiar and comforting. Something I've missed.

Deepening the kiss, Dustin grinds into me. I whimper into his mouth from the contact, my body desperate for more. I swear that bulge is not only bigger but harder than it was just a second ago. Not that I'm complaining. I want more of it. More of him. Dustin Wilder is a drug, and right now, I'm in need of a fix. So I do the only thing I can think of, grinding my own hips in return, trying to up the friction.

That move earns me a deep growl, his mouth moving to my jaw, nipping his way toward my ear. He's soft and gentle, more open-mouth kiss than actual bite, sending goose bumps down my arms. That is, until he gets to his destination. The graze of his teeth on my earlobe catches me off guard, the intensity of pleasure from that little move overwhelming. So much so I jerk underneath him, his hard chest stopping me from launching myself across the aisle.

"My sexy little librarian likes that, huh?" His voice is rough, full of gravel, a tone I almost don't recognize from him.

I manage to move my head up and down, the gesture feeling awkward and incorrect. My lack of response is amusing to him though. He lets out a single chuckle, his warm breath dancing over my neck. Oh, fuck. Wetness pools in between my legs, my body responding nonverbally to something that I can't even name. I don't think I have ever been this turned on.

"You have no idea the fantasies I had in high school of what I wanted to do to you in between these stacks," he continues, hand inching its way up my body, leaving a trail of heat I feel through my clothing. Stopping right at my breast, he runs his thumb along the underside, the movement searing into me. At this point, I wouldn't be surprised if I looked down and saw that there was a burn mark left in its wake. "Watching you yesterday, in that adorable green sundress clinging to these perfect tits of yours, brought them all back."

His thumb moves again, this time over my already taut

nipple. I whimper, wanting him to do it again. But he doesn't. Just works his hand right back down my body.

"Then you were up on that step stool, and my mind went blank, thinking about running my hand up your bare legs. Wondering what I might find there," he continues, mimicking the movements he mentions.

Fuuuuuuuuuuck…

"Please," I moan, cursing myself for not wearing another dress today. My choice of leggings and an extra flowy long blouse seemed like a good idea this morning. I was even thankful for the coverage while we were sitting on the log, but now…now they seem like the worse thing in the world I could be wearing.

"I do like when you say please."

His mouth moves to my neck, searing open-mouth kisses down to the sweet spot at the base. The spot he knows will drive me crazy. I don't wait for him to get there though. His teasing is all well and good, but I need friction. Pure, unbridled friction.

Wrapping a leg around his waist, I try to angle myself to get what I want. No, what I need. For the insane hardness in his pants to make contact with my aching core. My efforts are met with a thrust, his erection hitting me right where I need it. I yip with excitement, his mouth homing in on my neck as he does it again and again. Oh fuck.

I have died and gone to heaven.

Who knew that the gate to heaven was dry humping. Not me.

"Dusty," I moan, feeling my climax start to build.

In a flash his mouth is on mine again, kissing me harder and deeper. He's picked up his pace. Now he's on a mission. What that mission is, I'm not sure, but I don't care as long as he doesn't stop.

Until he does. At least with his hips. His mouth never

leaves me as he unhooks my leg from his waist, letting it down slowly. What isn't slow however, is him finding his way up my blouse, toying with the hem of my leggings.

Yes, Yes, Yes...

"I think it's time I find out if your pussy feels as good as I remember," he growls.

Slipping his hand inside my pants, he effortlessly finds my center, my panties already damp from his attention. Casually grazing his finger back and forth, he toys with the cotton, briefly making contact with my clit. I buck each time he glides over the bundle of nerves calling his name, making him laugh into our kiss.

"My little naughty librarian wants something, doesn't she?"

YES!

I silently scream, knowing I can't do more than let out unintelligible sounds right now. I'm too worked up. Naughty librarian has never been a fantasy of mine, but right now I'm all in. Hot, wet, and raring to go. Whatever it is Dustin wants from me, he can have it. As long as he keeps this up.

He isn't showing any signs of stopping though, enjoying this tease just as much as I am. Maybe more.

Long, grueling seconds pass by, my body heating up with each one, until I'm sure it's a million degrees in this building. My orgasm is brewing just below my overheated surface, just waiting for Dustin to push me over the edge. An edge he's kept me dangling on forever.

A split second later, that changes. My brain is too clouded by lust to follow his movements, but in a flash, one hand is in my panties, fingers dancing through my damp curls, the other holding the back of my neck, as he kisses me like his life depends on it.

"You're nice and wet for me, aren't you, Kenzie?"

"Mmmhmmm."

"Such a good girl. Makes it really easy to do this…"

His words are punctuated by a swift flick of his wrist, fingers brushing over my clit as they slip through my folds. I shudder from the contact, but he doesn't slow down. Not until his thumb is right where I need it, hovering over the slick, sensitive bud. Two more thick digits slip inside of me.

"Gaaaaaah!" I scream, the sound vibrating through the silence.

"Shhhhhh," he whispers. "This is a library after all. Wouldn't want us to get caught."

I shudder, my body not sure if it's hot or cold, all my nerve endings on high alert. Each one of them is right at the surface of my skin, firing at will. Dustin's fingers continue to slide in and out of me, tapping the hidden spot inside me that only he has ever been able to find on each downstroke, thumb circling my clit nice and easy, like rubbing a wishing stone.

I'm so close, the orgasm that has been building in me is hovering right there, threatening to release itself. All I need is…

"Come for me, Kenzie."

And I do.

I scream, not caring who hears, my eyes slamming shut, fireworks going off all around me. Inside me. He captures my outburst with his mouth though, my pussy clamping down on his fingers. He never lets up, carrying me through my orgasm, making sure that I feel every last millisecond of it.

And I do.

Forget the best kiss of my life. That was the best orgasm of my life.

Dustin steps back, removing his hand from my panties. His eyes are dark, still full of lust, lips swollen. He looks like a man possessed, chest heaving, proud of his accomplishments.

Raising his hand to his mouth, he lazily drags a finger across his lower lip, before sucking them clean, savoring my taste.

Holy hell...

He smirks, eyes dancing up and down my body. I must be a sight at this point—rumpled, flushed, hair all a mess, pushed up against the shelf. Taking a second to catch my breath, I realize just where we are—the romance section. Staring back at me are the titles I put up for display last week, hoping to entice people to try out these new additions.

Emily Silver, SM West—hope you ladies enjoyed the show...

"You have no idea how beautiful you are," he tells me.

I snort. "Ha. Right now I'm—"

"Fucking gorgeous."

My cheeks flush, this time from embarrassment rather than lust. Dustin might be my ex, one of my oldest friends, and the person who knows me better than anyone. But he's still a star. And I'm still just a small-town girl. Hearing him tell me I'm beautiful seems so foreign and undeserved. I love hearing it, nonetheless.

"It's probably getting late. We should lock up and get home," I say, changing the subject. "Tomorrow is a big day. Sound check, festival prep, all that."

"Can I take you to breakfast first?"

"Breakfast?"

My voice catches. He wants to take me to breakfast? He just gave me a toe-curling orgasm, in my place of employment, after telling me it was his teenage fantasy, and now he's thinking about breakfast? Must be a man thing.

"I've been craving Dolly's blueberry pancakes for months. So, what d'ya say? I'll pick you up at eight?"

"I can meet you there."

"No, baby. That isn't how this works, remember?" He winks, letting loose those butterflies all over again. "I'll pick you up at eight."

CHAPTER THIRTEEN

DUSTIN

Oh five two five.

I stare at Kenzie across the booth at Dolly's, watching her eyes skim over the menu, like it hasn't been the exact same for our entire life. Hell, based on how tattered the thing is, I wouldn't be surprised if that was the exact one I'd held the last time we were here.

The morning I left.

I push that memory from my mind, focusing back on the four digits that stumped me since Kenzie said them last night. The meaning of them is right on the tip of my tongue. I know once it comes to me I'm going to feel like an idiot, but right now I can't place it. I would've bet good money her code would have been the same as mine—oh five one oh. Especially since she'd entered it into my phone without thinking. So what the hell was the significance of oh five two five?

Kenzie lets out a sigh, two of her fingers aimlessly twirling her hair. She's dressed down today, at least by Kenzie standards, in a pair of jeans and an old Rhythm and Brews T-shirt, her long chestnut hair flowing over her shoulders. There's a hair elastic on her wrist, just waiting and ready for when she gets frustrated with her hair in her face and piles it on top of her head. Given how warm today is supposed to be, I give her about an hour—ninety minutes max—before that happens. Either way though, she's beautiful.

"You look perplexed," I say.

Looking up at me, she gives me a coy smile, the same one she gave me last night before slipping inside her door. Being the gentleman my mother raised me to be, I insisted on not only driving her home, but walking her to her door. I was then the man my mother probably doesn't want to think about and proceeded to kiss Kenzie for another half hour, until neither of us could breathe.

"I can't decide if I want French toast or the frittata."

"So why not get both?" I shrug, problem solved.

"Because I won't be able to eat both."

"Did you forget?" I lean back and pat my stomach. "Bottomless pit. I'll finish whatever you don't."

"Someday that will catch up with you."

"And when that day comes, I'll slow down. Until then, my girl gets to order two breakfasts."

I float the "my girl" thing out there just to see what Kenzie will say. She either doesn't care, or it doesn't register, because all she does is giggle. The sound goes straight to my dick, the semi I'm already sporting getting even harder. Thanks to the myriad of sounds she made last night in the library—and then again on her front porch—I've been hard for what feels like twelve hours straight, with only a few minutes of relief thanks to my hand. I'm like a teenager with out of control hormones all over again.

"See, I told you!" a thick, syrupy southern accent exclaims loudly, overtaking the buzz of conversation in the small diner. I look up to find Mrs. Chamberlain, our high school math teacher, barreling our way. The look on her face is self-congratulatory, mixed with mischief. Like she was waiting for just this occasion and can't wait to tell the world. "I just knew y'all would reconnect!"

"For the love…" Kenzie mutters under her breath.

Uh-oh. One doesn't have to be a genius to feel the tension that is suddenly radiating off Kenzie. Seems like our nice relaxing breakfast is over.

I stand up, holding my arms open for a hug, cutting off Mrs. Chamberlain before she can get all the way to our table. "Hi, Mrs. C."

"Dustin Wilder, look at you, all grown up!" She squeezes me tight, swaying to and fro just enough, putting extra emphasis on the gesture. "And just as handsome as I remember."

"Thanks, Mrs. C. You look even younger than you did when I was in high school, if that's even possible."

She titters. "Oh, you charmer you! I am so sorry I didn't get a chance to stop by the library the other day while you were doing your thing, but there's just so much to be done for the festival and all. Speaking of, I won't keep you, just wanted to say 'Hey!' and make sure you know just how happy we are that you're here. I was just telling Kenzie the other day how exciting it is! And how much I knew you two would be looking forward to reconnecting. Anyhoo, I know both y'all have a big day ahead what with sound check and getting everything set up. It's so good to see you two together again!"

Turning on her heel, Mrs. Chamberlain waves over her shoulder, no doubt gloating in whatever mess she thinks she's made. Or is about to make. The latter probably more likely.

Our waitress sidles up to the table as I slip back into my seat, taking our order. Flustered, Kenzie stumbles through her choice, at the last minute adding on her second choice as well. I give her a wink, hoping it helps soothe whatever is eating at her.

"I have five dollars that says I will have a voicemail or text from every member of the planning committee by the end of this meal," Kenzie says, eyes trained on the door as the waitress walks away.

"I'll take that bet. I don't see Mr. Murphy getting in on the gossip." The history teacher and town archivist is a lot of things, but that was never one of them. His wife, however, she's right up there with Mrs. Chamberlain.

"Mr. Murphy retired last year. They moved up to Seattle to be closer to their grandkids."

"Well then, would you like that fiver in cash or can I buy you a beer later?"

Kenzie throws her head back with a laugh, her whole body getting in on the action. Including her perfect breasts, which I did not get to spend enough time with last night. As much as I want a round two, I'm not holding my breath. I may just have to rely on memory where her boobs are concerned.

"Has there been a lot of it?" I ask, curiosity getting the better of me.

"Gossip?" I nod. "Some. Lots of excitement. Which you saw the other day with the meet and greet. I haven't really had anyone mention it directly, though. Other than Mrs. Chamberlain. She was in the library the other day, very clearly trying to get me to spill the tea."

"There's tea?"

"They…they don't know what happened." Her voice is soft, her sweet brown eyes vulnerable as she swallows hard. "You left, and we didn't break up because you were going to come back. But then you got your record deal and you didn't. And we were still together, I think. I thought. But, I wasn't sure because you were off becoming Dustin Wild. I kept waiting for the call, you know, the one where you said that we'd grown apart or whatever. But it never came. Every time you called, or I would call you, it was the same as it had always been. Until one day, two years into all that, it was clear that you weren't coming back, ever. And that's when I knew."

The words flow out of Kenzie rapidly, as if she has a time limit to say as much as possible. Each one hits me like a bullet. A reminder of what a jackass I was.

"I didn't know what to tell people when they asked. Because it was pretty obvious to the world you had moved on, but…I dunno. It was a mix of me not wanting to talk bad about you, because it's not like you really did anything wrong —you chased your dream. I encouraged you to do it. But I also…" Closing her eyes, Kenzie lets out a long, stuttered breath. "I also didn't want to look like a loser. You know what the rumor mill in this town is like. So it was just easier to keep it vague, and tell them something like 'we're just doing our own thing right now.' Eventually, people stopped asking."

My stomach rolls. Every horrible emotion on earth washes over me, my regret over how I handled things escalating to an extreme level. I want to apologize again, but I don't know where to start. This might be easier if my actions had been purely selfish. Don't get me wrong, they were selfish enough, but that wasn't the main reason behind what I did. No, that was stupidity. Because it wasn't that I was simply thinking of myself—it was that I wasn't thinking at all.

"I'm sorry."

"Dustin, I don't—"

"Kenzie," I cut her off. "Don't tell me that you're not saying this to make me feel bad. You're allowed to make me feel bad over this. Because I was an asshat. I didn't mean to be, but I was. I know that. I should have been a man and had a conversation with you. Whether we ended it or tried to make it work...I dunno. But that should have been something we decided together, rather than just letting it sit in the background until life had gotten so far in the way that it made the choice for us. I chickened out, that's all there is to it. And in doing that, broke both our hearts."

Tears fill Kenzie's eyes, her arms stretching out across the table. She takes my hand in hers, squeezing it. We sit like this for a moment, all our hurt laid out on the table, the world buzzing around us like the raw emotion of our past isn't there for the world to witness. There's something freeing about it though. Getting it out there finally, the two of us knowing how the other has been feeling for the last seven years.

"I owe you an apology too."

"You don't."

"I do. Because we always promised to be honest with each other, and I wasn't. I didn't tell you that I was hurting or ask what was going on between us."

"You shouldn't have had to," I tell her, a lump forming in my throat. "I, one...should have known and two...should have asked. So again, this is all on me. You're blameless in this, Kenzie."

"Hardly, but thank you."

The warm, serene smile that takes over her face lights me up inside. It's almost as good as my name on her lips last night as she came. Almost. Definitely more important though. Between last night and now, we feel like Dustin and Kenzie again. And fuck, does it feel good.

"One last thing," she continues with another squeeze of my hand. "And then I vote we move on. But, I'm sorry I missed your show in Atlanta. It was right after..." She makes a circling motion with her hand, indicating what we just talked about. "And I just couldn't bring myself to go. Figured I'd catch the next one. Had I realized there wouldn't be a next one… Well, anyway. I'm sorry for missing it, and I'm looking forward to finally seeing Dustin Wild in all his glory this weekend."

A pang hits me as the memory of that Atlanta show floods my brain. I don't know what it was that made Kenzie realize that things had faded between us—and I don't need to—but for me, the day the Keller twins showed up to the venue in Atlanta by themselves was the nail in the coffin for me. I had held out hope that maybe all wasn't lost, that when I saw her at that show, everything would be magically okay. But she didn't come. I didn't blame her then, and I don't now either. The sting has lessened over the years but is something I know won't ever go away. A feeling Kenzie seems to understand all too well.

"I hope he lives up to your standards."

"So far, every performance has received a standing O, soooo…" Kenzie winks, sitting back in the booth.

You most certainly did, beautiful…

"Busting out the puns and it's not even nine a.m."

"I enjoy being punny, at all hours of the day."

"Well, there's plenty more where that one came from," I tell her, hoping the nuance isn't subtle. Or overt for that matter. Last thing I want is for her to think that all I want is sex. Because that couldn't be any further from the truth. *She* is what I want. Every last bit of her smart, sweet, kind self.

"Puns?"

"O's."

"Oooohhhhh," she says, drawing out the word, exaggerating the shape of her mouth. Yeah, she did that on purpose. And I fucking love it.

She gives me a knowing smirk as the waitress drops off

our food. Those pretty pink lips upturned like that are going to be the death of me, making my dick twitch all over again. Seriously, if I make it through this day without requiring medical attention for an erection lasting longer than four hours—or whatever the time limit is per the TV ads—it will be a miracle. After this meal is over though, and we are safely in my truck, there is a kiss with her name on it.

Kiss.

Oh five two five.

"Our first kiss," I say, just blurting it out. How could I have forgotten? "I took you to the Slice on May tenth, but your dad was sitting on the front porch waiting for you to get home, so I didn't kiss you."

"He was actually waiting on Moira. She was grounded but had snuck out, so…"

"It took me two weeks to grow a pair, finally finding the nerve at the drive-in after the parade."

"I was wondering how long it was going to take you."

Too fucking long…

"Best kiss ever, right?" I joke, quoting her from that night.

"Second now."

"Second?"

She nods. "It got demoted last night."

CHAPTER FOURTEEN

DUSTIN

SOME THINGS—SOME feelings—become a part of you. No matter how long I've been away, the energy and the excitement that come with the Rhythm and Brews Festival are unforgettable. What I did seem to push out of my mind, though, was the intensity and the sheer insanity of this event.

From the second Kenzie and I arrived on site at Newton Field—Hickory Hills's community athletic space—we were sucked into the whirlwind that started last night. It takes hundreds of volunteers to turn the gravel track, soccer fields, basketballs courts, and picnic area into a space that will play host to thousands of people tomorrow. Random groupings of tables and chairs, some under tents, some out in the sunshine, weave around the food trucks and other vendors in the open area usually occupied by sporting event equipment. Southern Brothers Brewing, who is now the major sponsor of the festival, has taken over the entire basketball court for their operation, with the stage at the opposite end, allowing festival goers to overflow into Ward's hay field.

It's an all-hands-on-deck situation, the majority of the town closing down for the day to make sure that everything is set up. Tomorrow will be a busy day for every local business, and no one is willing to let anything be risked by chance.

"Feel like you never left?" Ken asks, taking a case of bottled water from me. A quick slash with the boxcutter in his hand splits open the plastic wrap holding it together, allowing him to dump it in the cooler at his feet.

"It does. I try and not let the whole musician thing go to my head, but nothing will knock you down a few pegs like your old homeroom teacher hollering instructions at you like you're at boot camp."

He chuckles. "The more things change, the more they stay the same."

I sneak a glance over toward Kenzie, who is pacing in a circle, scrolling on her phone. I can't help but smile as my eyes land on her curves, my hands aching to hold them.

That's for sure...

"Ready for sound check? Or have we worked you too hard? Wait, no, I'm sure you have spent most of the day taking more selvsies."

"I have not softened that much," I reply, giving him a shove. Ken chuckles again, his deep, hearty voice a soothing sound. "And actually, for the most part, no one has asked. I don't know if they all just got to me the other day or everyone is so focused on setup, but the only screaming of my name I've heard so far today is Mrs. Chamberlain bossing me around. As for being excited, I am. I've never played on that stage before. I did throw my hat in the ring once in college, but Mrs. Burch just smiled and politely told me 'maybe next year.' Ironic that she was the one to reach out and ask me to play this year."

"Hattie Burch suffers from selective amnesia, so I'm sure she has zero recollection of ever turning you down."

Now it's my turn to laugh. Selective amnesia. I'm going to have to remember that.

"I, ummmm, I know I haven't really acknowledged it," he continues, clearing his throat. Nerves radiate off him, his posture turning in a bit. The man is like a father to me, but he's also not one for showing his emotions. He kicks at the dirt, a telltale sign that those emotions are about to make a rare appearance. "I do really appreciate you coming back here for this. Don't get me wrong, I still hate the whole thing. It should be about the high school; that's tradition. But it means a lot that you're doing this."

"Could have saved us all the trouble and just let me pay," I offer, trying to lighten the mood, knowing he'll have none of it.

Ken scoffs. "And miss this town up in arms over a celebrity coming to town? Don't deny an old man his entertainment. Speaking of, what time are you up for sound check? Want to make sure I don't miss it."

"Whatever time your beautiful daughter tells me to get my ass on stage. We're dead last, since they're going in performance order, making sure to get transitions correct, so it'll be a few hours yet. But, my band said they should be here soon, along with the merch cart," I say, glancing quickly at my phone to check the time. "They know who to talk to once they are here to get the few things they are bringing set up, and we should be good to go."

I sneak another look at Kenzie, who is wearing out a path in that small circle she keeps making. She's nervous about something. Given everything we've accomplished in the hours that we've been out here since our breakfast at Dolly's, and everything there is still left to do, it could be any number of things. Still, I'm tempted to walk over there and kiss the nerves out of her.

Turning back to Ken, I catch the shit-eating grin on his

face. Busted.

"Do me a favor, would ya, son?"

Son. I love that he still calls me that. Sure, it's partially a nickname, the kind of filler most southerners toss out on the regular, but Ken only ever used that one with me. The Keller twins, his nephews, any of the other guys around town—none of them were ever "son." Only me. The fact that he still uses it means a lot.

"Anything."

"Go turn that frown of hers upside down. I'm sure you've got a trick or two up your sleeve."

If you only knew...

I nod, walking backward for a minute, then turning on my heel and making a beeline for my girl. Yes, my girl. In some way, Kenzie always has been, and always will be, my girl. Even if just for the next few days.

Or maybe longer.

Kenzie doesn't look up as I approach, continuing in her path, lost in whatever she's muttering. That is, until I step right in front of her, forcing her to come to a halt. Her steps anyway. Her mouth continues on its pace.

"Founded in 1823, by Miles Knox, Hickory Hills was created to be a pit stop for those traveling through the area that is now referred to as the Magnolia Midlands. Almost dead center between Macon and Tifton, it wasn't until the Civil War that our beloved town became known for more than just a comfy bed and a hearty meal," Kenzie recites, her voice even and full of southern charm. "Home to the Hayes brothers, Augustus and Llewellyn, who found favor with a Confederate general, who commissioned them to supply the newly founded army with weapons. Unfortunately, Llewellyn passed during the Battle of Atlanta, while delivering supplies to troops there. However, Augustus carried on the family tradition, passing it down from generation to generation, making Hayes Industries what it is today and keeping Hickory Hills on the map."

"You sound like Tour Guide Barbie," I tease when she finally takes a breath.

"I'm sure she had better material."

"Oh, I dunno, the history of Hickory Hills is riveting. How they haven't made a TV movie about it yet, I will never understand."

"Shush!" She gives me a playful shove and I stumble backward, pretending to be hurt, laughing. It feels good to play around with her like this.

"Hi, sorry to interrupt," a high school-aged kid I don't recognize says. "Miss Noble, there is a problem with the dunk tank, and Miss Forde said to come see you about it."

"What am I going to do about it?" Kenzie asks. The kid shrugs, obviously not thinking past following instructions.

"I can go take a look," I say. "I assume there's a set of tools over there?"

"Errr, yeah," the kid answers. His eyes go wide as he realizes who I am. "But you're…you're Dustin Wild."

"I am. I can still handle a wrench though. Lead the way."

The kid nods furiously, stumbling over himself as he heads back in the direction of the dunk tank. Grabbing Kenzie's hand, I follow his lead. She interlaces her fingers in mine as we walk, a tingle racing up my arm, like this is the most natural thing in the world. Which is exactly how it feels.

"What exactly is wrong with it?" I ask.

The tank is in need of a fresh coat of paint, but otherwise looks just as it should, a hose draped over the side, slowly filling up. I peer over the side, noting just how low the water pressure is. No wonder they started filling it now. At the rate it's going, it'll be tomorrow morning before it's full.

"The button won't work."

"Define work," I say, sounding a lot like Ken used to when I first started at the garage. Work was a relative term and could mean almost anything in this kind of situation. "And where's Sylvie? Err, I mean Miss Forde."

"She said she'd be right back."

"Okay then. Kenz, up you go."

"Excuse you? No." Shaking her head, Kenzie crosses her arms, pushing her perfect breasts upward. My dick strains against my pants witnessing the little bounce they do, wishing this high schooler wasn't here so I could tell her just how incredible they look when they do that. Instead, I bite my tongue, letting her finish. "I am not getting up there while the tank is filling. That's crazy talk."

"The button doesn't work," I remind her, banging the side of my fist against it. Sure enough, the button doesn't engage and the seat remains perfectly perpendicular.

"But you're trying to make it work."

"The safety lever is on, Miss Noble," the kid says. "The one so that the seat won't tip even if you hit the button. Mr. Keller installed it last year so he could repair things without the seat falling all the time."

"See, you're all set, baby. Up you go."

Kenzie glares, sticking out her tongue at me, but does what I ask. She's hesitant, and I can't blame her, but I'm glad she trusts me. Once she's settled on the seat, I lean over the side, beckoning her closer with my index finger.

"Hi."

"Hi," she says back, waggling her eyebrows.

"You look adorable up there on your throne."

Her cheeks flush pink, a giggle starting and then stopping just as quickly, eyes flicking to something behind me. I look over my shoulder and find exactly what killed the moment. The awkward teenager. He's still standing there, hands in his pockets, up to God knows what. Actually, I have a pretty damn good idea what, since that's the kind of thing I would have done at his age—staring at Kenzie, hoping no one would notice.

I roll my eyes, pushing back from the tank and turning my focus to the task at hand. I slam my open palm against the button a couple more times, just to make sure. Nothing. And I need to stop that, or else my hand is going to hurt too much to play later on.

Grabbing a wrench from a tool kit that I recognize—an item donated by Ken to the high school forever ago—I set to work on the mechanism, trying to figure out the culprit. Everything looks to be in working order. Nothing too tight or too loose. Nothing rusted over. In fact, it looks like some of the parts have been replaced since the twins and I originally built this thing more than a decade ago. More than anything, it probably just needs some WD-40.

I reach back into the tool bag, knowing that if Ken is in charge of upkeep on this kit, there is a can in there. One of the first things he taught me was that "you really only need two tools in life—duct tape and WD-40. If it moves and shouldn't, duct tape. It doesn't move and should, WD-40." His theory didn't apply as soundly to the cars we repaired, but in everything else, it hasn't failed me yet.

I spray the pin behind the button, standing back to look at my handiwork. "That should do it."

I toss the can to the side, smile triumphantly at Kenzie, who I can tell is holding in a laugh, and smack the button again. The button does exactly what it's supposed to do. Which is exactly the problem.

Kenzie's shriek fills the air. I lunge toward her just as the plank drops, sending her into the partially filled tank. She hits the ground with a thud, the few inches of water doing nothing to catch her, but splashing plenty, soaking her.

"Kenzie!" I shout just as the kid behind me says, "Miss

Noble!"

Face scrunched together, out of pain, embarrassment, or something else I'm unsure of, Kenzie looks up at me. "The water is really, really cold."

Relief washes over me that she's not hurt. Her stressing about how cold it is sends my eyes straight for her chest, catching her pebbled nipples through her now borderline see-through T-shirt. I hold back a groan, licking my lips, all sorts of naughty thoughts racing through my mind. There are so many things I want to say to her, but we have a chaperone.

Instead, I help her out of the tank and pull her in close, wrapping my arms around her. She shivers against me, no doubt feeling my erection. I don't try and hide it though. There's something about this moment, public or not, that is completely personal. Intimate. She snuggles into me, letting me know she feels it too and that she has no plans to end it.

"We should get you into something dry."

"I don't have time to go all the way home to change. Sound check is going to start soon and we have to run through all fourteen acts."

"We can grab you something from my merch cart," I tell her. "Assuming you don't mind walking around with my face on your chest for the rest of day."

"I'd rather it somewhere else on my body," she replies, lowering her voice so only I can hear it. "But I guess that'll work for now."

Fuuuuuuuuck...

"But," she continues, "pants."

"Pretty sure I have an extra pair in Old Blue."

"You just have an answer for everything." I nod, leaning down and kissing her softly on the forehead. She mewls faintly, another shiver running through her. Looking up at me, she smiles. "Lead the way, cowboy."

Ten minutes later, she's all dried off and looking sexier than I ever thought possible in a pair of my old jeans and the sky-blue fitted tee with my stage name written across her glorious chest. If it can't be me hanging out nestled between her boobs, my name isn't a bad second. Just as quickly as we got her into something dry, we're both pulled in different directions—her to get sound check under way and me by my band, needing directions on where everything goes, along with some last-minute set list prep.

When I told Kenzie last night that I could do this with my eyes closed, I meant it. My band and I have this routine down. At least we did when I wasn't distracted thinking about the prettiest girl I've ever known walking around, literally in my pants, without panties.

Panties that are currently stashed in my pocket.

I force myself to concentrate. This is work. There will be plenty of time to play later. Next thing I know, hours have passed, my crew long done with the sandwiches Mama brought over for them as dinner, and it's our turn on stage. My crew doesn't hesitate, hopping up there like this is any old show. To them it is. To me, it's more than that. This festival—this town—makes up so much of who I am, even if I haven't been back in years. Hickory Hills is the small town and dirt roads that I sing about. And for the first time ever, the girl I sing about, the one that every one of my songs is about, will be out there watching.

No pressure.

Sucking in a huge amount of oxygen, I let it out slowly, stepping up onto the stage. It's a surreal feeling, similar to the first time I stood before a crowd in Nashville. Only this time, I'm not as worried about being booed off the stage.

The opening notes to "Silhouette Stetson," my usual show opener, surround me, my band kicking into performance mode. The few people who are still hanging around Newton

Field all seem to stop at once, turning to face the stage. Bright smiles and excited faces, along with a few people who are already moving to the beat, make my heart want to burst. Especially when I catch a glimpse of that sky-blue T-shirt and a pair of way-too-big jeans.

Trying to focus on the lyrics, I adjust my in-ear monitor. It's no use though. My mouth might be singing the words, but my brain is elsewhere. Back in that dive bar in Hurricane Shoals, sunburned from a long day in the sun, mic in hand as I serenaded the small crowd with Tim McGraw's "Southern Voice." That song was my karaoke go-to—and still often makes an appearance in my shows now—and I hadn't even considered singing anything else. We were celebrating. It was Spring Break, and we didn't have a care in the world.

"You're good," a voice had said as I stepped down from the stage, handing the microphone back to the attendant. I turned to find a middle-aged man with shoulder-length blond hair standing there with his arms folded across his chest, appraising me like a judge at a 4-H show. "You ever think about doing it for real?"

"Doesn't everyone?" I responded, brushing him off.

As I headed to my seat, the guy followed, holding out a business card.

"I mean it. I think you've got something. And I know what I'm talking about. Name and number's on that card if you change your mind."

With a simple nod he walked away, not waiting for me to respond.

Part of this moment feels just like that one. Difference is, instead of being in the seat next to me, Kenzie is leaning against a folding table, looking like an angel God has sent just for me.

"Hey Kenzie," I say into the mic, ignoring the rest of the song. My band fades the song they're playing, taking the opportunity to make whatever adjustments are needed. I, on the other hand, am on a mission. "Got any requests?"

She shakes her head, pretending to be shy. She'll probably smack me later for doing this to her—she never did like to be the center of attention. But she is absolutely the center of my world right now. Every last one of my fantasies is built around her. No one else has ever come close. No one. None of the women I've met at meet and greets, none of the female musicians I've collaborated with, and most certainly not any of the publicity dates I've been sent on.

I need to find a way to show her that.

And I think I know just the song.

"None? None at all?" I taunt.

She shakes her head again, brushing me off. I can see the coy smile tugging at her lips though, stirring desire in me. Fine, if she won't make a request, then I will take matters into my own hands. Leaping off the stage, I head straight for her, all eyes on us. I can feel the tension building, everyone waiting to see what happens.

"Then I shall need you to join me on stage."

I hold out my hand, bowing slightly, as if I'm Romeo and she's Juliet. The faint giggle I hear as she places her hand in mine tells me my plan is working. Leading her back up on stage, I nod to Joel on the bass, who follows my thought process and grabs her a stool. Once she's situated, I step back, letting the moment soak in. It's killing me not to kiss her right now.

"I'm sure you've figured this out by now," I say, running my fingers along the strings of my guitar. "But I wrote this one about you. *For you.* I've wanted to sing it to you for a long time."

Kenzie sucks in her breath, holding it, her eyes already glassy with emotion.

Here goes nothing...

CHAPTER FIFTEEN

KENZIE

Because all I want...is to be back chasing falling stars, with you...

I am a puddle.

A big, wet, oozing pile of goo. Forget swooning. Forget melting. I have experienced whatever that scientific process is where something goes from solid to not-solid instantly. That is a scientific process, right? I'd make a mental note to ask Sylvie, but my mental capacity for doing anything other than falling ass-over-tea-kettle in love with Dustin Wilder is gone.

The familiar melody envelops me, weaving its way into every nook and cranny of my being. I've ignored this song for so long—changing the station, leaving rooms, talking loudly over it all so that I didn't have to hear it. So that it wouldn't take me back to memories that simultaneously fill my soul and tear it into pieces. The two of us, in the back of Old Blue, a couple of blankets and whatever we could find to drink, parked up on a hill on my dad's property, watching the night sky. Nowhere to be, no agenda. Just two kids so in love that nothing else mattered.

Sitting here now, the song hits different. It's not a painful memory, but a promise. A promise of a life we could still have together. Dustin's smooth as whiskey voice soothes every nerve and worry I had about being pulled up on stage, the entire world melting away. The band, the festival, the handful of remaining volunteers are all a distant memory. The only thing that remains is him. His sandy hair, ice-blue eyes, insanely kissable lips, and a five o'clock shadow that is more than working for him.

Oh, and my desire to feel that five o'clock shadow on my bare skin.

Dustin steps in closer, eyes trained on me. If I wasn't already lava, such a gaze would end me. Absolutely end me. Or so I think, until Dustin whips the guitar over his head, handing it off to someone, and closes the gap between us even more, never missing a beat.

My stomach does somersaults, my heart singing right along with him, making the same promises in return. We have no business saying forever. Hell, we have no business saying *right now*, but that's tomorrow's problem.

"Like my heart…it's yours," Dustin sings. He's so close to me now we're all but touching. I start to reach for him then stop. We have an audience. Dustin doesn't seem to care though, finishing my movement for me, taking my hands in his. I can feel the small indents on his fingertips from his guitar strings, making me tingle. In fact, my whole body is getting in on the action. If I were still wearing my panties, they'd be ruined, without question. Much more of this, and his pants might not survive. "Because all I want…is to be back, chasing falling stars with you. Kenzie…"

He adds my name in at the end of the lyric almost like it was always meant to be. A silent part of the song that has always gone unsaid. And I'm done.

An overwhelming sensation I can't name takes over. My

heart swooning and squeezing, the somersaults my tummy has been doing are now an entire Olympic floor routine, and my lady bits…well, they are all in. Forget butterflies, this is next level from that. Because that fluttery, tingly feeling has taken over down south too.

Clitterflies.

That's what this is. Clitterflies. And I never want this feeling to end.

I don't wait for Dustin to say anything, launching myself at him. He's prepared though, catching me, letting the stool fall backward behind me. My lips are on his almost instantly, my legs wrapped so tight around his waist I should probably worry about cutting off circulation. But I don't. Because my need right now is his kiss.

Dustin is meeting that need epically—his strong lips leading the way as he deepens our contact. His tongue meets mine and it's like we have found all of those falling stars we spent years chasing. Every. Last. One. I feel it everywhere, his hands tightly gripping my backside, neither of us showing any signs of letting up.

Except, I need to stop.

Need to figure out a way to control myself. I cannot climb Dustin Wilder like a tree on stage, which is what I'm about half a heartbeat away from doing. Except he's not Dustin Wilder right now. He's Dustin Wild, making it that much worse that I'm about to dry hump his brains out in front of the entire town.

"Dusty," I say breathlessly, pulling back just enough to speak. Our foreheads are pressed together, heavy breath mixing. It's a good thing he's still holding me, because I can feel how useless my legs are right now.

"Did you like your song, baby?"

I sigh, my already limp body slouching into him more. He doesn't balk though, just tightens his grip, chuckling. The way his exhale moves across my skin tickles, upping the ante on how turned on I already am.

"I need you to take me home, *right now.*"

"I can absolutely do that."

Kissing me again, even harder this time, Dustin starts toward the edge of the stage. He pulls away in just enough time to descend the few stairs, calling over his shoulder to his band to finish up without him. I'm sure there will be talk tomorrow about how he just walked out of sound check—with me clinging to him like a koala. This will give the gossips in this town something to talk about for years to come.

Good, they need a change of subject.

Next thing I know, Dustin has me loaded in his truck, driver's door slamming shut behind him. We're on the main road a second later, heading away from Newton Field. As we approach the center of town, he slows, which is the exact opposite of what I want him to be doing right now.

"When you said home," he says, his voice sounding unsure. "Yours or mine?"

I start to answer, realizing very quickly the conundrum—neither of us has a place of our own. Our choices are his childhood bedroom in his mom's house, or mine, in my father's. Fuck-a-doodle-do.

Mentally flipping a coin, I blurt out an answer. "Mine."

Hitting the gas, Dustin veers right at the town Civil War monument, heading down Broad Street toward the farm. He reaches over, squeezing my thigh just above my knee, and giddiness fills me all over again. I couldn't be any more like a teenager if I tried, my thoughts centered on one thing and one thing only—getting Dustin naked.

The clitterflies swirl through my core again, images and memories taking over. My hands ache to touch him, not wanting to wait until we get back to my house. I look over to my left, a sneaky smile tugging at my lips, drinking in the profile of his square jaw. A naughtiness I didn't know I possessed takes over, my hand acting all on its own, reaching for the bulge I can just make out in the dark.

I rake my fingers over the thick denim of his crotch. Dustin hisses as I do it again, gripping the steering wheel harder. Changing it up, I angle my hand differently, palming the hardening bulge.

"Kenz…" Dustin says through gritted teeth.

I can't tell if it's a plea or a warning, but it doesn't matter. Because I'm not stopping. Single-handedly, I flick open the button, slowly pulling down the zipper. I toy with the elastic on his boxer briefs for a few seconds before slipping my hand inside.

Jackpot.

A shudder rushes through me, the feel of him in my hand overwhelming. Lazily, I run a single finger down the hard length, just to be a tease. We're not far from home, so I can't get too involved, but I want him to know how badly I want him. Want this. Want *us*.

The jerk of his hips lets me know we're on the same page, as does the rev of the engine as Dustin guns it even more.

"You keep doing that, and there's gonna be hell to pay, baby."

"Doing what?" I ask, all coquettish and innocent. But innocent is the furthest thing from what I am. Wrapping my fingers around his cock, I gently squeeze just under the head. Running my thumb along the tip, I feel a bead of precum and coat him in it.

Dustin growls, long and hard.

"Just you wait."

Yanking on the steering wheel, he takes a hard right into the drive, the back end of the truck fishtailing on the gravel. As soon as we're close to the house, Dustin slams on the brakes, throws it in park, and kills the engine. Two seconds later my door opens, I'm in his arms, and he's storming into the house.

"Shhhhh! I don't want to disturb Dad," I giggle.

"His truck's not in the drive; we're fine," Dustin answers, scaling the stairs two at a time. "And after the stunt you just pulled, baby, I promise you're going to be screaming my name so loud they're going to hear you at the state line."

Oh, shiiiit...

A shiver zings down my spine, straight to my sex, while the rest of my body heats up with an intensity I've never felt. The two sensations collide, and I like it. A lot. I don't remember Dustin being this much of a dirty talker before, but far be it from me to argue with this new version of him. Dustin kisses me hard, kicking my bedroom door closed behind him. The harsh thud of it crashing to a close is borderline jolting, but Dustin doesn't let up. If anything, he kisses me harder.

Yeah, this version of Dustin can abso-fucking-lutely stay.

Unceremoniously, he drops me onto the bed, the mattress swaying underneath me. His eyes are dark, resembling a swimming pool at night, so full of lust I can feel it radiating off him.

"As good as my name looks splashed across your tits, this needs to go," he says, a long nod up my body. He wastes no time reaching for my T-shirt, whipping it over my head. His breath catches as his eyes land on my boobs, heaving up and down from my own heavy breathing. He's not done though, his hands moving just as quickly to the fly of my—well, his— pants. "These too."

A quick tug of the soft denim and they slide down my hips, as I unhook my bra, tossing it onto the floor with the rest of my makeshift outfit of the day. Dustin's eyes go even darker, an animalistic sound rumbling in this throat as he licks his lips.

"No panties. I love that you've been like this all day."

"They were wet," I croak, eyes going wide as he moves closer to the bed.

Placing one hand by my head, Dustin leans over me, his other hand on my hip, tracing its way south. "Wet, huh?" Continuing his path, he dips his hand between my legs, dragging a finger through my slit, collecting my arousal—slowly, deliberately, carefully—narrowly avoiding my clit. "Not the only thing that's wet…"

He raises his finger to his mouth, licking me off him, just as unhurriedly as before. Sweet fuck. That might just be the most erotic thing I have ever seen. It's a vision that will be living rent free in my head for the rest of my life, making a regular appearance in every dirty fantasy I have from here on out.

"I've had a sample, and it's just as good as I remember," he whispers, starting to kiss his way down my body. He pauses briefly to flick each one of my already taut nipples, my back arching, looking for more. "But I think it's time I got a *real* taste."

A few more searing kisses along my belly and Dustin settles in between my legs. He gives the tender skin of the inside of each thigh an open-mouth kiss, anticipation pooling within me. I can feel myself growing wetter by the second.

Then, a flash of nerves hits me. Dustin Wilder is between my thighs. Holy hell.

"Gaaah!" I cry out as Dustin's tongue flicks my clit, not giving me time to overthink or let those nerves settle in.

Good thing too. Soon enough I'm overcome with everything he's making me feel. All of it good. No, better than good. Sensational. He licks and sucks, swirling his tongue in all the right places. Like he still has my body memorized. Long licks paired with teasing nibbles have me on the edge of something incredible. I don't know whether or not I'm chasing this pleasure or it's chasing me, but we're about to crash right into each other. A crash that I know will be so consuming, I may never recover.

I wiggle my hips, trying to force contact between the little bundle of nerves calling out Dustin's name with his tongue, but he wraps his arms around my thighs, holding me in place. A devious chuckle emanates from him, those captivating blue eyes looking up my body at me.

"Not yet, baby, I'm not done."

O...M...G...

True to his word, Dustin continues. More nibbling, sucking, teasing. He lets go of one leg, snaking his arm back around. Cool air hits my skin from where he was holding, another new sensation taking over. Every nerve ending in my body is on high alert, ready to respond to whatever move comes next. Ready to show me just how good this can all feel, helping me get lost in the moment.

Slowly, Dustin slides a finger inside me. I mewl, my hips bucking. It's only one finger—although quickly followed by a second—but it's exactly what I need to tip the scales that much farther. An explosion is building inside me, barreling toward the surface.

"Dusty...I'm..." I start, unable to finish my sentence as he takes my clit in his mouth and sucks. Hard. I scream, my hands flying to the back of his head, holding him in place. Not that he's going anywhere—all his efforts make that perfectly clear. "Don't stop...right there...yes, yes...I'm gonna..."

My orgasm slams into me like a tidal wave, taking out any and all sense of what's going on around me. A bomb detonates inside me, my fingers, toes, all my limbs briefly going numb as fireworks flash behind my eyelids. I thrash hard, my hands gripping Dustin's hair so tightly I won't be surprised if he has a newly formed bald spot. That doesn't stop him though. He continues to focus on me, not letting up until I stop moving completely, totally and utterly paralyzed from his oral efforts.

"That's my naughty little librarian," he whispers, sliding up my body and kissing me. I can taste myself on his lips, the tanginess lingering on his tongue, fueling my desire even more.

"I need you inside me. Now."

Dustin doesn't say anything, pushing to his feet and whipping off his clothes faster than I think I've ever seen him move. My eyes dance up and down his body, drinking in all the hard ripples of muscle. His smooth chest gives way to a lightly colored happy trail, framed by the most perfect hip V I've ever seen. Forget all those dudes on the cover of romance novels—they have nothing on this country star.

In a flash, Dustin pulls a condom from his pants pocket, sheathing himself before returning to me. The hardness of his cock feels good pressed against my belly, and I reach down to grab him.

"I'm all yours, Kenzie."

I guide him to my entrance, lining him up as he utters those words. All mine. And I'm all his. A shift of my hips, and Dustin slides inside me. We both let out a groan, the feel of him inside me almost too much.

"You're so fucking tight," he mutters. "Feels so fucking good."

"So do you," I return, moving my hips more. Dustin takes the cue, slowly withdrawing from me, then thrusting back in hard. "I really have missed you inside me."

"I'm here now."

He picks up the pace, finding the rhythm neither of us

seems to have forgotten. Our bodies are doing the talking now, picking up right where we left off. Like no time has passed. Each new movement makes both my body and heart sing. It's a song that I've kept silent for way too long, but still know all the lyrics to.

Resting his forehead on mine, Dustin kisses me, this time nice and slow. Despite the power in his hips, his strong, thick cock hitting me in all the right places, every movement is unhurried and purposeful. We've ticked horny, lust-fueled grab-ass off the list. Leaving only one remaining item on the agenda. Coming together. As one.

We're a tangle of kisses, caresses, grunts, groans, and moans. I want this to last forever. To spend the rest of time in whatever bubble this is, wrapped in Dustin's arms, our bodies conjoined, fitting together like they were made as a matching set. My body is betraying me though, another climax building, this one even stronger than the last. As if that were somehow possible.

Dustin can sense it too, his hips changing their angle to go deeper inside me. I meet him thrust for thrust, throwing my head back, unable to fight what is coursing through my veins.

"That's it, baby," Dustin croons, his silky voice even more of a turn-on as he fucks me. "Come for me. Come on my cock."

His words are magic. But so is his thumb on my clit, and that's all I need to send me soaring, straight into the atmosphere. I can see stars and planets as my body goes rigid, my pussy clamping down on Dustin, holding on to his dick for dear life. A few more hard thrusts and he's right there with me, my name on his lips as his own orgasm takes over.

Dustin collapses on top of me, the weight of him another comfort I didn't realize I missed. His sweaty body against mine feels like heaven, my limbs too heavy to move. To even think of moving. I am beyond blissed out, my heart racing so fast it's a good thing it's in my chest, or it would be halfway to the county line by now.

My mind, though, is serenely blank, which is not something I can say very often. This moment is just too wonderful to be anything else though. All the other worries in my life—the festival, my dad's health, the fact that I just fucked my celebrity ex-boyfriend—are all tomorrow's problems. Far, far away from the here and now.

Shifting off of me, Dustin rolls off the bed, walking over to the small desk in the corner. He grabs a couple of tissues, returning with them to clean me up, then tossing them into the trash can along with the condom. I steel myself, ready for him to make an excuse, to pick his clothes up off the floor and make his exit. Instead, he pulls back the covers on the bed, slipping both of us underneath them and kissing me.

Flipping me to my back, he runs his hand along my breasts, toying with my nipples. "I'm sorry I didn't get to spend any time with you beauties," he says, gaze locked on my chest. "Next time, promise."

"Did you…" I giggle. "Are you apologizing to my boobs?"

"I am. I neglected them. I promise to never make such an oversight again."

I laugh more, snuggling into him. The heat from his body is warm and welcoming. Just what I need to lull me to sleep, into sweet dreams of him and me. Of what the future might actually hold for us.

Because Dustin Wilder just said, "next time."

CHAPTER SIXTEEN

KENZIE

Here's the thing about saying that something is tomorrow Kenzie's problem—tomorrow Kenzie is now today Kenzie, and she doesn't want to have to face it either. Or maybe ever.

That, however, is not an option.

Because the thing I don't want to face, the thing that is currently gnawing at me with concern, has his arms wrapped tight around me, holding me against him, like I am the most precious thing in the world. And I like it. I really fucking like it.

I can feel Dustin's lips curl into a smile, the soft sound of him inhaling and his embrace tightening sending a new rush through me. A rush I'm not used to feeling this early in the day. His morning wood twitches against me, his hand sliding upward, curling around my bare breast, fingers immediately toying with my nipple. An involuntary moan escapes me, electricity shooting straight to my core. My lady bits are awake and standing at attention.

"Morning, beautiful."

"Morning," I return.

The words are breathier than I intended, but at least they

don't betray the wild ride of emotions that I'm on right now. My heart is beating out of control, but I can easily blame that on the sneak attack to my nipples. Or so I hope. Because the last thing I want is to have to admit that I don't know where my head is at about everything.

Sex with Dustin was incredible. There is no doubt about that. It wasn't just the sex though—it was all the emotion tied to it. All those things I'm still feeling. That I still want but know I can't have. As much as I tell myself that I'm just enjoying him while he's here, that's not who I am. Who I am is Kenzie. And Kenzie loves Dustin. Pretty sure that's actually still written on the underside of a bleacher at the high school.

Difference is, this time I know he's leaving. I know that this won't last forever. Probably won't make it hurt any less when he does leave, but I'm a big girl and know what I'm getting into. I just don't want him to see anything other than the confident, collected Kenzie that I am most of the time.

Also, please dear Lord, don't let him think last night was a mistake. I'll find a way to recover from him walking away. I did the first time, and I will the second. What I won't be able to come back from is him regretting this. Regretting me.

"I don't want to get up," he groans, voice hoarse from sleep. "Staying in bed all day isn't an option?"

"It is not. Especially not on festival day."

He grumbles, rearranging us so we're now facing each other. His hair is a mess and there is a small patch of dried spittle in the corner of his mouth, but damn, is he sexy first thing in the morning. Forget sunrises, this is the perfect thing to wake up to.

"Kenzie, about last night," he begins, his eyes turning serious.

My heart drops, my stomach churning the nothingness that is in there. Here it comes. I should have known. The writing was on the wall, and I let that damn song get to me.

There's a reason I've avoided listening to it for all these years. Now I remember why.

I swallow hard, nodding. I close my eyes so that he won't see the tears that are already starting to form. I can handle this.

"The condom," he continues. "I stole it from Nash. I don't want you to think I was being presumptuous…or slutty."

The condom? That's what his first concern is this morning? I bark out a laugh, the once sad tears turning into happy ones, rolling down my cheek.

"What so funny?" he asks. He glides the back of his forefinger across my face, wiping away a tear.

"That's not where I thought you were going with that, that's all." I swipe under my eyes, catching the remaining tears and drying my face. The condom. Only Dustin. "And I don't think you presumptuous, or slutty. Just don't think either of those things of me, for the one that I snatched off Willa. It's in my…" I trail off, realizing that I don't know where the purse with said prophylactic is.

"Your purse is still in Old Blue," Dustin answers, as if he can read my mind. "Speaking of, we should move your car. Bring it back here, or at least park it in a shady spot at the library. Don't want your insides to melt."

Too late…

"We can just bring it back here. That is, if you have time. I don't know what your plan is for the day."

"To hang out with you."

Swooooooooooon…

"One, following me around as I work this event is not going to be fun. And two, won't people recognize you?"

"You'd be amazed at how unrecognizable I am with a baseball cap and a pair of sunglasses. People aren't expecting to see me out and about, so they don't. I get told I look just like Dustin Wild a lot."

I chuckle, my heart so full as we lie here and talk. The idea of staying like this for the rest of the day doesn't sound so bad. Upgrade that to the rest of time, and I'm here for it. Life beckons though. This time, via the alarm on my phone, chirping that it's time to get my ass in gear.

"We both need showers." I roll away, but Dustin's hand grips my hips, holding me in place. The impish look on his face, paired with the waggle of his eyebrows, spells trouble, and I know exactly what suggestion is coming next. So I cut him off. "Separate showers. All showering together is going to do is make us dirtier."

"Nothing wrong with that."

"Not this morning, cowboy. Maybe later."

"I'm gonna hold you to that." Digging his fingers into my skin, he kisses me, ignoring my morning breath. It's soft, sweet, and full of a tenderness that I've missed.

Dustin finally lets up on his kisses, the both of us rolling out of bed. He makes quick work of throwing on his clothes and heading for the door. I've always had mixed feelings about watching Dustin exit a room, hating to see him go but loving watching him leave. This morning is no exception, with that perfect ass wrapped nicely in jeans that manage to hug him like a second skin.

"I'll be back in an hour, maybe less," he says. One more goodbye kiss and he slips out the door, headed down the stairs.

I rush to my window, feeling as giddy as I used to in high school, wanting to wave to him through the large live oak that sits outside my bedroom. My foot lands on something cold and sharp, my eyes flying downward to see what I stepped on.

Dustin's keys.

Shit. He's not going to get very far without those. Grabbing my robe, I hastily slip it on, tying it around my waist as I fly down the stairs, praying I don't trip. That's the last thing I need.

I land at the bottom of the steps, just in time to hear my father's voice.

"Much easier than that through-the-window stunt you pulled in high school, huh?"

Busted.

I freeze, trying to figure out where exactly my father is, and to which one of us he's speaking. To my right, Dustin leans against the entryway to the kitchen, one leg crossed in front of the other, looking remarkably comfortable considering the way my dad just called him out. Slinking over to them, I stop next to Dustin, looking at him first, then to my dad, who is sitting at the table, coffee cup in hand, massive smile on his face.

"Morning, MacKenzie."

My full name. Ohhhhhh boy.

"Morning, Dad."

"You knew about the window?" Dustin asks, not bothering to look remorseful or embarrassed. Glad one of us isn't.

"That one limb on the live oak always looked a little funny. And paired with the scuffmarks and tattered screen on that window, the math wasn't hard," Dad answers, taking a long sip of coffee.

And now I want to die.

"Errr, you dropped your keys," I mutter quickly, handing them to Dustin, eager to make my escape.

"Thanks, baby." He takes them from me, kissing me on my forehead. My chest fills with butterflies, my cheeks heating up. I'm not sure if the latter is from Dustin's attention, or the embarrassment I'm feeling as this all goes down in front of Dad. While I'm in my robe.

"You want breakfast?" Dad asks.

What?!

"Kenzie made this quiche casserole thingy; it's good. Let me grab you some."

"Dad," I interject before Dustin can respond. "We have a big, long day. We need showers, and have to shuffle cars, and get to Newton Field—"

My father cuts off my word vomit with a smile. "Big, long days require a good breakfast. Sit down, son. Kenzie can go shower while we eat and then you two can be on your way."

I open my mouth to object, but Dustin grabs my hand, squeezing it, and all my thoughts leave me.

"Go shower. I'll have breakfast with Dad, and then we can get going." He kisses me again, for real this time. My knees wobble a bit, forgetting where I am and the audience we have. Pulling back, Dustin spins me around and gives me a pat on my ass to shoo me up the stairs. Oh, he's going to pay for that one.

After taking the world's fastest shower and getting dressed and ready at world record speed, Dustin and I are back in Old Blue, heading toward his mom's. Feeling more than a little awkward after the encounter with my father, I try and find a way to ask my questions without sounding like I'm freaking out. Except, I am freaking out, and there is no way around it.

"What did he say?"

"Your dad?"

"No, the garden gnome out front that Nash and Noel keep moving around even though I have tried to throw him out a dozen times. Yes, my dad!"

"Nothing."

"Nothing? You two just sat in silence while eating strata?"

My voice is shrill, making me wince. So much for confident and collected.

"Is that what that's called? It was really good."

"Thank you," I say, my heart fluttering with the compliment. "But, seriously, what did he say?"

"Let us men have our secrets, would you?"

Secrets? Ummm, no. The last thing I'm going to let Dustin and my dad have are secrets.

"I just wanna—"

"Kenz." He cuts me off, arm whipping across the bench seat, hand landing on my thigh. He slides it ever so slightly to cup the inside of the muscle, giving it a squeeze. Right where he'd placed a series of kisses last night. "Nothing like what you think went down. No interrogation, no threatening my life or limbs, okay? He told me I knew where the plates were kept and to cut us a piece of the casserole while he brewed more coffee. Past that, I'm not going to betray the confidence of a man who has never betrayed mine."

I'm not going to betray the confidence of a man who has never betrayed mine... My heart squeezes, loving that he loves my dad so much. They've always had a special bond. I guess I didn't realize that despite the space and years, that their bond was still intact. Okay, maybe the two of them are allowed to have their secrets.

My body relaxes, Dustin's hand still firmly on my thigh as we turn into his mom's place. I can't remember the last time I was out this way, since it's the opposite direction of town from Dad's, but the only thing that is different about it is the new rosebushes out front, no doubt courtesy of Keller Landscaping. Putting the truck in park, Dustin leans over, kissing me. I can taste the garlic on his lips from the strata, making me realize that while Dustin got breakfast, I did not. Damn it.

Sliding out of Old Blue, my thoughts still focused on my lack of breakfast, my eyes land on something unexpected. Noel's truck. Parked right next to Helena Wilder's SUV.

"You always hang around other people's mama's houses

this early in the morning?" Dustin shouts as Noel shuts the front door behind him.

"Toilet was leaking in her bathroom."

"You a plumber now too?"

"I can replace toilet innards," he replies, chuckling.

"I could have done it."

"That's what you pay me for. Besides, when you didn't come home last night, she wasn't really sure what the plan was," Noel retorts, a crooked grin on his face. "Hi, Kenzie."

My cheeks redden instantly, the warm morning air getting hotter by the second. So much for keeping this between us.

"Thanks for taking care of her," Dustin says.

"Of course. Plus, I got breakfast out of the deal." Noels pats his stomach, a satisfied smile taking over. "You hurry, the skillet might still be hot."

"I ate over at Kenzie's. Although,"—Dustin turns to me, taking my hand—"you didn't get to eat, did you?"

I shake my head, my response caught in my throat like the cotton wad shoved into a pill bottle, keeping the words from moving.

"Better get inside then. I'll see y'all over at Newton in a bit," Noel replies.

With a nod to imitate the tip of a cap, he walks past us toward his truck. Dustin and I head up the pathway, stopping as Noel calls out my name. I turn to find him walking back toward us.

"No need to blush, Kenzie. If anyone can keep a secret, you know it's me."

And just how does one respond to that?

The boys don't let me try to figure it out though, Noel returning to his truck and Dustin leading me into the house. The familiar scent of a hot, perfectly seasoned cast iron skillet greets us, my stomach grumbling its hello back. Some might tell you that there's no way a pan has that distinctive of a smell, but it does. Promise. Also, a perfectly seasoned, southern cast iron skillet isn't just any pan either.

"Well hey there, you two!" Helena's voice rings out. "Was wonderin' if I was gonna see you this mornin' or if I had to wait until the show tonight like everyone else."

Busted.

Twice in one morning. Wait, make that three times, since Noel called us out as well. That's a new record.

"Hi, Mama."

Dustin places a kiss on her cheek, Helena's wide smile as proud as can be.

"One of those wild nights you claim you don't have?"

"I'm gonna go grab a shower," Dustin spits out quickly, avoiding the question. I bite back a laugh, his mother's pointed look and pursed lips relaying that she knows that's what he's doing. "But Kenzie didn't get a chance to eat yet, Mama, so…" He trails off, eyes going wide, like he just stepped in a bear trap and is waiting for it to engage.

"We see each other once a week at Service Committee. It's still held at the library," Helena says. "Don't think you're special, Dustin. Just go shower."

I chuckle quietly as he scrambles out of the room, not bothering to look back. Helena, on the other hand, bolts across the room, throwing her arms around me for the biggest hug imaginable. She squeezes tight, rocking from side to side, barely audible squeals of joy bursting out of her.

"Okay, okay, I'm okay," she says when she finally lets me go. Stepping back, she smooths out her apron, obviously still trying to calm herself. "You've got a big day ahead of you, so sit down and let me make you some food. And while I do that, you can spill the tea that seems to have been brewin' last night."

I sigh, slipping into one of the chairs at the kitchen table.

"If I'm honest, it's been brewing for a whole lot longer than that. I don't know that I ever actually took the kettle off the stove."

"I could have told you that."

"Thanks?" I sputter.

"I don't mean that as a bad thing."

"I know you don't. I just…these last few days have brought a lot to the surface. It's given us a chance to say a lot of things that I think we meant to say a long time ago, but never did. But even with everything that's happened and how different things are, we still somehow picked up right where we left off."

"Do you not want to pick things back up?" she asks, the skillet popping and crackling as she works.

"I just said I left the kettle on, didn't I?"

"Just because it's on, doesn't mean you want to break out the fine china and host a party. Trust me, I know. My feelings for Dustin's father were around for a long, *long* time after that man disappeared from our lives. But I wasn't letting him back in, ever. Even if he had shown up on that step with a million dollars. And as you well know, there were a lot of times when y'all were growing up that I could have really used a million dollars."

I smile, the memories of how hard Helena had worked when we were kids flooding back. She'd been a bookkeeper at Hayes Industries for years, even after Dustin had hit it big. The Hayes family paid her well, but being a single parent still meant having to do whatever she needed to do to make ends meet, most often in the form of doing people's taxes in the evenings after work. She'd met Dustin's father, who Helena never referred to as anything but that, at work, six months before it was discovered that he was a conman, planning an embezzlement scheme. Helena had been the one to uncover it and turn him in.

He'd left town in the middle of the night when she called him on it…one week before she discovered she was pregnant.

"Do you ever regret him?" I ask.

She sighs, sliding the contents of the skillet onto a plate and placing it in front of me. Joining me at the table, she places her hand on top of mine. "I could never regret him completely. He gave me Dustin. But, to do over again, I'd do some things differently."

I nod, taking a bite of food. Big, bold flavors come alive in my mouth, taking over my senses. Helena Wilder is seriously the best cook in Hickory Hills. Maybe even all of Knox County. I'd bet money on it. We sit in silence, me shoveling food in my mouth like this is my last meal on earth, her just sitting there watching, a proud mama.

"Kenzie, no matter what, I will always love you like my own. All I want is for you two to be happy. Together, separate, whatever it ends up looking like. As long as you're happy."

"That's all I want too. I just wonder if I'm the only one."

"Oh, baby girl," she says, taking my hand in hers again, fully understanding my meaning. "Don't you dare think that it's one-sided."

"But how—"

"Ready?" Dustin asks, bursting into the kitchen. In a heartbeat, he's by my side, placing a kiss on top of my head.

Helena gives me a knowing look, as if that right there should answer my question. Standing up, she clears my empty plate.

"You two better get going. I'll see y'all over there."

Dustin hugs her goodbye, then takes my hand to walk me to the side kitchen door.

"Kenzie," Helena says as we step outside. "I just do. Promise."

Climbing into Old Blue, Dustin turns to me, brows knit in confusion. "What was that about?"

"Let us women have our secrets, will you?" I say, mimicking his comment from earlier.

"Hmmmmm. Well, at least you stopped blushing."

"We ran into every person possible making an early morning exit from my bedroom. Of course I was blushing! I don't know what was weirder, seeing that many people in such a short time frame or the fact that everyone was so nonchalant about it."

"Of course, they were nonchalant about it. What did you expect?"

I shrug. "Something different, I guess."

"There's nothing for them to react to, Kenz. You and me together, it's the most natural thing in the world."

CHAPTER SEVENTEEN

DUSTIN

KENZIE WAS WRONG.

Following her around while she bounces around from area to area, directing the chaos that is already ensuing, is a blast. If I thought watching her in her natural element of the library was sexy, then there are no words for what seeing her take charge like this does to me.

I'll give you a hint. It makes me want to let her take charge of me that way, resulting in very naughty things.

Keeping myself under control and the front of my pants from tightening every other minute is tough, but the stern look I got from a few of my former teachers when I playfully swatted Kenzie's behind is enough of a boner killer for me to maintain some decorum. At least outwardly. Inwardly, I am a teenager all over again, trying to work out a way to get my sweet, brown-eyed girl behind the field house.

The part Kenzie had been correct about is me being recognized. I don't think it takes five minutes before someone comes up to me and wants a picture. Followed by another, and another. By the time the opening ceremony and beer tasting contest—which I gladly volunteered to judge—are over, I can barely take a step without someone being right there, snapping a photo, whether I stop or not. It is surreal. Especially when I stop to think about how little I get recognized in my day-to-day life. Like so much else though, Hickory Hills hits different.

I also seriously underestimated how big the Rhythm and Brews Festival had gotten during my time away. We are barely an hour into open gates and there are already more people here than I remember ever attending. The first band is on stage, a cover of Hal Ketchum's "Small Town Saturday Night" wafting through the air. Talk about an oldie but goodie. The lyrics made me laugh, feeling each one of them deeply, remembering all the trouble we caused during our own small-town Saturday nights as teenagers.

"What's so funny?" Kenzie asks.

The back of her hand brushes against mine as she escorts me back to the VIP tent, where she informs me I will spend the rest of the afternoon. I have zero intention of following her directions, but also have zero intention of letting her know that. Her skin is soft, and my own hand aches to hold hers, lacing our fingers together as we walk, just like we used to. I have to keep fighting the urge though. She's already self-conscious from our walks of no shame this morning. Okay, I have no shame. Kenzie…well, shame might not be the right word, but it's clear she's still working out her feelings on the matter.

Her feelings for me are probably included in that. Something I'm trying very hard not to think about.

"I love this song, that's all. Brings back good memories."

"Of howling at the moon? Of shooting out lights? OMG, was there some girl named Lucy I didn't know about?" she teases, referencing the lyrics.

I laugh. "The only Lucy I can think of is Mama Keller, and I can promise you, there was nothing untoward going on there."

"Other than when she caught us kissing in the nursery behind that arborvitae."

"That was me being untoward with you, not her," I correct, smiling at the memory. "And I totally forgot about that."

"How could you forget? Nash and Noel taunted us with 'Dustin and Kenzie sitting in a tree, k-i-s-s-i-n-g' for months!"

I groan. How could I have forgotten? The taunts ring out in my head, the joined voices of the twins in surround sound, one on either side of me, clear as if they were doing it now. Our relationship wasn't secret—those two knew that I had been crushing on Kenzie for years before finally working up the nerve to ask her out. But it wasn't until the evening that their mother had found us behind that bush that we'd really been a couple in the eyes of our friends.

"Why were we even there?"

"That I don't remember," Kenzie says. "Or why we thought it would be a good place to make out."

"Probably because I couldn't keep my hands off you," I reply, grabbing her hand and stopping in place. Her arm catches as I pull her into me, wrapping my arms around her. "Much like I don't want to now—"

"Dustin!" a sharp voice calls out. A voice I cannot stand. I also hate that I know it, without question, across a crowded, open field.

A shiver runs down my spine—and not the good kind—as Kitty Cataway calls out my name again. I don't have to look up to know that her arm is extended high, her long legs fully on display in a too short skirt, beelining toward us. It's not very often that I don't want to interact with fans, but dealing with Kitty the other day left a sour taste in my mouth, one I don't ever need to experience again.

"Help me hide," I say, my jaw tense.

"From Kitty?" Kenzie's eyes go wide, full of questions that she doesn't know how to ask.

I nod, looking around for an escape route. There are people everywhere, which really should make this easier, but it doesn't. Only makes it that much more complicated to know where to go. Because all they are going to do is slow us down, letting Kitty and those damn legs catch up to us.

"She made a comment at the library that her offer from high school was still good."

"Offer from *high school*?" Kenzie chokes slightly on the last two words, eyebrows raised.

"Yeah…she offered to let me take her under the bleachers and show me how well she purred."

"How she purrs."

I nod again, starting to feel a little panicky. "She was offering—"

"I know what she was offering. The whole town knows."

Ain't that the truth…

Twisting all the way around, I see the fun house behind us. Yes, that's the answer. It's dark, full of obstacles and items that are meant to trick you or make you think you see something you don't, and some place Kitty certainly won't brave in whatever come-fuck-me-heels she's undoubtedly wearing. It'll be easy to get lost in there.

I grab Kenzie's hand, dragging her to the entrance. Her grip is strong, as is her giggle, our feet thundering up the metal stairs of the entrance. Relief washes over me at the sound of her laugh, glad she's in this with me and not throwing some fit about something that happened a long time ago. Then again, Kenzie has never been that type of girl.

At the top of the stairs, we're immediately greeted by a dark tunnel, the only light coming from a green laser cutting through the fog. The floor shifts beneath us, causing Kenzie to gasp, the undulation catching her off guard.

"I got you," I whisper into her ear, hands on her hips, guiding her in front of me.

"Says the man who is currently using me as a human shield."

"Do you not trust me?"

Stopping at the end of the tunnel, in a small space with psychedelic paint, Kenzie glances up at me. Her profile is framed perfectly by the door-sized entryway to the Hall of Mirrors, a distorted piece of glass reflecting the perfection that is her ass back at me. My mouth starts to water, the desire to sink my teeth into that peach staring back at me beginning to take over. Until Kenzie wraps her fingers through my belt loops, tugging gently, pulling me back into the moment and my gaze to her big brown eyes.

"I trust you completely."

My stomach flips, my chest filling with a warm sensation I can't name. She trusts me. After everything between us, after what I just told her about Kitty—she trusts me. Those four words were everything I didn't realize I needed to hear. The only thing better could be the infamous three words— but that would be getting ahead of ourselves.

I lead her into the Hall of Mirrors, careful as she steps backward over the small gap in the threshold. Placing her directly in front of the mirror that had been catching her from the side, I take some time to let this new angle sink in. I think I like it even better than the first.

"Are you staring at my ass in the…" She trails off, throwing a glance over her shoulder. "OMG, that thing makes it look huge!"

"Perfect. You pronounced *perfect* wrong."

Peering around me, she giggles. "Actually, my view isn't so bad either."

"You think you're funny, huh?" Grabbing onto her sides, I tickle her. What starts at giggles quickly morphs into squeals, and Kenzie slips out of my hold.

I look around, thankful there is no one around us. I figured we'd be lost in the crowd inside here, but won't complain about having the place to ourselves. We play in front of the mirrors for another couple of minutes, laughing and making faces at each other as our wacky reflections stare us down. When we get to the last mirror, Kenzie shakes her head, letting out a huff. Like all the others, the glass looks normal, but there is something to it that gives the reflected person an exaggerated hourglass shape.

"I look like one giant set of boobs," Kenzie mutters before trying to step away.

"Oh, no you don't."

I catch her wrist, pulling her back in front of the mirror, her back flush with my front. I have no doubt she can feel my growing erection pressing up against her, but I can't help it. The view of her like this is sexy, but the sound of her laugh and her playfulness while we've been in here is really what did it for me. Lord help me if this fun house has one of those sections with the air jets in the floor and she leaps into my arms startled. I won't be able to help myself.

Not that I'm doing a very good job of holding back right now.

"I happen to really like your boobs," I continue, my fingers playing with the hem of her fitted tee. Slipping up underneath, I run my palm along the smooth skin of her tummy, watching the skewed image in the mirror. Desire arcs through my veins, unable to stop myself even if I wanted to. Kenzie sucks in a hard breath as I run a thumb over her nipple, eyes glued to our reflection. "And I do recall promising them some more attention."

Kenzie wiggles against me, her ass seeming to know exactly how to stimulate my dick through all this denim. Fuck me. Two can play this game.

Grabbing hold of her breast, I squeeze, just hard enough to earn a moan. I lean down, my lips finding the sweet spot on her neck, the one I know will make her lose her mind. Nipping at it, I grip her breast tighter, my other arm firmly wrapped around her waist.

"Hey you two, enough playing grab-ass!"

Fuck...

Letting go of Kenzie, I whip around, hands flying to my hips, partly out of aggravation, partly as a way to hide Kenzie as she straightens herself up.

Nash stands there, a shit-eating grin on his face, not an ounce of remorse for interrupting us. At least he didn't stand there and watch. Noel appears behind him, an equally knowing smile on his face as he nods at us.

"Out of the way!" Willa says, pushing the twins to the side as she and Sylvie pile into the room.

"Well, at least the gang's all here," Kenzie mutters, stepping around me.

"Whatcha doin'?" Nash taunts.

I roll my eyes, not bothering to hide it. I love the guy—he's my best friend and has been my whole damn life. But fuck, is he an instigator. It's no wonder Willa wants to smack him most of the time.

"I was just about to knit a sweater," I reply through gritted teeth.

"Unless that's a euphemism I don't know about, this is probably the wrong light for that," Noel says, completely straight-faced. "Not to mention, you seem to have forgotten your needles."

Fuckers, both of them.

I sneer at them, their almost identical faces holding back their laughter. Someday, it'll be their turn, and when those days come, I hope they know that payback is going to be a bitch.

"Stop being so…" Willa trails off.

"So what?" Nash asks, his voice sharper but just as provoking as a moment ago.

"So *you.*"

Her narrowed eyes and the snarl on her lips as she turns to Kenzie are borderline deadly. Nash bumps the outsides of his fists together like Ross on *Friends*, the mocking gesture meant the same way as on the show—a politer way of giving her the finger. Now it's my turn to hold back a laugh. If Willa saw him, she didn't react—which leads me to believe she didn't. Instead, she loops her arm through Kenzie's, leading her into the next part of the funhouse.

Trailing behind the girls as they cautiously go from room to room, the guys and I hang back a bit, enjoying the view in front of us. As easy as it would have been to pair us all off with one another, Kenzie and I were the only two that ever went there. But just because there was never anything more than platonic feelings toward Sylvie and Willa, didn't mean we were blind. The three of us knew exactly how beautiful each one of those women were back then and even more now. We also know we're lucky bastards that they even give us the time of day, much less call us friends.

When we emerge from the funhouse, I cautiously look around, scanning the crowd. The last thing I need is for Kitty to be waiting at the exit for us. There seems to be twice as many people as there were before we went in, making me pull my cap down even farther.

"Something the matter?" Sylvie asks, her head whipping back and forth as she tries to figure out what I'm looking at.

"No," I answer, starting to feel confident that Kitty isn't lying in wait somewhere close by. "Just trying to avoid someone."

"Oh, who?" Willa's ears perk up, eyes alight with the thought of potential gossip. "Someone we know?"

"Kitty Cataway."

"What did Slutty McGee want this time?"

"Willa!" Sylvie scolds. "There are children present."

Willa shrugs, not a care in the world that she might be overheard.

"We didn't get that far," Kenzie offers. "She screamed his name and we went running."

"That's all it took? Her voice is enough to strike fear in you?"

"Jealous much?" Nash comments.

"Not of her." Turning on her heel, she marches away, leading us toward the VIP area we'd been on our way to. My stomach grumbles, letting me know that the food certainly waiting there is probably a good idea.

Weaving our way through the crowd, I take my time, trying to enjoy the feeling of being here. The event might be bigger than I remember, but it still feels the same. A small town, friendly people, and a relaxing afternoon of food, beer, and music. Can anyone really ask for more than that?

We pass by the "Mess Hall," the nickname a former police chief gave the series of tents that are home to empty tables and chairs for visitors to sit and rest, snuggled between the beer tent and the food vendors.

A long line wrapping around the inside of a large green tent leads to three long tables full of volunteers manning cash boxes and handheld credit card machines, taking BBQ orders. Despite the long line of fancy food trucks that show up every year, the highlight is always the BBQ. Hickory Hills Police and volunteer Fire Departments take great pride in many things—and at the top of that list is their meat. No pun intended.

A deep, raucous laughter pulls my attention over to a group of men standing next to the smokers, massive hunks of meat on chopping blocks in front of them. In the center of the group is Jack Keller, the twins' dad, wearing a bright red apron with a pig's backside, curly-Q tail and all painted on it, surrounded by the words *I like my butt rubbed and my pork pulled.*

"Things I never needed to know about your dad," I mutter to Noel, nodding in the man's direction.

"Tell me about it."

My attention still locked on the smokers and the amazing smell wafting our way from them, I trip over my own feet, stumbling forward. I catch myself before I crash to the ground, but not before Kenzie grabs ahold of my arm in an attempt to stop my fall. My skin tingles from her touch, the air crackling between us. I'm still turned on from almost getting to touch her in the funhouse, all the other feels the festival is giving me fueling that fire.

"Careful. Can't have my headliner canceling because he took a tumble."

I open my mouth to comment, but stop myself. The cheesy romantic in me is dying to tell her that I fell a long time ago, but I know that will come off wrong. Instead, I go with something I should have said earlier.

"It was freshman year, before I found the stones to ask you out."

"What was?" Her face pinches in confusion.

"Kitty and her offer."

"I wasn't worried."

"I know," I say, taking her hand and interlacing our fingers as we walk. "But I needed to say it. Need you to know. Because I promise you, Kenz, the only girl I've ever been interested in making purr is you."

CHAPTER EIGHTEEN

KENZIE

"MISS NOBLE," a small voice says, an equally small hand patting my thigh.

I look down at Justine, the younger of Jake's two nieces beaming up at me with excitement, her eyes wide with wonder. There is a question on the very tip of her tongue, ready to burst out at any second, her whole body bobbing up and down.

"Uncle Jake says that you know Dustin Wild," she continues, not waiting for me to respond. "Is that true? Do you really know him?"

I crouch down so I'm eye level with her, trying to match the size of her smile with mine. It's a tough task though. I'm not sure there is any competing with her right now, all dolled up in a bright pink sundress, matching jelly shoes, and her platinum-blonde hair curled, about to meet her favorite singer. As far as she's concerned, life doesn't get any better than this. Oh, to be six again.

"I do. And I'll let you in on a secret, so does your Uncle Jake."

"He does?" Corinne, Justine's older sister, asks. She looks

just as adorable as her sister, opting for a pair of jeans, sparkly cowgirl boots, and a matching hat pulled over her French-braided hair.

"He does," I confirm. "We all went to high school together."

I leave out the part about how their uncle was a bit of a bully at times, all cocky about being quarterback of the football team, looking down on those who didn't play. He and my cousin Zachary were a year ahead of us, never passing up a chance to taunt me for being the baby of the family. That was petty, small-town teen drama that we're all long past, and not something these two sweet little girls need to know about a man they adore. Their eyes grow even wider as they register the news, a new level of excitement unlocked. I can practically feel them vibrating with the anticipation. I chuckle, enjoying their reaction immensely.

"Thank you again for doing this," Jake says.

I push to my feet, taking a moment to look at him. His wavy brown hair flutters in the slight breeze and his brown eyes are full of warmth, the one corner of his mouth upturned in a small smile. I know how much these two little girls mean to him—he talks about them constantly. And despite his often being a jackass in high school, adult Jake is a good guy. Smart, hardworking, loyal. The kind of guy that any girl would be lucky to have steal her heart. I'm simply not that girl.

"It was all Dustin."

"Pretty sure he agreed because of you."

The band on stage ends their song, a round of applause followed by silence taking over and filling the space between us. The comment wasn't meant to be awkward, but that's certainly how I feel right now. Things were never serious between Jake and me—at least not on my part. But that doesn't make it any less weird that we're standing here, waiting on my ex—who may or may not be quite so ex-like after the last few days—with the guy that I "see sometimes." There should be a name for this feeling. Or maybe not, because truly, I don't wish it on anyone.

The sound of the door to the "green room"—also known as Mrs. Chamberlain's RV—opens up with a creak, pulling our attention to it. The old RV needs some TLC, but the AC works and the toilet flushes, making it good enough to park next to the VIP tent so that the performers have a place to cool off and bathrooms to use other than the porta-potties strewn around the event before they go on stage. I banished Dustin to hang out there after the funhouse, wanting to make sure there wasn't some kind of riot if he was spotted.

"Who are these two pretty ladies?" Dustin asks, sauntering toward us.

"OMG," Corinne gasps.

Justine is too overcome for words though, her mouth dropping open, both hands flying up to cover it. I can see a tinge of pink on her cheeks, the fact that Dustin is standing right there, talking to her, almost too much for her little soul to take.

I feel you, girl...

"This is Corinne and this is Justine," I answer for them. "Ladies, I'd like to introduce you to Dustin Wild."

"Hi there."

Dustin crouches down, extending a hand to Corinne first. She takes it, shaking his so furiously you'd think she was trying to pump water from a well.

"My favorite song is 'Silhouette Stetson,'" Corinne offers. "But I also really like 'Chasing Falling Stars.' It's really romantic."

"I think so too."

"Should I worry that at nine she even knows the word romantic?" Jake whispers, leaning over so only I can hear.

I shrug. "Eh, I'm sure she picked it up from her mom. She has yet to leave the children's section in search of the romance section, so I think we're okay for now."

"Please let me know the second that changes. Wait, no, I'm not sure I want to know."

I nod, happy that the awkwardness is easing. The band on stage finishes their set, piling into the tent from the far side entrance that's connected to the stage. Checking my watch, we are right on time. A ten-minute break before the next group takes the stage, and then one more break until it's Dustin's turn. My stomach fills with butterflies at the thought of seeing him on stage again. I'm excited to see him up there, with the lights and his band, for more than just a sound check. At the same time, I don't know that I want to share him with the crowd.

The moment we had last night as he serenaded me was special. Special and not to be repeated. Instead, tonight he'll be singing our song to whatever cute girl in a short skirt is in the front row flashing her tits at him. I might be the only girl Dustin Wilder has ever been interested in making purr, but *Dustin Wild*, well, I don't have insight into his brain.

And reconciling the two of them makes my head hurt.

"How was pizza the other night?" Jake asks, pulling me from my thoughts. Dustin is still crouched down, listening to the two little girls in front of him ramble on a mile a minute. Justine seems to have found her words just fine, her wild gestures causing Dustin to have to lean back every few seconds.

My heart squeezes, my insides swooning at the sight. Dustin interacting with kids is more than my senses can handle.

"It was the Slice, same as always," I deflect, not wanting to go down this road. The awkwardness had dissipated, so why are we jumping back in with both feet?

"You two look good together. Like you fit."

We fit?

"Jake…I…"

"Kenzie, it's a compliment. Take it."

"Thanks."

"I've always known you weren't mine. When Z asked if I would take you out to dinner because you needed some cheering up, I thought why not. I didn't expect it to be more than just that one night."

"You didn't?"

"Nope. I think we've both always known, at least subconsciously, that we were just killing time until your real life circled back around." Jake subtly nods toward Dustin, his serene, knowing expression lightening the weight I feel pressing against my chest. He really is one of the good ones. I just hope there is a girl in this town worthy of him. "I will say, it was nice being the one you passed the time with."

I bark out a laugh, the harsh sound briefly catching the attention of the girls, who dismiss it just as fast. "I don't know that anything has circled back around, and I may soon be in need of cheering up again. You never know."

"Well, if that's the case, you have my number. And I know where the Whippy Cone is."

"Uncle Jake, take our picture!" Corinne says, more a demand than a question, her hand jutting backward toward us, wrist twirling to get our attention.

"At your service, milady!"

Jake tips his head at me, stepping toward his nieces. He pulls out his phone, getting them all lined up for the photo op. I stand back, letting it all play out in front of me, still feeling like I could burst. The girls are still a pile of giggles, taking turns posing for the camera with Dustin, lining up shots where they are hugging him, pretending to kiss him, and even one where he's giving them a piggyback ride. If these two were on social media, they'd go viral in no time with these photos. Instead, they're getting the better end of the deal, making memories with someone they idolize. The photographic evidence for bragging rights later on is just icing on the cake.

"Y'all are staying for the show, right?" Dustin asks as they finish up.

"Yes!" both girls exclaim.

"Miss Noble saved us seats right up front actually," Jake adds.

"Really?" Corinne asks, rushing toward me and wrapping her arms around me as I confirm. Justine is right behind her, the force of her plowing into me and her sister knocking us all back a step.

"Well, y'all better go get settled. I have to go warm up with my band. But I'll be looking for you, okay? I need someone to sing 'Chasing Falling Stars' to."

The wink he gives me makes my tummy do somersaults. I guess that answers that question—Dustin Wild might just be as singularly sighted as his small-town alter ego. And I'm here for it.

———

"Where'd the twins go?"

Willa, Sylvie, and I are standing in the wings of the stage, watching as Dustin wows the crowd. I haven't seen either Nash or Noel since before Dustin went on, making me worry slightly.

"Helena grabbed them to help with crowd control," Sylvie says. "Apparently there is record attendance, so she wanted a few extra bodies just in case."

"She have enough people?"

"I think so. Every cop is here, plus all the boy cousins and

Willa's brothers who aren't working the beer tent. She even grabbed Camden Tyler out from the dunk tank, so she's exhausted all her resources."

"Camden was in the dunk tank?" Willa asks.

"Yes, he volunteered."

"I'm sure that took a lot of convincing."

"He *volunteered*."

"I have no doubt. Just like I also have no doubt that he wishes you were in there getting wet with him."

"Shut up!"

I snicker, unable to hold it back. Sylvie's voice is already flustered, from that one little comment.

"You could give him a chance," I offer. "He's so sweet."

"He is. But I'm not interested. And neither is he."

"What planet do you live on?" Willa asks. "He's looked at you like you control the moon and stars since we were eight. Trust me on this one. When have I ever steered you wrong?"

"Extreme clit cream comes to mind almost instantly."

Sylvie glares at Willa, dropping that bomb of a memory like we're the only three people in the world right now, and not in the middle of a concert. Everyone around is oblivious though, in their own little worlds enjoying the show. I can't blame them—he does look damn good on that stage.

"That was one time."

The two of them continue to bicker, Sylvie launching into her well-rehearsed story about how she couldn't feel her lady bits for days after a severe reaction to this cream that Willa had found online and purchased for a laugh. It was funny then, and it's even funnier now, because of course if there was one of us who would have an adverse reaction to something that was supposed to heighten awareness down there, it would be Sylvie.

Their voices fade into the background, the music coming from onstage taking over. It's like each note is being played just for me, Dustin's familiar voice wrapping around me like a warm blanket, the rest of me starting to react like I just used some of that extreme clit cream. Tingles work their way down my body, and goose bumps start to form on my arms, the warm fall air failing to stop them. How could it? There's the sexiest man I've ever seen on stage with a guitar, singing about a brown-eyed girl.

Song after song he continues, glancing over here every now and again, our eyes locking for the briefest of seconds. My mouth waters, wanting to kiss him more and more with each nod or wink I receive. No, more than kiss him. I want him to push me up against these speakers and have his way with me.

The crowd roars as he launches into "Outlaw In My Blood," another one of his massive hits. Looking out at the sea of people, watching them sing along, I wonder how many of them know the history of the song, or that the chorus was made up right here in Hickory Hills, in a mechanic's bay in the heart of town. Each word he sings takes me back to those days, the silly lyrics he would make up and sing as he worked on Old Blue.

I sigh, my heart full and overflowing, my brain still working overtime with dirty fantasies about all the areas we can sneak off to when this is over. The little alcove of large speakers and storage crates right behind the stage comes to mind first, but there is always the Green Room. Then again, I'm not sure the door on that RV locks, and that's the first place everyone is going to look for him. And I am desperate for him to finish what he started in the funhouse this morning. I wish this feeling could last forever—that Dustin and I could last. But I know it's not possible. We lead two very different lives, and at the end of all this, he's leaving again. I'm just going to have to make the most of it while I can.

"Just don't burp while you're swallowing," Sylvie says.

Errr...what? My head whips toward my friends. I have clearly missed something while I was daydreaming.

"Swallowing?" I choke out.

"You know..." she replied, waving her hand in front of her. "*Swallowing...*"

"No, Sylvie, I don't know. Enlighten me," Willa taunts, keeping her voice low.

"I know you know what I'm talking about. You taught me how to do it. I'm not saying it out loud! Especially not here."

"You burped while swallowing?" I ask, needing clarification. Forget how we got here, or anything happening on that stage—this requires my full attention.

"It's not something I recommend."

All three of us burst into laughter, just as a song is ending. The sound carries more than we intend, catching the attention of the guitar player, who signals to Dustin. He turns our way, leveling me with a panty-melting smile.

"Y'all, I haven't performed this next song in a long time, but something about tonight just feels right. A big thanks to the king, the great George Strait, for letting me borrow this one when I was a newbie. I hope y'all enjoy."

Another wink in my direction and a nod of his head, then the band launches into a slow ballad, the twang of the guitars as distinct as the melody. My knees wobble, my breath catches, and my heart races as the song continues, Dustin's smooth voice lulling the chaos inside me. I can't remember the last time I heard this song, but I still know all the words as if it were yesterday. Singing along, I fight back tears as we get to the title of the song.

Nobody in his right mind would've left her...

CHAPTER NINETEEN

DUSTIN

My whole body is thrumming, electricity shooting through my veins as I look out over the massive crowd. The field is jam-packed as far as I can see into the hay field and I'm sure even farther than that.

Scanning the audience, I wonder if this is what Garth Brooks felt like when he played Central Park. He must have. It's an overwhelming feeling of joy and gratitude. I'm honored every time I'm on stage—no matter the venue—that they chose me. There are a lot of things that people can spend their hard-earned money and beyond valuable free time on, and it's never lost on me that it's my show, and my music, that they are choosing.

Tonight is different though. Because tonight is bigger than me.

I glance down at the set list taped to the stage right next to my mic stand. We just finished up "Chasing Falling Stars," which is normally what I save for my encore. But like I said, tonight is different.

"Y'all, I'm not gonna lie…you might just be the best crowd ever!" I declare, the whoops and hollers starting before I even finish my sentence. "You sure do know how to welcome a guy back home!"

More shouts and cheers erupt, joined by more than one wolf whistle. There's even a "we love you, Dustin!" thrown out from somewhere. There's so much going on, it's hard to know which direction it came from.

"This is the part of the show where normally the lights would go down, my band and I would disappear for a minute, and try to fool you into thinking the show is over, even though we all know that it's not," I continue, slinging my guitar around so it rests against my back. "But we're not going to play that game tonight."

Another wolf whistle slices through the air, followed by more cheers. I turn to Joel and nod, giving him the signal we had arranged earlier. He disappears to the side of the stage, putting it in motion.

"The Rhythm and Brews Festival has always been one of my favorite times of the year. Even as a kid, long before I could partake in the brews part, there was something about this event. And for those of you wondering, I will not confirm or deny if I took part in the brews portion before it was legal. Chief Myers is standing right there."

I point down to the police chief, laughing along with the crowd as he holds up his hands as if to say he wasn't going to bring it up. He and I both know exactly how old I was the first time he busted me—right along with Nash, Noel, Kenzie, Willa, and Sylvie—out in the woods by Rocky Pond. Pretty sure Mama did his taxes for free a number of years in a row as a thank you for all the times she didn't get a phone call from him or one of his deputies.

"But this year's festival is extra special. Because this year, we are honoring a man who means more to me than I can ever put into words. Any of y'all who were singing along with 'Small Town Star'—well, you were singing about him. It is my pleasure to introduce you to Ken Noble!"

Turning to the side, my heart swells as Joel pulls a reluctant Ken onto stage. Right behind him is a teary Kenzie, grasping onto Sylvie's hand, a smile on her lips brighter than the moon. God, do I love that smile. Even better knowing that I was the one who put it on her face.

"What we're raising money for tonight is this man right here. A man who has never thought twice about helping out a member of this community. He's the most honest, loyal, and dedicated human being I have ever met. He's who I want to be when I grow up." The whoops and screams start up again and Ken hangs his head, hating all the attention. That's not stopping me though. "So, here's what I'm gonna ask of y'all. My team is putting a number up on the screen right now, and I hope y'all can see it. If you can't, ask anyone in a Rhythm and Brews volunteer shirt and they'll give it to you. By texting this number, you're donating five dollars to 'A Noble Cause.' Text as many times as you like. There's no limit."

Ken's head snaps up so fast I'm not sure he didn't give himself whiplash, turning to look at me. The love in his eyes almost brings tears to mine, but I hold them back. If I start, he'll start, and cause a chain reaction that might just flood this place. Instead, I pull him in for a bear hug. He squeezes me back just as tightly, expressing everything we feel but can't say at the moment.

When he lets go, he starts to step backward, inching off the stage. I laugh, throwing an arm around him and leading him backstage, giving the crowd time to make their donations. My band plays on, each one of them having made their own donations earlier after getting the chance to meet the man I "talk about all the damn time" according to them.

Giving me another hug once we're out of view of the crowd, Ken pats me on the back. "I owe you big, son."

"We're not even close to even after everything you've done for me."

Another nod and he steps away, quickly replaced by his daughter, throwing her arms around me. Kenzie's body feels like heaven against mine as I hug her back, lifting her off the ground. The need to kiss her fills me, but I know I can't. I need to get back out on that stage and finish my set. Just one more song to go though, and then she's all mine.

"I'm going to do such dirty things to you," she whispers in my ear.

Holy shit...

My dick is instantly hard, my whole body revved up and ready to go in a flash after those words. That was not what I was expecting her to say. I won't complain one bit, however.

"Then I better go sing this song."

Setting her down, I tug on my guitar strap, thankful I have it to hide the massive erection I'm now sporting. I give her a wink and head back out on stage.

"Alright y'all! I wrote this song about growing up here in Hickory Hills, so if you know it, I hope you sing along!"

Five minutes and a few extra choruses of "My Dirt Roads" later, we're winding down. The crowd is still rowdy, wanting more. The temptation to stay and give it to them is there. But there is a bigger temptation standing in the wings, biting her bottom lip, making eyes at me. For as great as tonight has been, Kenzie wins out.

"Do you have any idea how hot it is watching you?" she greets me, grabbing me by my T-shirt and kissing me hard.

Her lips are sticky and sweet, reminding me of ice cream. Sucking lightly on her bottom lip, I savor the taste as she moans, pressing herself into me even more. My dick twitches, still rock-hard from her comments a few minutes ago.

"The lights are pretty warm, but you get used to them," I reply, barely pulling back from the kiss, teasing her. I learned a long time ago that Kenzie keeps herself fairly even-keeled in public, only letting her real self out among friends. And only letting a completely different side out around me. But there is a brazen, risk-taking, dirty girl deep in there, and right now, I can tell she wants to come out to play.

"You think you're so funny."

"I do."

Giving me a shove, Kenzie steps back, shaking her head. There's a fire in her eyes that tells me exactly what she's thinking, and fuck, do I like it. There are too many people around though, already fast at work to close out the night. We might feel like the only two people in the world, but we most certainly aren't. And I need to get her alone.

"So…" I start, turning up the charm. "Hypothetically, where would the rock star take the pretty little thing who's been making eyes at him all night for some one-on-one time?"

"That depends. What are his intentions?"

Flames flicker up my arms, my balls tightening with need.

"Nothing good," I growl, yanking her into me and grinding my hips against her so that she can feel exactly what she's doing to me.

"Then follow me."

Kenzie grabs my hand, leading me through a maze of boxes and crates behind the stage. An eerie half silence greets us the farther we get from the action, the buzz of it all still in the background, turning into white noise. The lights from the stage give the space just enough glow to make out Kenzie's gorgeous form in front of me, my eyes glued to her ass. When she comes to a sudden stop, I bump into her, earning myself a wiggle against my erection.

Fuuuuuuuck...

Spinning around, Kenzie grabs the hem of my shirt, lifting it and slipping her hands up underneath. The tips of her fingers against my sweaty skin feel like icicles, my body shivering from her touch.

"How long have you been keeping the donation thing a secret?" she asks, moving to my belt.

Undoing it with ease, she looks up at me, licking her lips, fingers deftly undoing the button. I suck in a breath, trying to find my composure to answer.

"Since that night you called," I answer honestly. Kenzie doesn't let up, sliding my zipper down, running her flat palm along the bulge in my skivvies. "Hearing you say that you'd been thinking about me, and had been on the edge of calling. I knew I needed to do something more."

"Hmmmmmmm," she hums, toying with the elastic on my boxer briefs.

The teasing doesn't last long though, her hands slipping beneath the elastic and gripping me tight a second later. My hips buck, the softness of her skin the best thing I've felt since…well, since the last time she touched me. Reaching up, I cup her face, kissing her hard. She matches my efforts, both with her lips and her hand, the two of us a tangle of limbs, lust taking over.

But then Kenzie stops.

Letting go of me, she leans back, once again pushing me away. Worry races through me that I did something wrong. That she's hurt or upset. I scan her up and down, trying to figure out what changed. Except, I can't.

Sexy as sin Kenzie is still standing before me, looking at me like I'm a four-course meal and she hasn't eaten in a week. Slowly closing the gap between us, Kenzie's hands land on my shoulders, walking me backward until I'm resting against a large wood crate marked fragile in big red letters. She continues to move silently, running her hands down my chest, thumbs catching on my pants, working them down my thighs. When she reaches my knees, she lets go, and sinks all the way to the ground.

One hand grips my cock again, stroking it hard. Licking her lips again, Kenzie looks up, and my mind goes blank.

Oh, fuuuuuck...

I can't think, I can't speak, and I can't even make any unintelligible noises as Kenzie takes me in her mouth, her tongue running along the underside of my shaft. My whole body goes numb, all the blood in my veins and every last nerve ending I have all huddled right there. Each new movement she makes sends a wave of pleasure through me that I can't describe. It's that first bite of your favorite food, paired with hugging someone you haven't seen in forever, topped with the comfort of your own bed. But better. And with each bob of her head and stroke of her hand, Kenzie kicks it up a notch.

It shouldn't be possible to feel this good. Or so I think until Kenzie circles her tongue around the tip of my cock, smiling up at me as she does it. I almost come right then and there, the small bead of pre-cum on her tongue too much to handle.

"Fuck, baby," I groan. Not the most eloquent expression ever, but again, the only thing I can manage.

Reaching down, I pull her up. I need her. Now. Need her legs wrapped around me, our bodies pressed together as I fuck her mouth with my tongue. My hands fumble with her jeans, too focused on getting her naked to actually be successful at it. Somehow we manage though, getting one shoe off and one leg out of her pants. Her panties are still in the way though.

Sliding my hands between her legs, I gather the already damp fabric in my hand and tug. The lace gives way easier than I thought, and I let them drop to the ground. Kenzie yelps as I dip my fingers back into her wetness, sliding them across her clit. I love how responsive she is to me. The thought of how she's this wet just from sucking me off turns me on even more.

"Don't tease me, Dusty," she groans.

"I have no plans to."

Whipping a condom out of her bra, she rips it open and has me covered in no time. Just as fast, I have her off the ground, spinning around so that it's her turn up against the crate. I kiss her long and hard, lining myself up at her entrance, giving her a chance to change her mind. I have her shielded so that if anyone does walk back here they won't see it's her, but I still want to make sure she's sure. As hot as this moment is, semipublic sex is new territory for us.

"Dusty," she moans again, and that's all I need.

I sink into her slowly, letting the both of us adjust to this position. She's tight and wet, her pussy welcoming me home. Forget about her mouth. Yes, the blow job was incredible, but nothing will ever beat this. Nothing will ever be better than the feel of Kenzie surrounding me.

My hips draw back quickly, then slam forward, driving into her. Kenzie's nails dig into me, spurring me on as I pick up the pace, losing my control. All the electricity that was coursing through me earlier is back, this time sparking between us with each new buck of my hips. Kenzie meets me thrust for thrust, her whimpers and moans echoing in my ears.

Throwing her head back, Kenzie shifts in my arms, angling her hips forward. She's close, I can tell by the way her pussy is gripping me, and my girl wants to come. More than that, I want to make her. I want to hear my name on her breath as she loses control. So I'm going to give her exactly what she wants.

"Are you gonna come for me, naughty girl?" I ask, slipping a hand between us, fingers finding her clit. It's a tight fit with the way our bodies are pressed together, amping up the friction. Kenzie whines as my thumb circles the tiny bundle of nerves, her breathing growing heavy. "Be a good girl—come."

Eyes flashing wide, Kenzie careens forward. I continue to pump into her, not letting up as her pussy starts to spasm. I can feel her orgasm start, increasing the pressure on her clit.

"Dusty!"

Biting down on my shoulder through my shirt, Kenzie doesn't disappoint, with muffled screams of my name as her climax rips through her. Mine's not far behind. My spine starts to tingle, my balls tightening as her pussy clamps down on my cock like a bear trap, milking me for all I'm worth. I empty myself into the condom, holding back my own roar.

I continue to hold her pressed against the crate for a long moment, our mingled, labored breathing the only sound against the buzz of the festival in the background. My whole body is satiated, the high rushing through my veins unparalleled. But more than that, my heart is happy.

I don't know what any of this means. All I know is that I've never been as happy or at peace as when Kenzie is in my arms. That this—whatever this is—will never feel right with anyone else. I don't even have to try to know that.

Too bad it's not that easy.

"That's the second pair of panties that you have ruined," Kenzie says, resting her forehead against mine.

The move is simple, sweet, and full of so much trust and love that my already overwhelmed heart isn't sure it can take any more. I sigh, letting the feeling sink in.

"Second? What was the first?"

"The ones from yesterday."

"Those are still very much intact. They are just not being returned."

Kenzie laughs. "Either way, I'm down two pairs."

"That much less laundry you have to worry about."

She shakes her head, apparently unable to come up with a response. Lifting her head, she pushes her hair off her cheek, a self-conscious look on her face.

"Can I ask you something?"

"Absolutely anything."

"Does what we just did…am I now just one of many groupies to blow you backstage?"

My stomach drops with her question, hating that's where her mind went. What she and I just did, what we shared, was not some casual fuck. At least not to me.

"No. This was a first for me."

"Oh." The smile she gives me is addictive, making me hard all over again. "I like being the first."

Oh, my girl…if you only knew the truth…

CHAPTER TWENTY

DUSTIN

THE CHIRP of my phone ringing cuts through the morning air, my body bolting upright at the disturbance. My heart jackhammers, moving faster than my already racing mind, panic setting in. The only reason for someone to call this early would be an emergency. Especially the morning after a show. I do my best not to disturb Kenzie as I fumble for my pants, finding my phone in the back pocket.

"Hello," I answer in a whisper. Glancing over at Kenzie's bedside clock, I realize that it's not quite as early as I thought, but my priority remains—let Kenzie rest.

"Why are we whispering?" Eric asks.

"One sec."

Putting the phone down, I grab my skivvies and slip them on, before making my way into the hallway. I gently close the door behind me, sneaking one last look at the beautiful brunette tangled up in the sheets. My heart is full, my soul at ease after another night spent wrapped up in each other, talking and laughing well past bedtime. Getting to finally spend that quality time with her breasts wasn't a hardship either. This is what I want every night to be like.

"Sorry," I reply, closing the bathroom door and perching on the side of the tub.

"Everything okay?"

"More than. Everything's perfect." I can hear the smile in my voice and wonder if Eric can as well. There's no hiding it. This is the lightest I have felt in a long time.

"Let me guess, 'Heartbreak Country Song'?" he asks, naming one of the first songs I wrote after moving to Nashville. It's a title very few people know, since it was never released or even made it onto an album. It's one of the best songs I've ever written, but after recording it I decided it was too raw—too personal—for the world to know about. Instead, "Chasing Falling Stars" got the nod.

"Among other things."

It's an evasive answer, but I don't care. It's none of Eric's business. At least not until I figure out how I feel. No, that's a lie. I know how I feel. What I need to figure out is how to make this work. If Kenzie even wants to make this work. If she does, then I will find a way. Getting back to Hickory Hills all the time won't be easy, but lots of musicians make stops at home in between tour dates. If they can do it, so can I.

"I take it that means the show went well then? I'm looking at the donation numbers from the texts, and damn, dude, you must have done something right to pull in this kind of cash."

"That's a small town for you."

"You want to know the number?"

"Nope," I answer, shaking my head emphatically like he can somehow see my reaction. "I'll hear the total number later today."

"You don't want to know how much you're matching?" His voice is incredulous, same as it was when I told him I was going to match whatever was raised from the text donation one hundred percent. He's never said it outright, but I know he disagrees with my choice. Again, I don't care. Eric's given me a lot of great advice over the years, and it'd be hard to argue that I would be where I am without him. But I also know he doesn't understand why this is as important to me as it is.

He doesn't understand that this is about supporting family. Whatever happens between Kenzie and me, her father is the reason I am the man I am. He's the reason for so much in this town. Mama wasn't kidding when she said that everyone has a Ken Noble story. He and that old tow truck of his, always at the ready to go save the day.

"Just make sure Mrs. Burch has the final total number. Where it all came from is irrelevant."

"If you say so." He huffs out his annoyance, but I ignore it. Let him be annoyed. We'll make more money. And if not, then so be it. "Next item of business. I need you back here earlier than you currently have planned."

"How much earlier?"

"Tomorrow."

Tomorrow? Hell, no. I purposely blocked out this whole week so I could spend it here. I want—need—more time with Kenzie. With the twins. With Mama. Everyone was in such a tizzy last week prepping for the festival, so this week is supposed to be about relaxing.

"Nope. I took this week off. We talked about this."

"That was before network TV came calling."

Network TV…?

"Who came calling?"

"I've been chatting with an old friend of mine," he says. I roll my eyes, because everyone in Nashville seems to be "an old friend" of his. "And he's been in talks with a couple of different networks about a new singing competition."

Eric continues, droning on in way too much detail about

a battle between the networks over all sorts of things I don't care about. I tune him out for a bit, the sound of the stairs creaking catching my attention. Based on the sounds of the footfalls, my guess is that Ken's awake, headed for the last of the strata. My heart squeezes, happiness flowing through me that the Nobles have welcomed me back with open arms. Even if I am currently hiding in the hall bathroom in my underwear.

"What does this have to do with me?" I ask, cutting off the long-winded story. I need to get going. I want more snuggle time with Kenzie before we have to head back to Newton Field, and this is cutting into that.

"They want the focus of the show to be on people from small towns. Little, itty-bitty places that no one knows exist but are harboring someone with huge talent. Someone like you. And they want you to be the primary judge. If you agree, they are looking to name it *Small Town, Big Star* after your song."

"That's not what the song is about," I reply before I can stop myself. That song is about Ken—about everything he does for almost no recognition. He's the big star, not me.

"The song is about whatever the listener wants it to be about, Dustin. And really, that matters very little at this point. This is huge for your career. And their starting offer is a shit ton of money."

"I can't be back tomorrow." Counting the days out on my fingers, I sigh, hating that I'm even considering this. But Eric's right, this would be huge for my career. Help launch me into markets I haven't even scratched the surface of. I might be a name in country music, but this would make me a household name, period. "Wednesday, at the earliest. I still have things here I need to take care of."

"Fine, Wednesday."

We say our goodbyes and I drop my phone onto the bathmat. It hits the ground with a soft thud, landing facedown. Briefly, I think about flipping it over, but I stop myself, instead running my hands over my face.

Fuck...

What was I thinking? So much for being resolved on finding a way to make this work with Kenzie. No, this isn't the end to that. It's just one more thing I need to work out in the schedule. Filming this can't take up that much time, can it? There's no guarantee that a network will even actually pick it up and turn it into a show. At least I'm pretty sure that's what Eric just said in his little monologue.

Still, I don't need to add anything else on my plate. I need to focus on what is important. My music, and…and what? Gah, I don't even know. I don't want to say relationship, because I don't know that this is a relationship. Kenzie could just be using me, getting me out of her system one last time. Counting down the days until she can say she's done with me for good.

Her smile from last night, her body still wrapped around mine, our foreheads pressed together, flashed through my mind. *I like being the first.* That's not something you say to someone you're simply using.

She likes being the first. I like her being the *only*. Maybe I need to find a way to tell her that.

Pushing up from the tub, I grab my phone and sneak back into Kenzie's room. She's rolled over onto her side facing the door, the sheet draped casually over her torso, showing off all her stunning curves, like she's posing for a Renaissance painting. My own personal angel of the morning.

I slide back under the covers, wrapping my arms around her soft, naked body, pulling her up against me. The sleepy coos she lets out make my dick twitch against her ass, and I know she feels it, the gentle rocking of her hips a giveaway.

I hold her like this for a while, enjoying the moment, my

heart aching. This is how I want to wake up. How I want to fall asleep. I want Kenzie to be my future. I just have to figure out how.

There's an easy answer dancing around my brain—ask her to move to Nashville. I know that's not possible though. Maybe she would have considered it seven years ago had I not been a jackass and manned up. But now, too much has changed. With Ken being sick, there is no way she would leave now.

The answer is out there though. I know it.

Waking slowly, Kenzie shifts in my arms, then rolls onto her back, looking up at me. She runs a hand along my morning scruff, her fingertips leaving my skin tingling.

"Morning, beautiful."

"What time is it?"

"Early."

"Then who was on the phone?"

"Just Eric," I answer, running my hand along her smooth skin.

"Is everything okay? Do you have to go back?"

"He would like me to go back early, yes."

Kenzie swallows hard, the muscles in her throat contracting, her eyes turning worried. My stomach rolls, hating the disappointment that is written all over her.

"Oh."

I kiss her forehead, then the tip of her nose, and finally her mouth, gently at first, deepening it soon after. I want her to know I'm here, and that I'm not running.

"I told him I couldn't leave yet. That I still need to be here."

"For?"

You, Kenzie, you...

"You didn't really think I would miss out on Sloppy Seconds, do you?" I chuckle. "Mrs. Higgins's mac and cheese, with some pulled pork and that sauce that Sargent McRae makes—which we all know is better the second day. I wouldn't miss that for anything."

Her eyes widen at the mention of food, and I can tell she's on board with my thought process. Because as amazing as the Rhythm and Brews Festival is, every local knows that the next best thing—or maybe even better than, depending on who you ask—is the tradition of Sloppy Seconds. The affectionate—if not borderline inappropriate—name for the event was allegedly coined sometime in the late eighties, although no one remembers by whom. Everyone in town, however, knows to be there for it. Once all the booths are torn down, the leftovers are busted out, with a few new dishes to round them out, and the biggest semipotluck you'll ever see is held.

I smile in return, finding her lips with mine. Moaning into our kiss, Kenzie wraps a leg around me. Sparks shoot through me from her touch, but not because I'm turned on. Or well, not just because I'm turned on. My heart is in this just as much as my body, maybe even more. Those sparks are fueling something in me that I can't name. A melody that is still a mystery to me, but is somehow stuck in my head. One that I am dying to figure out. Get down on paper and play for the whole world.

The sound of Kenzie's phone interrupts us, both of us grumbling as we part. It's the reminder that we need to get going, even if all I want is to stay like this forever. Quickly tapping back an answer, Kenzie looks at me with a devilish grin.

"I know I said no yesterday, but what would you say to conserving water this morning?"

"Conserving wat—" I stop halfway through the word, her hidden meaning smacking me in the face.

I'm out of bed and scooping her up before she can react, bursting out of her room. The bathroom is all of five steps away normally, but I do it in three, depositing her on the counter. Her laugh rings out, filling up my insides. This is the happiest I've been in a long fucking time, and there is no way I can let go. Not again.

I'm going to find a way to make this work.

CHAPTER TWENTY-ONE

KENZIE

One thing we most certainly did not accomplish this morning? Conserving water.

Not one ounce of me is sad about that though.

Standing in line for food, a shiver runs through me, a serene smile taking over as I play back the events of the morning in my mind. We might have wasted more water than needed—and taken twice as long as we should have—but it's a memory that I'm going to tuck back into my mind, to pull out whenever I need a pick-me-up. I know I don't have long until Dustin leaves again and whatever this is between us ends, so I am going to savor every second.

Let's not lie here; picking back up with Dustin was silly. There was just no resisting him. My feelings for him are still too strong. All I can do now is hope that this one last fling together will help get him out of my system. That I'll be able to move on.

Watching him as he loads up his plate, Chief Myers's wife beaming back at him, I can't stop my heart from clenching, the whole of me wishing this could be different. That this could be an all the time thing. He might have told his manager that he can't come back yet, but *yet* is the key word there. He has another life. One that doesn't include Hickory Hills.

"Who's that?" Dustin asks, jutting his chin in the direction of a tall, thin guy with a mop of dark curls on his head.

"In the electric-blue shirt?" Dustin nods, leading the way to the large round table where the rest of our friends are already seated. "That's Parker Michaels. KatieRae Gates's husband. They got married like a year and a half ago?"

"He looks familiar."

"He's the captain of the Atlanta Rising Football Club. And the reason like half the team was at the festival yesterday."

Dustin snaps his fingers with his free hand, setting his plate down on the table. "That's where I know him from. Wait, a year and a half? I thought it was her bachelorette trip they were on when I saw her and Moira in Nashville. And what happened to Chip?"

"Just a girls' trip. They didn't really do a bachelorette because she and Parker had this insane whirlwind romance before eloping. But with both her and Moira pregnant, they decided a girls' trip was needed."

"And Chip…" Willa adds, waving her fork. Her eyes gleam with excitement over getting to share this gossip. "They broke up like two years ago. She caught him with a redhead named Bernice, who was one of the moms of her preschool kids. It was this whole big thing—KatieRae fled to Atlanta to escape the gossip and somehow ended up as a nanny to her now hubby, after he ended up with sole custody of his kid when baby mama abandoned them at the hospital after giving birth."

"How do you even know all this?" Sylvie asks, voice filled with admonishment.

"How do you not?"

"Because some of us have real jobs, Willa," Nash retorts, a mouthful of pork.

"I have a real job. You, on the other hand, play in the dirt."

Nash flips her the bird, Noel side-eyeing her, not bothering to comment. I manage to hold in a laugh, finding comfort in their exchange. Everything about this moment feels good and normal.

"How did teardown go?" I ask, changing the subject before a real fight can break out.

"The whole process is a well-oiled machine," Nash offers. "Some packing up left to do, but not a single problem to be had."

"Speak for yourself," Sylvie comments. "The arm on the dunk tank broke again. I think the whole thing has seen better days. My physics kids might need to come up with a new building project."

"I can look later," Noel says.

"If you can. If not, no worries. Camden was trying to fix it."

"Camden?" Willa playfully elbows Sylvie, egging her on.

"You left the town vet to act as mechanic?" Nash asks.

"He offered!"

"He seems to offer to help you with a lot," Dustin says, a knowing smirk on his face. I kick him under the table, trying to get him to stop. The impish looks he gives me is all the response I need though. He's jumped on this bandwagon along with Willa, ready to join in the fun.

And this feels too damn good...

Sylvie rolls her eyes though, not giving in. Good for her. Although I have ten bucks that says she won't last another five minutes if they continue to push. Thankfully though, they let it rest, silence taking over as we shove food into our mouths. The peace doesn't last long though.

"Look who it is!" Willa's sing-songy voice cuts through

the air over the buzz of conversation filling the tent. "Doctor Camden Tyler, how are you? Join us!"

She gestures to the open seat between Sylvie and Nash, her pageant smile plastered on. Sylvie, on the other hand, is shooting daggers at Willa, who is either oblivious or much better at acting than I have ever given her credit for.

"Thank you, Miss Willa." A gentlemanly nod in her direction and he's taking a seat, turning his attention to the flustered teacher next to him. "Miss Sylvie."

"Oh, this reeks of trouble," Dustin whispers, leaning in and pressing a light kiss just behind my ear. My hand finds his thigh, fingers gripping tight as his breath tickles my skin.

"Would you expect anything less out of her?"

"Nope. I've missed this."

My heart squeezes at Dustin's admission, because I've missed this too. The six of us together, living the small-town life, just like I had always pictured us. I remind myself that this isn't real though. That in a few days, Dustin will leave, and we will never get another Rhythm and Brews Festival together again.

"How about some truth or dare?" Willa suggests. The gossipy gleam in her eyes has now turned into an evil sparkle, her excitement palpable.

Lord help us...

"Now?" Noel grunts, lifting one eyebrow, judgment written all over him. He may be a man of few words, but damn does he know how to make them count.

"Yes. Camden, you're our guest, so you first. Truth or dare?"

The poor guy freezes, the stereotypical deer in the headlights, fork in midair, coleslaw hanging off it. My gut roils, wishing I could help him somehow. But I'm not fast enough. Thankfully, Dustin is.

"That's not fair, he just sat down to eat. Let him get a couple of bites in first. I'll start—truth."

Willa sighs dramatically, making a point of her disappointment. "Fine. Have you ever stolen anything?"

"You mean other than Kenzie's heart?"

Heat instantly pricks at my cheeks, my whole body flushing with embarrassment. Did he really just say that? Prouder than a peacock, Dustin winks at me. He sure did. I smack his chest with the back of my hand, soft enough for him to know that I don't really mean it. Inside though, I'm dying, knowing that I'm in this way too deep.

Because yes, Dustin Wilder has stolen my heart once again.

"That's the only thing of consequence," he continues. Willa nods, accepting the answer. Dustin turns to Noel, his effort to keep the focus off Sylvie and Camden obvious. I squeeze his thigh again, a silent thank you I hope he understands. "Noel, truth or dare?"

"Truth."

"Last time you got laid."

Noel grunts again, a noncommittal answer if there ever was one. Taking a long drag of his beer, he shrugs, still not answering. My brain starts whirring, trying to remember the last time Noel dated anyone. No, dated would be the wrong word. Neither of the Keller twins "date." Nash used to have some kind of secret arrangement with a lady friend he won't name, and Noel…well, Noel is an enigma.

"I do just fine, rock star," he mutters finally. "Could ask the same of you."

"No!" I say, way too quickly, my response jumbled with Sylvie's, "I think we all know the answer to that."

Dustin inches toward me in his seat, the folding chair wobbling as he moves. The warmth of his hand on my back, stroking up and down, is soothing, making me want to curl into him even more. This isn't the time or place for that.

"Right, so Camden, back to you!" Willa says. The shy veterinarian grins awkwardly, his blue-green eyes looking nervous. He's come a long way from the weird, lanky kid from elementary school, growing into his frame, his now square jaw making him resemble a poor man's Henry Cavill. His dark hair is still usually a mess—mostly likely from the nervous habit of running his hand through it—and his stutter will make an appearance every now and then. "Truth or dare!"

"Truth, I guess."

"First letter of your crush's name."

"Willa," I hiss.

It's an unfair question. We know the answer and we have since we were eight years old. Forget my wanting to die earlier—right now, Sylvie looks like she could keel over any second.

"Fine. What's your guilty pleasure?"

"I-I…I love the movie *Hoodwinked*," he admits, grinning sheepishly. "I know it's for kids, but it's really clever, and no matter how many times I watch it, I laugh. It's not very popular, but it's a great movie."

Out of the corner of my eye, I see Sylvie perk up ever so slightly, like she's taken aback by the answer. I hope that inside she swooned a little—his more-than-perfect answer cracking the wall she's put up where he's concerned. *Hoodwinked* is one of her go-to comfort movies, often playing in the background as she grades tests or works on lesson plans. She has a whole rant about how incredibly underrated it is, and every year petitions for it to be down at the local drive-in over the summer.

Sylvie smiles, turning to Camden to reply, but she's cut off by the big, booming voice of the high school principal.

"Miss Forde!" Principal Wagner bellows, ambling over to our table.

Sylvie pops up out of her seat, the plastic chair toppling over behind her. "Principal Wagner, hi!"

"Good news, Miss Forde! The robotics team is fully funded!"

"What? How?"

"An anonymous donation. From someone who wants to simply be known as Mr. T."

"Mr. T," Sylvie responds. "As in…"

"I pity the fool," Nash interjects, doing his best impression.

"He said if you want or need more, just to ask."

"Oh my God. I mean…holy shit!" Sylvie squeals, doing a little dance. Willa and I immediately join her, the excitement overwhelming. I know how worried she's been about this, even though she insisted that they would be fine. It's also weighed heavy on me. Pulling her in for an embrace, I laugh, the relief letting itself out. She pulls away, swiping at the happy tears that have settled under her eyes, and turns back to her boss. "Is he here for me to thank?"

"I don't believe so. But he did give me some contact information to pass along if you need anything. I'll make sure to get that to you this week."

With a curt nod, Principal Wagner turns to go, leaving us to giggle and squeal more. I can see each one of the four men at the table wince a little from the high-pitched noise, but this is too happy a moment for me to care.

"Dustin, was this you?" Sylvie asks, snapping back to reality.

"Don't look at me. You told me not to, and I respect that." I throw a look at him, knowing damn well he does not respect that kind of thing. Just look at what he did with the text donations. When Dustin Wilder wants to find a way, he does it. "What's the look for?"

"You know," I tease.

"Okay, fine. I was going to, but this Mr. T beat me to it. Honestly, it wasn't me."

Leaning down so I'm eye to eye with Dustin, I wink, then kiss him. The perfect combination of soft and strong, I make it known that I'm claiming him in this moment. That he's mine, making me happier than I can express. The way his hand slips to the back of my neck, holding me to return the kiss, tells me the same thing in reply.

"Might I suggest coming up for air?"

My father's laugh as he asks catches me off guard, my heart skipping a beat. I quickly pull back, flashbacks to high school whipping through my mind, mortified that we've been caught. Only, I shouldn't be—not after yesterday's display in the kitchen. Wow, was that really only yesterday? Tamping down my unease, I turn to face the man I already know is grinning ear to ear, happy to see us happy.

Sure enough, that smile is bigger than I thought.

"Just came by to tell you that Mrs. Burch gave me the final donation number."

"What? I thought she was waiting until the meeting on Thursday."

"I'm sure that's what she said, but you know that old bat, can't keep her mouth shut for nothing."

I giggle at my father's use of "old bat," the roll of his eyes pushing it over the edge. He loves this town and everyone in it, but he also knows exactly what—and who—he's dealing with. Kind, steady, and always ready to lend a helping hand, Ken Noble also has a secret opinion about everyone. And only a lucky few of us get to hear it.

"And?" Dustin asks, standing to join us.

Stretching out his hand, Dad offers us a small slip of

paper wedged between his index and middle finger. I take it from him, unfolding it. On it is a number. A very, very large number. One that I'm not entirely sure I'm processing properly.

"Holy hell!" Dustin exclaims, stealing the words from me.

Holy hell is right...

"I still feel a little funny about taking this, but there is no doubt that it will cover pretty much everything."

"And then some, Dad, and then some," I say, throwing my arms around him and squeezing tight. Tears prick at my eyes, threatening to spill out. I can't believe it. "So this means we don't have to sell the land, right?"

My hopes skyrocket, my whole body starting to tingle thinking about how much this changes everything. Every worry my father has had—all those he's said out loud, and even more so the ones I know he's kept to himself—are soothed now that we don't have to fret over this.

"About that, kiddo."

Uh-oh...

"Dad…"

"I already made a deal with someone."

"But—"

"No buts, Kenzie. A deal is a deal. I feel that I got a reasonable price for it, and it's not like we need the land. It's just sitting there."

"Did Atlas buy it?"

"Nope, someone else. Atlas agreed it was a deal I couldn't pass up, so he stepped back."

My head is spinning. There is no way I'm hearing this right. He sold the land to…to a stranger?

Dustin's hand on my lower back steadies me, my body betraying me as I try to process it all. It never occurred to me that he would sell to a stranger. I hated the idea enough when I thought it was to Atlas, but someone we don't know?

"Kenz," Dustin whispers, pulling me in close. The rest of the world falls away—the tent, the town, all the conversations, all of it—the only thing left is us, but not in the romantic way I want it. This time it's like he's holding me as the room spins around us, like that stupid carnival ride. "Kenzie."

"That's…that's our spot," I choke out, all my emotions hitting me at once. I have no idea where they came from, but suddenly they are front and center. "Someone else is going to own our spot."

"It'll always be our spot," he assures me, his voice calm and even. "But how about this—what do you say to one more night out there? You, me, and Old Blue. Huh? Sound like a good time?"

I nod, unable to do anything else.

"Good. Then let's finish our sloppy seconds, make the rounds to fuel the rumor mill, and then we can go. And later on tonight, we'll go chasing falling stars."

CHAPTER TWENTY-TWO

DUSTIN

THE LAST TIME I was this nervous, I was picking up Kenzie for our very first date.

Dusk settles around me as I put Old Blue in park, killing the engine. My palms are clammy, nerves hurtling through me like a stampede of wild animals. I can't even begin to count the number of times I've walked up this gravel path to the rust-colored front door that seems a bit ominous right now. Dozens, maybe even hundreds of times, if we count all the years we were just friends. Still, tonight feels different from all those other nights. Monumental.

Because I have something I have to tell her.

Not about the show, which from the paperwork Eric emailed me while we were at Sloppy Seconds seems like it's far from a done deal. I'm still not sure that it's even something I really want to do. There is no denying it would probably be great for my career. But what it wouldn't be so great for is leaving me time to get back here during breaks. And that is my new priority.

I lift my hand to knock, but the door swings open before I can complete my movement, startling me. I take a step back, stunned as Kenzie steps outside, looking more perfect than I've ever seen her.

Her long chestnut hair cascades down her back, and the ruby-red tank top highlights the beautiful curve and soft skin of her shoulders. The sides of the tank are open, leather shoestrings laced through the fabric holding them together. I flex my hand, my fingers aching to tug on the end of a string, letting it unravel and seeing what happens. Skimming down the rest of her, my mouth waters as I savor her long legs in a jean skirt that hits midthigh. It's like she's an angel that God created just for me, and I'm not sure that I can handle it.

"Hey there, cowboy," she says, her normally sweet voice turned sultry, highlighting her southern accent even more.

My cock thickens, lust taking over for a moment. As much as I want to grab hold of her hips, march her right back up those stairs and have my way with her until we are both too spent to move, that is not what I came here for. That's not the point of tonight. I have bigger plans.

"Hi, beautiful, you look…" I trail off, trying to find the right word. Stunning? Incredible? Good enough to eat? My brain short-circuits, the only word I seem to have available stumbling out. "Beautiful."

Kenzie giggles, her smile bright enough to light up this whole town. Fuck, I am one lucky dude.

"You look pretty good yourself," she replies, eyes dancing up and down my body, drinking in my jeans and old UGA T-shirt. "I've been looking forward to this all afternoon. I thought about maybe inviting Dad and Moira to join us, have a family moment, but then I decided I wanted to keep you to myself."

I smile, my heart jumping at the thought that she wants me to herself. Because that's exactly what I want. "Tonight, the only thing I am is yours."

She slips her hand in mine, allowing me to lead her back

to my truck. Helping her climb in, I take a minute to admire her ass, holding in the groan I so desperately want to let out. It's like she wore this outfit on purpose, just to drive me insane.

In the blink of an eye, Kenzie's childhood home is in the rearview mirror, Old Blue slowly rolling over the hills of the back pasture. The lush green grass looks soft, even in the dim light, like a large welcome mat. Cresting the top of Hideaway Hill, I squeeze Kenzie's hand, silently telling her not to move, that I'll come to her door. Thankfully she still speaks my silent code, sliding into my arms as I open the door, kissing me before her feet even hit the ground.

"Give me one sec to get the bed ready," I tell her, pulling away from her kiss.

"That sounds dirty."

"Blame whoever named the parts of trucks."

"Blame them or thank them?"

"Maybe both," I offer, lowering the tailgate and hopping up.

I make quick work of spreading out the blankets and pillows that I scrounged up from around my mom's, arranging them the same way I used to in high school. Memories flash and my chest warms as I go through the motions, as if the last time I did this was yesterday and not almost a decade ago. When I finish, I hop down and turn to Kenzie. The bright smile is still on her face, mine growing to match it. Grabbing her hips, I lift her up into the bed, hating letting go of her.

"I haven't been out here in a long time," Kenzie says, resting against a pillow. I have one arm around her, our legs stretched out in front of us, taking in the scenery. You can see what feels like forever from up here—Hickory Hills in one direction, the rest of Knox County in the other—all sorts of farms, homes, and businesses nothing but small dots of light along the landscape. "It feels good to be back."

"It does. Things are simpler out here, that's for sure."

"No cancer, no medical bills. No worrying about how we're stealing money from the high school."

"That's not an issue now."

"No, it's not," she sighs. "Promise that wasn't you?"

"Promise. I told you, I was going to secretly do it next week once things had settled, but I got beat out."

"I'm so relieved that they are getting the money. I hated —*hated*—that the festival money wasn't being given to them. Working with those kids is Sylvie's dream, and she deserves to have the money to do everything she can with them."

"What about your dream, Kenzie?"

"What?"

Twisting in my arms, she looks up at me, eyes wide with confusion. Like she doesn't understand where I'm taking this.

"What about your dream? Last I remember, it wasn't being the town librarian."

"No, it wasn't."

She sighs again, this time a little more exaggerated, her whole body sagging against me. I pull her close, her soft curves forming to my body. She's always fit so perfectly against me, and I'm amazed at how time hasn't changed that.

"So?"

"So, what?"

"So, has the dream changed? Traded in the elementary school for the library?"

"I don't know. Please don't get me wrong, I love what I do. I love that library, and keeping it alive is so important to me. That's why I took the job after Mrs. Cassum died. But, it's not where I saw myself, and sometimes that's hard to reconcile. Especially when all your friends achieved exactly what they always said they wanted to. Willa was Miss Georgia. Sylvie teaches science. Nash and Noel have the landscaping business. You're a freaking rock star! I'm just the town librarian."

"First off, you're not *just* anything," I tell her, my voice turning serious. "You are very, very important to everyone in Hickory Hills. I know because I have witnessed it firsthand over the last week. They would not have done what they did with Rhythm and Brews if you weren't."

"That was Dad."

"That was you too. I don't think we went anywhere where there wasn't some kid shouting 'Miss Noble' and waving at you or coming over to say hi. That's a big deal, Kenz, because people saw Mrs. Cassum and ran the other way. So, you're doing something right." I pause, wanting to make sure I get this next part right. Help her see how special she is. "The way I see it, it's not that you didn't achieve what you said you wanted—it's just that it looks different. So you're not standing in front of a classroom leading kids in the ABC song, but you're helping them apply that skill with all the books you help them fall in love with."

"When you put it like that, I have no rebuttal."

Good, no rebuttal required...

"Then tell me, if you could do anything, anything at all, what would it be?"

"I'd write a book where the plot is basically 'The Night the Lights Went Out in Georgia.'"

"Really?"

"Yup. Reba McEntire leaves you with a lot of questions when you actually listen to the lyrics. Like, if little sister was around to shoot the guy, then why didn't she have time to own up to it before brother was executed? Also, dude was only gone for two weeks and his wife slept with at least two other men? Bit extreme."

"That's like a weekend for Kitty Cataway." The words are out of my mouth before I can stop them. I can see them floating in the air, wishing I could shove them back in my mouth. Despite my extreme distaste for the woman, I don't need to be disparaging. My mother would kill me if she'd heard me say that.

A loud guffaw bursts from Kenzie, her whole body barreling forward as she laughs. She covers her mouth as she sucks in a breath, still cackling.

"I didn't say that."

"Oh, yes. Yes you did," she manages in between bouts of laughter. "And it might be the best thing I have ever heard you say."

"That's the best thing you've ever heard me say?" I ask, mocking insult. "None of the encouraging words I've offered over the years, or the sweet nothings I've whispered? Or even the really dirty words I know rev your engine?"

Kenzie shakes her head, smile as wide as the Flint River. My heart squeezes, my stomach doing flip-flops as the sound of her laugh echoes through the night air.

"I apparently need to up my game," I mutter, Kenzie settling back into my arms, her body still shaking with her laughter. "'The Night the Lights Went Out in Georgia,' huh? Not 'Fancy'?"

"That will be my wildly successful follow-up, duh!"

"I should have known."

"Thinking of songs, do you have a favorite that you've written?"

"In a pond made of tinkle, sat Arnie Fossenwinkle," I recite, not skipping a beat and managing to hold my own chuckle in. It's been a long time since I sang that one, and how it came to mind so quickly I'll never know, but here we are. It's also probably not one I should be all that proud of.

"You did not write that!" Elbowing me playfully, Kenzie squirms in my arms, my grip tightening around her.

"I had some help from my coauthors the Keller twins, but I sure did. Don't you remember when he peed himself while we were watching *The Magic School Bus* and he had to wear those sweatpants from the nurse's office for the rest of the day?"

"I very clearly remember, since they were way too small for him, and we saw everything. I guess I just never realized you were behind that taunt."

"Not my proudest moment, but indeed I was. I didn't think it would catch on quite the way it did and that people would be singing it basically right up to graduation. Arnie Fossenwinkle. Now there is someone I have not thought of in a very long time."

"He runs swamp boat tours out of the Okefenokee Swamp now. Last I heard, he was also doing taxidermy on the side."

"So, still weird, good to know."

"Other than the Arnie Fossenwinkle song, what's your favorite?"

I suck in another breath, holding it for a moment, trying to figure out just how honest I want to be here. No, not honest. Vulnerable. But if there was ever a time to prove to Kenzie just how serious I am about her, and how she's a priority in my life, this is it.

"It's called 'Heartbreak Country Song,'" I say, letting the words hang in the air. "I recorded it, but never released it and have never played it live. Only a few people have ever heard it."

"Why?"

"It is too personal. Too…I don't know the right word. Writing it was like I had reached into my own chest, ripped out my heart, and put it to paper. It's beautiful, but not something I could share with the world."

"You shared 'Outlaw in My Blood' though."

"Much easier to write and sing about a man I've never known than…"

"Than what?"

"Than breaking your heart."

Kenzie shifts, a mix of surprise and amazement on her face. I can see the thoughts whizzing through her mind, the rest of her trying to keep up.

"Can I hear it?"

I nod, reaching into my pocket to pull out my phone. As I scroll, looking for the file, Kenzie climbs into my lap, straddling me. I look up at her, our eyes locking, a weight settling in around us that is not as uncomfortable as I would have imagined. Instead, it pulls us closer.

Hitting play, I let the strum of the guitar chords fill the air, overtaking the gentle sounds of nature that had been our soundtrack until now. Soon enough, the lyrics start, my every thought and feeling spilling out. How much I loved her, how I worried that leaving wasn't the right thing to do, how I worried we would end up being nothing but a heartbreaking, country song—the kind someone going through a breakup would listen to on repeat until everyone around them was ready to scream.

Listening to it, the irony that I was so worried about this, and yet I let it all play out the way it did, isn't lost on me. My gut churns, watching Kenzie as she takes it all in, the same guilt I had when I first got back to Hickory Hills returning. But I can't let that get to me. I have learned from my mistakes. I know better now, and I won't let it happen again.

That is, if she'll still have me.

Kenzie leans forward, resting her forehead against mine.

She sucks in a shuddery breath, a tear slipping down her cheek. Fuck, I hope that's not a sad tear.

"Dusty," she whispers as the song winds down.

"Kenz. The last thing I have ever wanted to do was hurt you. And I'm so sorry that it all went down the way it did. But here's the thing, Kenz. You're it. You're my priority. I might not have done a good job of showing it back then, but I want to now. It won't be easy, I know that. I will make this all work. That is, if you'll let me."

A sob escapes from Kenzie, her tears flowing faster now. I still don't know if those are happy tears or sad ones, just that whatever emotion is behind them was fueled by my impromptu declaration. More than anything, I want—no, need—her to tell me what she's thinking. The longer she's silent the harder it is to breathe, even with the cool breeze blowing.

"Kenzie, say something."

Pulling back, she swipes at her eyes, drying them. Her beautiful brown irises shine, the serene look on her face giving me hope.

"I love you."

CHAPTER TWENTY-THREE

KENZIE

THE WORDS ARE out of my mouth so fast that I couldn't stop them if I tried. Not that I want to. They've been sitting on the very tip of my tongue since he walked back into town.

I love Dustin Wilder.

It was true then, true now, and I can't imagine a time in my life it won't be true.

"I love you, Kenzie. That's one thing that's never changed."

"You really think we can make this work?" I ask, my voice catching. My heart is on the verge of bursting at the thought, my brain trying hard to reel it in. But staying rooted in reality isn't easy. Not when the only boy you've ever loved is holding you tight and telling you he's always loved you too.

"I do. I'm committed to it. To you. You, MacKenzie Rose Noble, are my priority. It will be tough, especially at first while I figure out some scheduling stuff, but there is no reason I can't come back here in between shows and my other commitments."

"You have no idea how badly I want that."

Wrapping my arms around his neck, I kiss him hard.

Harder than I think I ever have before. Certainly with more purpose. It's not the first time we've said these three little words to each other. But they carry so much more weight now. More than I think either of us ever realized they could when we said them the first time. Our teenaged selves had no idea what that really meant—and all the other emotions that are tied up in that one word. We do now though. It might have taken almost a decade and a ton of hurt to get us here, but I'm not sure I would trade it for anything.

"I think I do," Dustin replies, pulling back from the kiss. My lips tingle, missing him instantly, wanting more of him. "Because it's all I want too. You are my one and only."

"One and only, huh?" I tease, my insides turning to goo. I have zero doubt that it's the truth, but I can't help myself in ragging him. Knowing that we still belong to each other after all this time is bringing out a different side of me—the playful one that only Dustin ever saw. "Don't let all your other girls hear that."

Dustin chuckles, playfully tickling at my sides. "I'm not exactly leaving a trail of broken hearts."

"Oh, I know that's a lie. I am sure that Corinne and Justine will be devastated."

The big, booming laugh Dustin lets out makes my tummy flip, launching those same clitterflies as the other night. My whole body responds, heat pooling in my core, loving this.

"I think Corinne and Justine will understand." He kisses me again, his fingers toying with the lacing on the sides of my tank top. The callouses on his fingertips are rough against my skin, sending tiny shock waves through me. I roll my hips, my center making contact with the bulge already forming in his jeans. He moans, letting go of my lips with a nibble. "Admission time. Kenz, when I say only, I mean *only*."

I freeze, that one word stopping my heart. Only. As in no one else. It takes a minute for it to click...he's kidding, right?

"O-o-only?" I sputter.

"Only," he repeats. His eyes are serious, the blue so deep you could drown in it.

"What about…" Names race through my head—all the different, stunningly beautiful women he's been linked to over the years in different articles. Bella Fontaine. CC de Milo. Hollie Berry.

"All fake," Dustin answers, reading my mind.

"So, the other night after sound check…that was the first time since…"

"Since the morning after Moira's wedding when we had that quickie in my truck as we were saying goodbye."

Holy shit…

I blink hard. I'm Dustin's *only*. My heart squeezes, all of me falling for him even more. A small part of me wants to ask him why, but the rest of me just doesn't care. I know he has some swoony, perfect answer locked and ready. The why doesn't matter though. What matters is that we're here together now.

"I hope I didn't just kill the mood," he says, hands traveling up under the hem of my shirt. The warm trail they leave fuels the fire within me, turning me on even more.

"Quite the opposite." I reply, swiveling my hips against him. My skirt rides up my thighs as I move, exposing more and more of my bare legs. I want him more than I ever have, his admission strengthening whatever this is between us.

Dustin hisses at the contact, his own hips bucking upward. Thunder softly rumbles in the background, threatening the beautiful evening sky. It can grumble all it wants though; I don't care. This is our last night on Hideaway Hill and I'm not cutting it short.

Our mouths fuse together quickly, tongues dancing with each other, our bodies doing the rest of the talking. We're past words at this point. Everything left to say is best expressed physically, our bodies in charge.

Moving one hand from under my shirt to my bare thigh, Dustin glides it up the bare skin, pushing my skirt up. The cool air feels good as I'm exposed, giving me more freedom to move against him. He moans into our kiss as his hand caresses my hip, discovering the missing fabric.

"Naughty, naughty girl," he says into the kiss. "You forgot your panties."

"Oh, I didn't forget." I nibble on his bottom lip, dragging my already wet sex along the stiff denim. It feels so good I want to do it again, but I stop myself, wanting Dustin's touch more. "I simply couldn't risk losing another pair. I figured you wouldn't mind."

"I dunno. I really like ripping your panties off you," he growls. His hand dips between my legs, a single finger parting my lips, toying with my wetness. I mewl, pleasure rolling through me. "But there is something to be said for this."

Just as quickly as his finger was there, it's gone. Dustin lifts it to his mouth, lazily sucking on it, his eyes going dark as he savors the taste of me. Oh, fuck. The one little move releases a tidal wave of need inside me, a whole new swarm of clitterflies taking over. I can feel myself growing wetter by the second, and there is no way Dustin is oblivious to it. I would bet good money there is a large wet spot on his jeans.

A devilish grin breaks out on his face, his eyes growing even darker. "Oh, my naughty girl likes that." Returning his fingers to my sex, he gently teases and toys with me, careful to avoid the contact he knows I'm craving. "Question is, baby, what do you want more? My fingers, or my tongue?"

I moan, unable to form an answer. I don't care; either will work, just as long as he doesn't stop. Gripping his shirt, I rock forward, seeking out the friction I'm desperate for. That devilish grin turns into a wicked laugh, Dustin's fingers slowing their efforts. I whimper my displeasure, but all that does is make him laugh more.

"Need something?"

"You," I say, my breath heavy. "I need you."

"I'm all yours."

Another roll of thunder sounds out as Dustin's thumb finds my clit, making me keen. I throw my head back, howling into the night like I'm trying to compete with the storm. With the way he's making me feel, the skies have no chance. I'm riding a high that can't be beat.

Two fingers slip inside me, the circling of my clit never easing up. Extreme pleasure pulses through my body in waves, each new one stronger than the last. I'm pretty sure it doesn't get any better than this, that it's simply not possible to feel any better. That is, until the hand holding my hip travels up my torso, finds my bare breast, and pinches my nipple. I gasp, my hips launching forward, Dustin's fingers managing to hold me in place with a move I didn't know was possible but feels so fucking good.

"No bra either? So, so naughty, Kenzie. So much so, I might need to punish you."

That's all it takes to push me over the edge I didn't see coming. My eyes slam shut, my spine stiffening as my orgasm shoots through me like an arrow. An unrecognizable sound cuts through the air, and it's a long moment before I realize that it's coming from me, the sheer amount of pleasure racing through me taking over me completely. I can't think, can't move, can't do anything but ride the wave.

"That's my girl," Dustin coos, kissing along my neck as my climax subsides. My limp body crumples against him, the warmth radiating between us comforting. The hand between my legs is still toying with me, only now it's softer, less mission focused than it had just been, stroking me through my aftershocks.

I take a minute to catch my breath, my heart still galloping as fast as it can go. The lust flowing through my veins isn't slowing down either though. That might be the best orgasm I've ever had—although Dustin's given me so many of those these last few days I'm not sure if that's a fair statement anymore—yet it's not enough. It's not him inside me. That's what I really need.

I claw at his shirt, yanking it upward, trying to get it off. He chuckles, lifting his arms to help. Moonlight dances on his surprisingly tan skin, the ripples of muscles calling my name. I run my fingers along the ridges of his abs, the soft hair leading into the waist of his jeans tickling my fingers. I've always been a sucker for this part of him—ever since I first noticed that happy trail when we were teenagers. Tonight is no different.

Flicking open the button of his pants, I ignore the droplets of rain I feel on my shoulders, thunder sounding even closer now. I am focused on one thing, and one thing only—the man I love. I slip my hand under the elastic of his boxer briefs, palming his hard length. His cock twitches in my hand, greeting me.

"I need to be inside you, baby," Dustin mutters through clenched teeth. I continue to stroke him, enjoying the hisses and moans it elicits.

"Please."

Kissing me softly, hand holding me by the nape of my neck, Dustin pulls me in close, lifting me just enough to wiggle his pants lower and free himself. A loud clap of thunder startles me, the rain starting to fall fast and heavy.

"Want to take this inside?" Dustin asks, voice gentle and full of love.

I shake my head. "Make love to me, Dusty, please."

He nods in response, lifting his hips again, reaching for his pocket. I grab his wrist to stop him, shaking my head no once more. Looking deep into his eyes, I can see the question there, just as I hope he can see my answer. After what he told me tonight, there is no need for anything between us.

Without another word, he lines himself up with my entrance, slowly pushing inside. I gasp at the feel of him, loving the new sensations without the barrier between. I shudder, a combination of Dustin and the coolness of the rain, my whole body enveloped in something I can't describe. We stay like this for a long moment, his hard dick throbbing inside me, my pussy holding on to it like a vise.

The storm continues to roll on around us, carrying on its ways, leaving us to do our thing. Unlike the ones we get in the heat of the summer, this storm doesn't have the anger behind it. Just like Dustin and me, all the hurt and pain is gone, leaving nothing but strong feelings and emotions. Holding on to him—our bodies fused together like this as the rain pours down, the soundtrack of thunder in the background—feels cathartic. The perfect start to the new us.

I start rocking my hips, needing to feel him deeper inside me, matching my emotions. Dustin holds on tighter, moving his hips in time with mine, the back and forth making my orgasm start to build all over again. The faster we move, the more I need it. The more I need him. My desire fueled by the thought that he and I are finally the us I've always dreamed about.

I hold on tighter, the telltale tingle growing in me. But my orgasm won't be enough. I need us to come together.

"Dusty…"

"Kenzie," he returns, his voice barely audible over the rain against the truck. Wrapping an arm around my waist, he leans in, pressing his lips to my ear. "Do you hear that? That's our love song, baby."

My heart explodes, love oozing out, tears burning my eyes as I bury my face in his neck. Our love song. It's so much more than I can handle. The only way I can answer is by picking up the pace, letting my body show him what my words can't. How much I love him. How I belong to him. How being his only means everything to me. Absolutely everything.

"That's it, baby. I'm so close. Fuck, Kenz, right there."

One hand grips my ass, the other flicking my clit, as Dustin pumps into me harder, hitting the secret spot inside me. A few more thrusts and I'm done. Once again, I'm screaming out into the night sky, rain still falling all around us, fireworks flashing behind my eyes. Every nerve in me fires all at once, my pussy clamping down on Dustin's cock as his own orgasm rips through him, his cries matching mine. I can feel him emptying himself into me, the unique sensation the catalyst for another climax, right on the heels of my second one of the evening, this one just as powerful as the others. Dustin captures my screams with a kiss, holding on and keeping up his efforts as I plunge over the edge again and again.

A long moment passes, neither of us moving, just holding on to the other for dear life as the storm subsides. There is so much I want to say, yet the only thing I can do is sit here, curled up into Dustin. He was my first. I'm his only. We're each other's forever. How can anyone expect to put that into words?

"I love you, Kenzie," Dustin whispers, breaking the silence.

"I love you, Dusty."

"You know, you're the only person who has ever called me that. Just one more way that you're my only."

I bite my lip, trying to hold back the childish giggle

bubbling up inside me. Something only Dustin can make me feel.

"Call me selfish, but I like knowing that I'm it. Makes having to share you with all those screaming fans a little easier to stomach."

"There's no sharing me, Kenzie. Not the real me. They're screaming for Dustin Wild. But Dustin *Wilder*, he belongs to you."

He belongs to me...

CHAPTER TWENTY-FOUR

KENZIE

I'M TRYING VERY HARD NOT to be that girl.

The one where everything is just absolutely amazing because she's in love and there is no convincing her that the sun isn't shining brighter, or that the birds aren't tweeting louder, or that there isn't some kind of magic in the air. Except, the sun is brighter today. And the birds? Yeah, their song is definitely louder than usual. As for magic in the air, I can't rule that out either.

So, I guess I am that girl.

Keeping her under control, though, is a different story. Because that part is nonnegotiable. I will not feed the Hickory Hills rumor mill any more than I already have. The fact that the library has been open for more than an hour already and no one has been in here asking me about Dustin is nothing short of a miracle. I half expected them to be lined up at the door waiting for me to start their interrogation, regardless of it being Labor Day and the library usually being closed today. Instead, the only person here when I unlocked the doors was the guy from the security company ready to install the new alarm system.

A sharp, high-pitched beep cuts through the air, making me wince as I sort through the books Mrs. Dent, my Friday volunteer, pulled out to use for our upcoming display. I try to ignore it, my heart still giddy over even getting a new alarm system. A top-of-the-line, state-of-the-art system with every bell and whistle you can imagine. Most of which I will probably never use. The oversophisticated system is out of place in a small-town library, that's for sure, but the message of love behind it isn't. It's being provided by someone who loves me and wants to keep me and the place I love so much as safe as can be. How can you argue against that?

The shrill beep sounds again, followed by a quick "Sorry!" from the installation guy. I wave it off, not allowing it to tamper with my good mood. Today is the first day of forever —of Dustin and me officially being "Dustin and Kenzie" again. And damn, is that a happy thought.

"I've done all I can for now," the installation guy says, suddenly appearing at my side. "I have to get the units installed over at the fire station and the police station in order for it all to be fully compatible. So, I'm gonna go do that, and then I'll be back to finish up here."

"Units at the fire and police station?" I question. "This doesn't just automatically do whatever?"

"Not without the receiver units. It's a quick install, I promise. I'll be back in a jiffy."

A tip of his cap and he turns to go, leaving me dumb-founded. I speed walk back over to the counter, reaching for my purse underneath and digging for my phone.

> Did you know that units have to be installed at the police and fire station? I thought it just sent texts?

DUSTIN

Yes

Yes what?

DUSTIN

Don't worry about it. Chief Myers and Chief
Phillips know about it. I told you I would take
care of this.

You left out the part about it being all kinds of
fancy

DUSTIN

Nothing is too fancy for my girl

I swoon, not bothering to hide the smile that is taking over my face. There is a part of me that wants to push back. To tell him this is too much and that we don't need this. But I know better. Instead, I bask in this amazing feeling.

"I know that smile," Willa comments, a knowing smirk greeting me as I look up at her. Much like the Cheshire Cat, there is a glint in her eye that she is up to no good, and that she likes it. "Chasing falling stars…"

"Oh, I saw stars…" I waggle my eyebrows, bursting into laughter.

"That's my girl!" She high-fives me, doing the Britney Spears shimmy. "So does this mean you got him out of your system?"

"No."

"No?"

"No." I shake my head, looking away for a second. Willa waits expectantly for me to continue, eyes growing wide when I don't answer right away. "We're, ummmm, we're back together. Going to try and make it work."

"Squeeeee!" Willa keens, throwing her hands over her mouth trying to dampen the high-pitched noise she's making. I shush her, my inner librarian showing, even though inside I'm squealing right along with her. "Kenzie, spill. Now!"

"Not until Sylvie gets here. I don't want to have to do it twice."

"Fine. Where is she? I expected her to beat me here. It's Labor Day, so it's not like she needs to escape school."

I look down at my watch, noticing that Willa is actually early—something we are not used to from her. When we agreed upon a time to meet, my two best friends insisting on a lunch date after they found out about my plans last night, we opted for a time that would give Willa plenty of wiggle room. It never fails that someone grabs her on her way out the door—holiday or not.

"She still has time. You're the one who is extra early. I thought you were running into the office to catch up on stuff?"

"Err, I haven't made it in yet," she answers, looking a little flustered. "Had things to do this morning, then came straight here."

I squint at her, wondering for what must be the millionth time what she's hiding, and if I can use my own news as barter for her to share. I open my mouth to ask, but am cut off by the squeak of the door. We both turn toward the noise, expecting to see Sylvie, but instead we are greeted by the town busybody.

"Oh, there you are, my dear!" Mrs. Chamberlain says, her breath heavy as she rushes into the library. "I was worried y'all would be closed today."

"Technically, we are." My voice is light, but clearly put on, not wanting to give in to her gossip. I know that is the only reason she's here, so she can dig for information. "But we have a new alarm system being put in, so I had to open up for that."

"On Labor Day? Impressive. I assume that's Dustin's doing?"

"The old system malfunctioned last week, so it required replacing, but yes, Dustin did help expedite the process," I answer as carefully as I can. I can't deny everything, and I suspect she already knows more than she's letting on.

"How sweet of him. Although all the more reason to wonder why you're here, working. Unless he's somewhere here with you. I would think you'd want to spend as much time together as possible before he goes. And, oh!" She gasps, hand flying to rest over her heart. "It's just so wonderful to see you two back together. Like I said, I've always thought the two of you had staying power."

Out of the corner of my eye, I see Willa roll her eyes. I bite back a laugh, not wanting to give her away. She needs to be careful, or Mrs. Chamberlain will turn on her and start asking her why she's not married yet. The return of Dustin has taken focus off the Hayes family for a short while, but Willa is fooling herself if she thinks talk won't go right back to her and her brothers—and the single status of each and every one of them—once Dustin and I are old news.

"What can I help you with today, Mrs. C?" I ask, trying to move this along.

"Oh, nothing much. Just wanted to pop in and congratulate you on a wonderful event. Your father must be thrilled at the amount that was raised."

"We are," I confirm. "It helps lift the burden of Dad's medical care, that's for sure."

"Well, that's all I stopped by to say. I should be off, have lots to do. Don't forget about our wrap-up meeting on Thursday."

"I won't. I will see you there."

With a saccharine smile and a waggle of her fingers, Mrs. Chamberlain turns to go. I let out a long breath, thankful that's all it was. I got off easy—the whole thing could have been a lot more painful.

"She just never lets up, does she?" Willa mutters, leaning against the counter to not be heard by the older lady.

"Oh! One more thing," Mrs. Chamberlain says, spinning on her heel.

"And there is it!" I comment.

"You'll be sure to give the town plenty of notice before you leave, right? We just want to make sure we aren't in the same kind of position we were after Arlene Cassum passed. We got lucky that you were willing to take on the job, but I highly doubt there is someone else just waiting in the wings to take over for you. We might have to hire an out-of-towner."

"God forbid!" Willa murmurs under her breath, her words laced with sarcasm.

I look at my former math teacher, dumbfounded. What on earth is she talking about?

"Just where am I going?" I ask, curiosity getting the better of me.

"I saw the twitters this mornin', sweetie," she answers, her voice hushed, like she's in on a secret that only a few know. Which is highly doubtful if she's referencing Twitter. "All about that new show Dustin is gonna be hosting. I just figure if he's touring and hosting a television program, that is going to take up most of his time and would mean that he wouldn't make it back here all that often. And since you two are so clearly back together, I just assume that means you're moving to Nashville with him this time."

Her words hit me like a wrecking ball, all but knocking me over. I manage to stand my ground, steeling my expression to not give anything away. Despite my solid outside appearance, my insides are chaos.

Because I have no idea what she is talking about.

I swallow hard, quickly running through the conversation Dustin and I had last night, curled up in bed after getting home and drying off. We talked well into the night, about what kind of future we saw and logistics to make it work. It isn't going to be easy—neither of our schedules are very flexible—but we are committed to making it work. He assured me that he could arrange things so he would be back here, in Hickory Hills, at least once a month. However, not once did he mention a TV show.

Plastering on a smile that is just as sugary sweet as hers, I wave off Mrs. Chamberlain. "Mrs. C, you know that I can't confirm or deny a single thing you just said. But I promise you that if I ever decide to leave this job, I will give the town plenty of notice and will help find a replacement."

"You're such a dear. We'll see you Thursday!"

I hold my breath as she leaves, Willa's hand reaching out and grabbing mine. The walls feel like they are closing in around me. How does our small-town gossip know more about what is going on with Dustin's life than I do?

I tell myself it's a misunderstanding, that she's wrong. Except, I'm not so sure she is. We've been down this path before. He left once, promising me all sorts of things, and he failed on every single one. Why I thought this time would be different is a damn good question.

"A source close to the project says that Dustin Wild is slated to host a new reality singing competition. No word on network details," Willa reads, her thumb scrolling across her phone. "I take it you didn't know about this?"

I shake my head, my words caught in my throat. There has to be a good explanation for this. *Has to be.* My Dustin wouldn't just keep this from me. Unless he isn't really *my* Dustin. Which, with each passing second, is starting to feel more and more possible.

"What's the matter? What'd I miss?" Sylvie asks, her voice

cutting through my thoughts. I look up, blinking hard as she rushes to us. Willa holds up her phone, showing her what she just read. "Okay, so?"

I need to get out of here. I need to talk to Dustin. Need to find out just what is really going on.

Dipping down, I grab my purse, throwing it over my shoulder.

"Kenzie, breathe," Willa says.

"I am breathing," I reply. Rounding the counter, I try and calm myself but it's no use. "Alarm guy will be back soon. If he needs something, give it to him."

I plow past my friends, ignoring them as they call my name, trying to get me to stop. I can't stop though. Not now. I feel like a fool. Because for all my worries about being that girl, that's apparently who I am. The girl who let her feelings get in the way of seeing the truth. Of seeing that nothing is different this time.

Fuck, I hope I'm wrong. The pit in my stomach tells me I'm not, but there is a sliver of hope anyway. All I know is that I need answers, and there is only one person who can provide them.

Dustin.

CHAPTER TWENTY-FIVE

DUSTIN

My hand flies furiously across the piece of paper I ripped off the notepad hanging on the fridge, trying to keep up with the speed of my thoughts. Judging by my barely legible chicken scratch, I'm not sure that even if my hand was keeping up that it's doing much good—reading this later is going to be a bitch. I can't stop though, the melody and lyrics are too clear in my mind and I don't want to lose them.

The flowery paper with the gentle reminder of 'don't forget!' scrolled in an even more flowery script on top isn't ideal for such a thought process—it's a far cry from the leather-bound notebook Kenzie gave me before leaving for Nashville—but in a pinch, it'll have to do. Now, if this old pen would just hold out long enough, we'll be in business. I hope.

"I was thinking 'bout you…and all the times we've shared…to dreams come true, and more…tonight, the only thing I am is yours," Mama reads out over my shoulder barely loud enough to be heard over the lawnmower outside. "I don't get it."

"I promise it makes sense in my head."

"If you say so," she replies, her voice sing-songy. She ruffles my hair, like I'm still five years old, sitting at the kitchen table doing my homework. The contentment on her face makes my chest swell, feeling a sense of pride. Knowing that she's happy makes me happy.

"I do."

"I'm a little surprised to see you going old school with a paper and pen. Would have thought you'd be typing this into your phone or something."

"Nah." Scribbling the last of my thoughts, my writing even harder to read than it was to start, I slam the pen down on the table with a loud thud. A new rush of pride washes over me, excited about the notes that are staring back at me. It's been a while since my muse felt the need to scream so loudly at me. I have zero complaints though. She is welcome to sing, dance, scream, shout, or throw a fit whenever she wants if it means ideas like this one. Leaning just enough to lift my one butt cheek, I reach for my phone in my back pocket, then slide it across the table toward Mama. "Call me old school all you want, but I rarely make song notes in my phone. The scratch of pen on paper is a melody all its own. All part of the process."

She nods, laughing silently, her attention turned back to the chicken salad she just pulled out of the fridge. I can see there is something on her mind; the way the corners of her eyes are pinched slightly is a dead giveaway. It's the same telltale sign she always had growing up whenever she had to mention something that had the potential to be uncomfortable. Never mattered how big her smile was, if that pinch was there, something was coming. To this day I still don't know which incident was worse—her telling me that my dog, Bandit, had been hit by a car or her trying to have the safe sex talk with me after Kenzie and I started dating. Either way, I know something is up by that look, so I steel myself, preparing for whatever it is. When she's silent for another beat, I decide to take matters into my own hands.

"Is there something you wanna talk about, Mama?"

"No. I just like having you home is all." She pats my hands, her soft, serene smile making the feeling of 'home' settle around me. "Can't I just enjoy this time with you here, not so secretly wishing that you came back here more often?"

You're about to get your wish...

"You sure? You have that 'this is going to be awkward, but I'm going to do it anyway' look. So I just want to make sure that you're not going to bust out some bananas and show me how to roll on a condom again."

"Dustin Randall Wilder, if you do not know how to put on a condom by now, I have failed you and your partners, in more ways than one."

I cackle, the sound bursting out of me like it had been waiting at the starting line for the gun to go off. Glad to know she feels that way. Shaking my head, I sit back in my seat, letting the memory of last night wash over me, the feel of Kenzie wrapped around me, nothing between us. It was a next level kind of moment, one that I know won't ever be surpassed. Just not one I need to share with Mama.

For a split second I do consider correcting her. It's partner—singular. But I stop myself. Also not something Mama needs to know. We're close, always have been. That might be *too* close though.

The hum of the mower outside cuts out, letting me know that I have ninety seconds at most before the side door bursts open and trouble tumbles in. Noel rolled in right behind me as I returned from Kenzie's, a knowing look on his face. He didn't say anything, but I could tell he was thinking it. And there is no doubt he'll give me hell here soon. For a man of few words, I have to give him credit for timing them well. Grabbing the piece of paper with my barely decipherable notes, I fold it in half, shoving it in my pocket so I don't lose it. Actually, so it doesn't get confiscated and then held hostage as I try to explain exactly what each one of those lyrics means and who inspired them.

Even though I think we all know damn well who the song is about.

Right on time the door flies open, crashing against the cabinet, Nash and Noel clamoring inside. Glancing over at the dueling fixtures, I make a mental note to ask Noel to do something about the gash in the wood left from years of us boys busting through the door without a care. It's poor design to have the door swing open in that direction, at least without some kind of doorstop, and thirty plus years of altercations have not helped anything.

"Mama!" Nash greets, making his way right over to her and placing a kiss on her cheek.

"Where'd you come from?" I ask, confused by his sudden presence. I could have sworn only Noel was out there. Then again, I was so focused on getting those lyrics out that who knows what else I missed. "Were you out there the whole time?"

"Thanks for noticing, rockstar!" He slaps me on the back, making his way to the fridge, pulling out the ever-present pitcher of sweet tea. "But since you asked, I had a special delivery this morning."

Noel grunts, rolling his eyes as he grabs the tea jug from his twin. Nash shoots me a shit-eating grin, proud as a peacock about whatever it is he's not sharing.

"Special delivery? What kind of euphe— Oh God, there's an angry husband out there somewhere, isn't there?"

"Fucking hope not," Noel mutters.

"Noel Joshua Keller," Mama scolds, a softness to her voice letting on that she wasn't *that* mad about the language.

"I'm the one who gets scolded? He's the one angering husbands…"

"There's no angry husband," Nash insists, Cheshire cat smile still plastered across this face. Noel and I exchange glances, the both of us knowing that he's up to something, but completely in the dark about exactly what. And it must be a doozy if even Noel is in the dark. "Promise."

"Nash, darlin', I'm not sure I believe you, but as long as you keep them off my property, your bad behavior is your own mama's problem. Now eat."

Nodding silently, Nash turns his focus to the chicken salad on the table, assembling a sandwich in record time. The cocky look is gone, taking the dressing-down handed to him like a man. There's still a glint in his eye though, and damn, I wish I knew what he was up to.

"How much longer are you here for?" Noel asks around a bite of chicken salad.

"And better question, are we going to see you at all during that time, or will it all be spent with Kenzie?" Nash follows up.

My mother's laugh catches me off guard, the snort-like sound coming from behind me, making me turn to look at her. A simple shrug is all she gives me in return, not even trying to come to my defense. Not that I have anything to apologize for.

"A couple more days, I think. And yes, if y'all aren't too busy at work I figured we'd hit the lake and fish or whatever."

"We got nothing tomorrow that can't be moved."

I nod and it's a done deal.

"So you and Kenzie," Noel starts, his voice cautious. I know what's coming next, and I'm prepared for whatever they throw at me. "You two on the same page?"

"Yes."

"Like the actual same page?" Nash prods. "Because I'm

pretty sure you thought that last time, and then you weren't. Cause, if we're gonna have a repeat, I might suggest you just buy the Whippy Cone outright. Save us a lot of hassle if we could just pay cost."

I sigh, trying to let my friends' ragging roll off me. It's not easy though, the guilt of what happened before still present and gnawing away at me, despite how amazing this last week has been. At the end of the day though, I love Kenzie. Always have, always will. Knowing that she still loves me too, that's just the cherry on top of the sundae. I can and will make this work. Even with everything else that life is throwing at me.

"Thank you for the investment advice, but I don't think that will be necessary this time." I pause, choosing my words very carefully. I don't want to say too much, but also know I can't hold back. These two know me better than anyone—save for the woman on the other side of the small kitchen working on her grocery list—so they know when I'm full of shit. "I love her."

"No shit."

It's Noel who says it, but both of them stare back at me with identical expressions.

"I never stopped loving her. And this time, I'm going to not be a jackass about it."

Nash's eyebrow quirks up, the skepticism clear as day on his face. He starts to speak, but is cut off by the rattle of my phone against the table. I reach for it, groaning to myself when I see my manager's name on the screen.

"Eric," I say, forcing cheer into my voice. This call is about one of two things, coming back sooner or the TV show. Neither of which I want to discuss right now. "To what do I owe the honor?"

"We have a network."

"What?"

I push up from the table and walk into the living room

for a little bit of privacy. This house isn't that big, and the only thing that separates the two rooms is a large arched opening in the wall, but it still gives me some room to talk. Sunlight streams through the windows, landing directly on the spot on the couch where I would normally park myself. So I opt for the overstuffed chair that Mama sits in when she knits, hoping I don't come into contact with the wrong end of a needle.

"We have a network," he repeats, voice going up an octave with excitement. "Nothing is final, but it looks like Adored is interested."

"Adored? As in the cheesy, made-for-TV, kissing movie channel that dumped Hollie Berry last year after she went to Vegas?" I clarify, sure I didn't hear him properly. There is no way this squeaky-clean network, who dumped their starlet after she was photographed at a bachelorette party in Sin City, is interested in a singing reality show. "They are aware we sing drinking songs, right?"

"They are. Apparently they are looking to loosen up a bit. Ratings haven't been quite as steady since Hollie left and her whole 'claim your coal' movement swept the nation, so they are trying to drop back and punt a bit."

"I'm not so sure I want to be their punter."

"Don't think like that. This is a real opportunity. Women eighteen to sixty-four is a key demographic, and the Adored Network is their catnip. Could be just what we need to level you up."

Level me up, what was that even supposed to mean? I throw my head back, trying to slow my thoughts down long enough to get a grip on them. This whole TV idea is crazy to me. Never something I thought I would want—and truth be told, I don't *want* it. But I also know I'd be crazy to turn down the chance.

There is another chance that it potentially jeopardizes

though—one that is significantly more important in the long run. My chance to make things work with Kenzie. It's already going to be tough enough to make it back to a small town in southern Georgia in between tour dates. My schedule is tight, and squeezing one more thing into it would mean that I would have *zero* extra time to even try to get back here. Hell, it would mean next to no time for Kenzie to even come visit me in Nashville.

Unless…

"What's the filming schedule? Can it be done in Atlanta?"

"Atlanta?"

"Yeah," I answer, not giving up any more details.

It's not any of Eric's business why Atlanta. But if we can film it there, on a consolidated schedule, this could maybe work. It would still be tough getting from Hickory Hills to Atlanta—which is at least a three-hour drive each way—but that's a hell of a lot better than Nashville. Or worse, LA.

"I can ask. Not ideal, but Georgia's got that whole East Coast Hollywood thing going these days, so I'm sure the production company could figure out something if that's going to a dealbreaker. Is that a dealbreaker?"

Sucking in a breath, I hold it, my lungs aching after a long pause. *Is that a dealbreaker?* Four words, one weighty question. My heart is screaming no. As in, say no to the whole thing. Tell Eric you're not interested because the only thing that matters is a sweet, kindhearted librarian in your hometown whose life's dream is to show kids the joy of reading. The same beautiful brunette that you see every time you close your eyes, in the front row of every show, and who still fills your dreams night after night. But my head says hear Eric out. Let him work his magic and see what he comes up with. Because just like before, it could be the chance of a lifetime, and change everything.

I exhale loudly. "Yeah, it's a dealbreaker."

"That's what I want to hear!"

"Eric, I'm still not agreeing to the show. I need more information. And maybe a better network than Adored. Understand?"

"I got you. But if we can do this in Atlanta, you'll think about it? And I mean seriously think about it."

"I will."

Eric whoops and hollers like his team just scored the game-winning touchdown in overtime. I hold the phone away from my ear, waiting for him to finish. It's a full minute before he does, clearing his voice before he starts talking again.

"Great. I'll get some answers and we can discuss over lunch tomorrow."

"Nope. I'm gonna be out on the lake with my two best friends tomorrow. Nothing allowed in the boat but rods, reels, and some beer."

"I feel like there's a song there."

I laugh. "There probably is. I'll think about it while I'm out on the water tomorrow."

"Good deal. Then Wednesday?"

"Eric..."

"Fine, fine...I'll respect your vacation. Everything still good?"

"Perfect. Everything is still perfect."

Eric clicks his tongue. "And that's why Atlanta. Got it. Well, let me get going and we will make this a reality. We're going to make TV history!"

"If you say so."

"C'mon, Dustin, say it with me. We're going to make TV history!"

"We're going to make TV history," I mutter, not feeling a single ounce of my manager's enthusiasm.

"You can do better than that! I know how your voice carries."

Sighing, I work up some excitement, knowing that I need to placate him if I'm ever going to get off this call. "We're gonna to make TV history!"

"Thatta boy. Talk at you later."

I hang up, throwing my head back and letting it all sink in. There's something nagging at me that this TV show isn't a good idea and that I need to just be honest with Eric. That it's not what I want. For a split second, I consider calling him back, but stop myself. Maybe they'll come back with Atlanta not being a possibility and I won't have to say a thing.

Fingers crossed.

"So it's true."

The sound of Kenzie's voice sends a chill down my spine. Throwing my eyes open I launch myself out of the chair and onto my feet, my gaze landing on her. She's standing under the archway, and the hurt that is laced into her voice is painted on her like a canvas. Her bottom lip is wobbling ever so slightly, her eyes shiny.

Fuck…

"Which…which means you lied to me."

CHAPTER TWENTY-SIX

KENZIE

I SUDDENLY UNDERSTAND exactly what Carole King has been singing about. Because staring at Dustin staring back at me, the indescribable blankness on his face does indeed make the earth move under my feet and the sky tumble down. My heart stutters rather than tremble though, making my stomach start to turn.

He lied.

The buzz of conversation behind me in the kitchen fades into background noise. The only sound I can hear is my own pulse and the silence between Dustin and me. A silence that might be the loudest fucking thing I have ever heard.

"Kenzie…"

My body involuntarily shudders at the sound of my name in that smooth as whiskey voice. It sounds so good, tempting me to betray all my emotions and run to him. Let him wrap his arms around me and tell me everything will be okay. But I know it won't. I've lived through this once and I promised myself I wouldn't do it again.

"You lied."

"I didn't lie," Dustin says, taking a slow step forward, his voice calm and careful.

"You completely failed to mention that you're adding a TV show to your already busy schedule," I state, my own voice a lot steadier than I'm feeling. Go me. "A lie by omission is still a lie."

"I didn't tell you because it's not final. I—"

"So you left it so that I could find out via Mrs. Chamberlain and Twitter. Didn't think that I deserved to hear that it was even a possibility from you."

Dustin winces, making me feel slightly validated. But only slightly. Because this is not something that I want to be right about.

"You told me that I was your priority—"

"You are!" he insists, cutting me off and taking another step toward me.

I hold up my hand, stopping him in his tracks. "But not enough of one that you felt you could share your life with!"

It comes out harsher and louder than I intended, the scrape of a chair against the kitchen floor alerting me that I now have the full attention of everyone in this house. I don't have it in me to care though. I'm too upset to think past the epic range of anger and hurt rushing through me.

"I was going to tell you."

"When? After it sucked all your time up and made you change your plans? Thought you'd mention it when it was the reason for breaking your promise this time around?"

"No, when it was a done deal. *If* it's a done deal. It's so far from being a thing it's really not worth mentioning."

"Just like you signing a record deal wasn't a thing. Until it was."

Dustin winces again, his shoulders sagging, face turning down in embarrassment. Because I'm right, and he knows it.

Memories of seven years ago swirl around me like fairy dust in an animated princess movie, taking me back to all the pain from the first time he left. All the things he said—promises he made—about coming back, and how nothing worth mentioning was going on out there. Until all of a sudden it was. Studio time, a real contract, paying gigs. And not coming back. If those things weren't worth a conversation then, of course he didn't think a TV show would be worth one now.

Tears burn my eyes, threatening to spill over as I fight back the hurt. I've wasted enough tears on Dustin Wilder; he doesn't deserve anymore. But that's not how this works. My heart has belonged to him for so fucking long that I don't know that I'll ever get it back. Not fully. So as long as he's around, telling me things I want to hear, I don't stand a chance.

That's my fault.

I'm the one who let him back in. Gave him my heart all over again.

"All your 'last thing I ever wanted to do was hurt you' and 'I hate the way it went down' is just more bullshit. Same way 'I'll be back for senior year' was," I choke out, a sob threatening. "I knew better than to fall for your bullshit, but I did it anyway."

"Hurting you *is* the last thing I would ever want. You can't actually think that I would do that on purpose."

"No. No, I don't," I acquiesce. "But I'm also not sure a leopard can change its spots, either."

Swallowing hard, I try and force the sob back down my throat, a tear escaping as my eyes flutter closed. Thorny vines strangle my heart, the hurt just too much. But my anger isn't just directed at Dustin. I'm just as much to blame.

What was I thinking that I could have one last fling with

him? Or worse, that we could make this work? I was a fool for thinking that he would come back. That I could still get my fairy tale ending with him.

"What are you saying?" he asks, face contorted with worry.

"I'm saying that I can't believe I fell for it again. For you. I knew better than to let you back into my life, and I ignored it. Instead, I let myself believe that I—*we*—could have it all."

"We can, Kenzie."

Dustin closes the gap between us in two large steps. His hands land on my hips, resting there so perfectly, making me want to lean into him. Let him hold me as I cry and tell me that I'm wrong. That's the last thing I need though.

"No, Dustin, we can't," I whisper, tears flowing freely now. "Not if you don't trust me enough to tell me about what's going on in your life. Whether it's a thing, not a thing, or a done deal, or even just a twinkle in someone's eye. If that can't come from you, then…"

I trail off, shrugging. There's nothing left to say. We're broken. Too broken to be put back together again. I've never thought that I would understand what Humpty Dumpty felt like, yet, here I am.

Stepping back, I try to pull away, but Dustin grips me harder. A mix of raw emotion flashes in his eyes, I'm sure mirroring my own. Ache coils in my gut, every inch of me feeling like I've been sucker punched.

"I know I fucked up before, but I'm not the same guy I was then. I know what I want and that's you, Kenzie. Let me show you."

I scoff through my tears. "There you go with that next level swoony bullshit again, Dusty." I tear myself away from him, his touch too much right now. I can't let him hold me, tethering us together as I say what I need to. He might not be the same Dustin he was, but I'm also not the same Kenzie.

This Kenzie isn't going to let herself be walked over and left behind again. "What you don't get is that you are. You are the same guy."

"I'm not."

"You are!" I shout. "You can stand here and tell me you aren't all you want. I'm sure you believe that's true. But it's not. Because if it were, I wouldn't have found out about this damn TV show from Mrs. Chamberlain! I wouldn't have had to stand there, in my own library, tap dancing my way through an answer so that I didn't look stupid for not knowing what's going on with you. All while the walls close in on me and I'm reminding myself to breathe because she knows something I don't. That the Internet knows things that the woman you claim is your priority doesn't."

I suck in a deep breath, my lungs stretching as far as they can before I slowly let it out, allowing my words to hang in the air. Dustin doesn't move, doesn't try to defend himself. I can't tell if that's because he's admitting defeat or he's just too caught off guard. Either way, it doesn't matter.

Because I'm done.

I won't do this anymore. Won't let there be a repeat of what happened seven years ago. I deserve better. No matter how much I love him. He doesn't love me back. At least not the same way.

"You should go," I say, my tone demanding.

"This is my house."

"I mean back to Nashville. I'm sure that your people there are counting down the minutes until you return, so you should just go."

"What about dinner with the family tonight?"

"*My* family," I correct him. "I'll tell them the truth. Something came up and you had to go. They'll understand; we've been through this before."

It's a harsh statement, cutting through the air like a razor.

Dustin takes it like a champ though, barely blinking as I hurl the ugliness at him. At least one of us can, because my own heartbreak is bubbling up again, and this time I know I won't be able to hold it in.

With a sharp nod of my head, I spin around, greeted by three spectators, all of whom instantly try to busy themselves to seem like they weren't hanging on every word. I acknowledge them with a nod as well, pushing past the group toward the kitchen door. It's a race against time and my own emotions and I know I'm going to lose. If I can only make it to the car—or at least outside—before breaking down again, I'll consider it a win.

"Kenzie!" Dustin calls after me, his voice cracking.

Grabbing my wrist, he spins me around, pulling me into him, until our bodies are flush. Heat engulfs me, butterflies letting loose in my tummy as his gorgeous blue eyes lock on mine.

Don't give in...be strong...

"Kenzie," he whispers, my name sounding like a prayer on his lips.

That's all it takes. I crack. All the anguish inside me spills over, a sob letting loose as the tears pour down my face. I wish that I could hate him. But I can't. The only hate I have is the fact that I hate that I love him.

"Goodbye, Dusty," I choke out, another sob cutting off the end of his name.

I wiggle free, making a beeline for the door. The bright sun blinds me, the light awkwardly refracting through my tears. Somehow, I manage to open my car door and slip into the driver's seat without injuring myself. A wave of nausea hits, only adding to the full body effect I have going on. I should have had Willa or Sylvie drive me here, so I wouldn't have to worry about getting back. Too late now.

I can do this. I'm strong, confident, and capable. Losing Dustin once didn't kill me. It won't kill me this time either. And this time, I'm going to get over him. For good.

Tomorrow is the first day of the rest of my life.

I just need to make sure I stop crying by then.

CHAPTER TWENTY-SEVEN

DUSTIN

Ache.

Pure, unadulterated, raw ache.

It's been hours since Kenzie walked out, letting the door slam, and I can still hear it ringing in my ears. And with each passing moment, the harder it is to breathe.

Add in a bottle of whiskey, and I'm about as cliché a country song as you can get.

I roll off the bed, pushing to my feet and shaking off the stiffness of not having moved for hours. I need to do something. Need to get out of this house. If there was a way to get away from my thoughts that'd be even better, but seems I'm stuck with those.

Grabbing my keys, I quickly make my way down the hall, tail hung between my legs. Mama said she was running to the store, and unless she got back without my hearing her, there shouldn't be anyone here, allowing me to make a clean getaway. That said, I also don't put it past either of my best friends to be sitting at the kitchen table, waiting for me. I haven't answered a single text or call all afternoon. There just isn't anything left to say.

Firing up Old Blue, I slowly back her out of the drive, turning left on autopilot. I don't know where I'm off to, just that I'm armed with the hope that the road will help clear my mind. And ease the ungodly weight on my chest.

At this point, I don't know what's worse—the pain from Kenzie walking away or the pain of knowing that I hurt her again. Either way, I want to scream. I want to find a way to make this hurt stop. For me. For her.

For us.

The us that I killed. Before we ever even got off the ground.

My phone dings with a text and I roll my eyes, wondering who it's from now. I know I should be thankful for friends who care enough to check in, but I can't right now. I need to be alone. To figure out where I went wrong. No, I know where I went wrong. I need to figure out how to fix it. If it's fixable, which I'm not sure it is.

ERIC

Good news! Production company says ATL is an option. Will keep you updated.

Atlanta isn't needed now...

Fucking Eric. I bang my hand on the steering wheel, my frustration coming to a head. I have a lot to thank that man for—namely my entire career—but he's also part of the reason I'm in this mess. A small part, since the lion's share is solidly my own stupidity, but a part, nonetheless. That stupidity never would have had its turn to shine if it weren't for this stupid show.

Or would it...

Pulling into the parking lot of the Whippy Cone, I have to hunt for a spot. Figures it would be busy. When I don't find one, I pull into the empty lot across the street and park facing the old, converted barn turned ice cream shop. I sit for a minute, watching all the happy families hanging out at picnic tables, enjoying the last of summer.

Very clearly not included in their numbers is Kenzie. It was stupid of me to think that I'd find her here, my subconscious full of a hope that it shouldn't have had. There is no way she's showing her face right now. And I can't blame her. She has to live here. I get to leave whenever I want, go back to that other life. But she's here, stuck with all the ghosts and memories. All the pain I've put her through.

I'm such an ass.

A green sedan pulls in next to me, drawing my attention away from the Whippy Cone. A guy I don't recognize gets out of the driver's seat, opening the back door. I watch them, hoping they don't see me, and my stomach rolls with what happens next. A little boy, probably not much older than Matty, tumbles out of his car seat, Dad hoisting him up onto his hip. I can hear his little voice declare "ice cream!" even through my rolled-up windows and the running engine.

Father and son.

As the two walk away, I have so much emotion caught in my throat that I don't know if I'm going to puke or cry. I want that. Kids, family, the whole nine yards. A little boy—or little girl—full of smiles and giggles, staring back at me with their mother's eyes. I want that so bad I can taste it.

And I want it with Kenzie.

Too bad that ship has sailed, my failure captaining the voyage.

"Fuck, Eric," I curse out loud. My phone chimes again, pinging my irritation. I have half a mind to toss it out the window, run it over with my truck, and then hurl it into Rocky Pond.

Unless it's Kenzie...

The hope floats to the top and is enough to get me to check my phone. My heart falls, though, when I see Noel's name on my screen instead of hers. Should have known better than to think it might be that easy.

NOEL

Silver Lake, 8a. Expect you there, no matter the hangover. Hair of the dog and breakfast biscuits will be provided.

I huff out a small laugh. Leave it to Noel. And maybe time on the lake with the boys is just what I need. Provide me with some clarity. Or some escape.

Although, truth is, I don't think there is an escape for this pain.

CHAPTER TWENTY-EIGHT

DUSTIN

"You know," I say, throwing my head back to get the last couple of drops of warm beer from the bottom of the can. Crushing it, I toss the can over into the empties bin, now close to overflowing after a long day out on the water. "When Kenzie called me last month, I had been thinking about that long weekend your parents took us to Lake Cumberland that the girls crashed. I don't know what made me think of it, but it made me laugh, then a couple of hours later, she called."

The memory hits hard, her sweet southern accent ringing in my ears, as if she were the one sitting next to me rather than Nash. She'd giggled when I admitted to thinking about the weekend, right before one-upping me with the memory of our make-out session in Baton Rouge, the rain pouring down, the Dawgs having dropkicked LSU earlier in the evening. Reminiscing with her, knowing that I'd been on her mind the same way she was on mine, had felt as easy and natural as breathing.

A vital life function that seemed to require way more thought than it should at this moment.

"And there we have it," Nash comments, looking at his watch. "Eight hours, eleven minutes, and forty-four seconds. Which means you owe me fifty bucks." He points to his twin, showing off a triumphant smirk.

Noel grunts in response, a slight shoulder shrug, his eyes never leaving the bobber he's reeling in.

"You rather I count empties? Because I'm pretty sure I got the over on that too."

Another grunt, this one accompanied by the middle finger, sends Nash into hysterics. I look between my two best friends, trying to figure out what they are going on about. Then it hits me.

"You two bet on how long it would take me to talk about Kenzie?"

My shock sounds more like anger, even though I don't mean for it to. Maybe that's because I am angry—at the situation, at myself, at Kenzie—and haven't expressed it. At all.

"You tend to be rather loquacious when you're all up in your head. Very much a verbal processor," Noel replies, stowing his reel. He wordlessly takes Nash's, then holds out his other hand for mine, quickly stowing them in the same place as his.

"What's that supposed to mean?"

"You word vomit, dude," Nash adds. "And we're happy to be the barf bags. We just made a little wager on the over/under of when you would reach that point."

"I don't word vomit," I defend, not believing myself for one second. Isn't that what every one of the songs I've written is? A way of externally processing it all?

"You do," Nash insists. "Remember when you didn't kiss her after that first date? You droned on for over an hour the next day about how you should have done it. And then continued to overthink it for two more weeks before finally growing a pair and kissing her."

I start to respond but can't. Because like always, my best friend has leveled me with the truth.

"So," Nash continues, casually turning the key in the ignition. The engine turns over with a smooth purr, the gentle rumble under our feet a comforting sensation. It's been a good day out on the water, regardless of how much we didn't catch. Warm sun, cold beer, and your best friends never make for a wasted day. Plus, it gave me plenty of time to throw myself a pity party without anyone asking questions. At least until now. "Out with it. You haven't said a word since she walked out that door yesterday."

"Because there is nothing to say. Y'all witnessed it. You heard her—there isn't a future for us."

"Ever think that maybe this just makes y'all even?" Noel suggests, swapping places with his twin. "You walked away once, now she has. Third times the charm, all that?"

"Not an expert on these things, but pretty sure that's not how it works."

Shrugging, he turns his attention back to the boat, turning the wheel and directing us back to the dock. I glance over my shoulder at Nash, expecting to find him texting or something, but I'm surprised to see him sitting back, eyes closed, obviously enjoying the feel of the wind on his face. Now that seems like a good idea.

I plop down onto the back bench next to him, letting my head roll back. The late summer sun feels good on my skin, the coolness of the spray from the wake enough to keep me from overheating. Not enough to distract me from my thoughts though.

My brain keeps bouncing back and forth between the phone call a month ago and yesterday's ambush. Talk about two sides to the same coin. The happy-go-lucky, giggling woman who called just to hear my voice was not the same one who stood before me yesterday, tears streaming down her face. But both versions of her are my girl. My Kenzie.

The one person I can't stand to lose but somehow did anyway.

Twice.

Truthfully, I don't know what is worse—the guilt I felt about drifting away from her years ago, or the guilt I feel now for not being the man she needs. For not being enough for her. I've run through this past week, moment by moment, trying to figure out what I could have done differently. What I needed to say or do to show her that she comes before anything else. Yes, I should have mentioned the show, but that can't be the only thing I did wrong. Kenzie is not an overreactor, so for her to walk away like she did, there had to be something else.

I just wish I fucking knew what that something else was.

"Did we have plans I forgot about?" Noel calls back to us.

"Huh?" Nash replies.

"Plans. Did we have some?"

"No."

"Then, are we expecting company?"

"Who could we—" The padding on the bench shifts as Nash leaps to his feet, a low, barely audible growl escaping from him. "What the fuck could she want? I mean, seriously. Way to ruin a fucking perfect day."

I open my eyes and peer over the side of the boat as Noel slows down, approaching the dock. Standing on the edge, arms crossed, hip cocked out to the side, with a scowl the size of Georgia, is Willa.

Oh, fuck...

"Willa!" Nash greets, his voice achingly sweet considering the cursing he was just doing. "To what do we owe the ball-busting pleasure?"

"I want nothing to do with your balls, Nash," she snarks.

"They want nothing to do with you either, darlin'."

"Stay out of my way, and they'll be safe. I'm here for Dustin."

I swallow hard, knowing what's coming. She and Sylvie might have been the only two members of our clan that didn't bear witness to yesterday's slaughter, but there was probably less than sixty seconds between the slam of the kitchen door and those two hearing about it. The fact that it took her this long to hunt me down means one of two things—either she's not that mad and finding me wasn't a priority, or she's spent all this time consoling Kenzie and now plans on skinning me alive.

My money is on the latter.

"Willa," I greet cautiously, climbing out of the boat and onto the dock.

She shifts, trading one jutted-out hip for the other, eyebrows raising in annoyed mock surprise. Yeah, she definitely wants to skin me alive.

"Did I, or did I not, tell you that if you hurt her again that no one would ever find your body?" she starts, sass boiling over like a pot that's too full. I remain silent, letting her question hang in the air, trying to decide if it's rhetorical or not. The way her face morphs with exasperation lets me know that it most certainly isn't. "Hmmmm?!"

"You did."

"Then what the fuck were you thinking?"

Now *that* is a damn good question.

To which I am not sure I have an answer.

What I do know is that I don't want to hear whatever it is she has to say to me. There isn't anything she could throw at me that I haven't already done to myself.

"Seriously, Dustin, what the fuck?" she continues, her voice going up an octave. "How fucking dare you just waltz back in here and disturb everything. Why couldn't you just leave well enough alone? Show up, play your stupid little show, and then leave. But no, you reappear after being gone for seven fucking years, acting like not a day has gone by. Like we're still those six small-town kids with nothing but big dreams about *someday*. Well, guess fucking what. We're not. You left and you didn't look back, leaving all of us in your dust. And now that you're some big, fancy country star, you think that we should all just be thrilled that you still want to be our friend. That you want to walk down memory lane with your high school sweetheart, promising her forever once again, without a care that you're going to break her heart all over again—"

"Stop!"

Something snaps inside me, the audible click in my brain loud enough I'm a little surprised no one else heard it. Long gone is the melancholy I was feeling on the boat, my heart no longer heavy with the remorse of losing the love of my life a second time. Now it's racing, thundering against my ribcage, indignation rising up in me. I love Willa like a sister—nothing will ever change that—and I know that hurling insults is her own defense mechanism, but I've had enough.

"Willa, did it ever occur to you that you're angry with the wrong person here? Or that maybe Kenzie isn't the only one hurting? She's upset, and heartbroken, and it's all because of me. I get that. But I'm upset and heartbroken too. You weren't there—"

"I didn't have to be."

"Maybe you didn't. But I also don't have to take this. Not from you. I know that you're her pit bull, and that you feel this is your duty, but it's not. If someone is going to yell at me, it should be Kenzie."

I storm past her, careful to avoid contact, heading toward the small gravel lot where our trucks are parked. My pulse is racing, my whole body overheating with emotion, the cool breeze coming off the lake doing nothing to cool it. My insides feel all out of whack, roiled and turbulent, with no signs of settling. I want to be angry. I want to scream, even though I know it won't do any good. Biting back at Willa probably wasn't the most fair reaction in the world, but neither was her ambush.

Slamming shut the door to my truck, I flex my hands, watching them tremble with my frustration. The urge to drive over to Kenzie's place and bang on the door until she opens up so I can ask her all the questions I have is starting to take over. That's an even worse idea than snapping at Willa. So I turn the key in the ignition and head to the one place I know will help me clear my brain.

THE ANGELIC VOICE of Carrie Underwood drifts out of A Noble Mechanic, lyrics about just what she's going to do with a Louisville Slugger at odds with such a sweet sound. Being greeted by the country station, rather than some sort of classic rock, leaves me guessing as to what Ken's mood is. Or if Ken is even the one working. He's mentioned a young guy that helps him at night sometimes and on days he has treatments. It didn't even occur to me that right about now might be the start of that guy's shift.

Please just let it be Ken...

"You just missed yourself on the radio," the familiar southern accent calls out from underneath a silver sedan. I look down just in time to see Ken wheel himself out from under the car, wiping his hands with a rag.

"Not 'Chasing Falling Stars,' I hope."

"'Few Beers Shy of Freedom.'"

"Huh, that's an oldie," I say, surprised by the answer. "How'd you know it was me?"

"You tap your toe on the lip of the concrete right under the garage door. Have since you were a little guy. I'd know that anywhere."

I chuckle, shaking my head. Leave it to Ken to notice something like that. Especially when I've never even noticed it.

"Sorry to just drop in, I…"

"You never need to apologize, son. You're always welcome in here whenever you want. Your key should still work too, just so's you know."

Son…

Fuck, hearing him call me that feels good. Probably better than it ever has. He was probably the next to know—right behind the girls—about what went down yesterday. He's never been one to take sides, but if there was going to be a first time for such a thing, this would be it. If I were him, I'd be turning my sorry ass out onto the street and telling me to fuck off. But not Ken Noble.

"Need to tinker?" he asks, pushing to his feet.

I nod. I shouldn't be surprised he knows, but it still feels foreign that I don't have to explain why this is where I turned up.

"Whatcha got?"

"Puttin' in a new starter for the Dohertys. Battery needs replacing too while we're at it."

While we're at it…music to my ears…

"Sounds good." I round the car, grabbing what I need off the bench.

"Good. Then we can chat about what brings you here."

I should have known. Yet, unlike the confrontation with Willa, this doesn't feel like the intake process at Gitmo.

"I'm sure you know," I offer, still wary about saying it all out loud.

"I know one side of the story. I'm sure there is another."

"I fucked up. And then Willa yelled at me."

Ken shakes his head, a long sigh making the wires he's hovering above flutter slightly. "That girl. Hard to believe somedays that spitfire was Miss Georgia. But, I guess that's the beauty of being in one's trusted circle; you get to know the real them and not the polish and shine the rest of the world sees."

"So it's an honor that a former Miss Georgia cussed me a half hour ago?" I quip.

"Something like that," he laughs. "As for your mucking up…you'll find a way to right it."

I stand back, taking in the man I've respected more than any other in my life, wondering if he's starting to lose it.

"Don't look at me like that," he continues, not even bothering to look up to judge my expression. "Just trust an old man now and then, would ya?"

I nod, trying to do just that. At the same time, the desire to say more, to let it all pour out of me—defend myself—bubbles up inside me. Word vomit, as Nash called it.

"I never meant to hurt her. It's never been my intention. I promise I would—"

"Dustin, you can't make that promise. There are a lot of promises in life you can make, but promising to never hurt someone isn't one of them. I'm not saying you go around tryin' to hurt people, but sometimes it happens, no matter how good your intention. Hurt is a part of life, the opposite side of the coin from love. What you can promise, though, is to do your damnedest when you do muck it up."

"I thought I was."

"Like I said before, you two will sort yourselves out. I have no doubt."

"That makes one of us."

Standing up to his full height, Ken shrugs, pulling a rag from his back pocket and wiping his hands. He winks at me, pulling his phone from his pocket, a wry smile taking over.

"Look at the time," he mutters, tapping on the screen hunt-and-peck style with his middle finger. "I promised AnnaGrace Davis I would meet her over at the Kountry Kitchen for dinner. I best not keep her waiting."

"You have a…a date?"

"I wouldn't say that, but call it what you like." He winks at me again, doing a little shimmy to show off that he's still got it. I laugh, unable to hold back. "Like I said, your key should still work, so just lock up whenever you're finished, son."

I nod as Ken slaps me on the back. I feel lighter already, letting his advice soak in. I'm still not as sure as he is that Kenzie and I will ever be back on good terms, but it's nice to know he and I haven't slipped. Much like installing this battery, it's a comfort to know that some things can be as easy as they always have been.

Too bad I can't tinker with my life the same way.

CHAPTER TWENTY-NINE

KENZIE

Laughter wafts through the air, the happy sound of kids playing tag in the open field adjacent to the library making my already aching heart burn even more. I force myself to smile though, letting the familiarity of it surround me, as if it's trying to give me some sort of comfort hug. Appreciated, even if momentarily trite.

Rocking slowly in one of the old wicker rockers that Mrs. Cassum kept on what we affectionately refer to as "the back porch" of the library—a long, covered strip of concrete that was added to the building when the foundation was redone in the 1950s—I suck in a breath, close my eyes, and try to let my mind wander. I desperately need a distraction. And for maybe the first time in my life, a book isn't cutting it.

"Oh, the Conrads got a new minivan," Sylvie says from the rocker next to me.

I open one eye just enough to see the three towheaded boys pile out and race toward the rest of the groups of kids in the field behind the library. Tuesday is Women's Club night at Hickory Hill Baptist, and the shared parking lot between the library and church is filling up fast.

"Yeah, the youngest one filled the gas tank with water, unbeknownst to either John or Stacey. Stacey drove it around for a couple of days before it started bucking and then just quit on her in the middle of Depot Road."

"Oh, that's a bad day."

"Yeah. Dad tried to save it, but he said the engine was just too far gone, and with that much water on the inside of the engine, they were at an extreme risk for rust and all sorts of stuff. The insurance company totaled it, so they got that fancy new thing."

"Is Moira, like, bowled over with jealousy?"

I nod, cracking a smile at my sister's reaction to her bestie's new ride. The two of them, along with KatieRae Gates, always did everything together—at least until Stacey married John straight out of high school and started in on the kids before Moira and KatieRae were even married. The three remained close, although there's some tension between them now. Or at least there is if you believe the town rumor mill.

"Hey ya!" Willa greets, hands full of goodies. Sylvie stands, grabbing both her chocolate-dipped cone and my pineapple split, allowing Willa to hold her milkshake properly, rather than squished between her forearm and her boobs. "Sorry it took me so long, Piña colada wasn't the flavor of the day, so it wasn't in the machine. But I told Micky it was for you and he promptly rectified that."

I dig my spoon into the dish, scooping up a large serving of sugary goodness. Piña colada soft serve, in between two large slices of pineapple, with a coconut-caramel sauce, macadamia nuts, and then slathered in whipped cream, this concoction is beyond comfort food. It soothes the soul like nothing else—even chocolate. The Whippy Cone adds it to the menu every year over Memorial Day weekend, letting it make an exit on Labor Day.

That is unless you're me, and it's required from time to time.

Actually, I'm pretty sure it's secretly known as the "Kenzie Noble Heartbreak Special" by the staff at the Whippy Cone. Which, let's not lie, is probably a pretty accurate title.

"Snickers is the flavor of the day," I offer, my mouth full of ice cream. "I had that double-dipped in butterscotch and chocolate for lunch."

"Good night, how are you not in a diabetic coma?" Sylvie asks.

"Or bouncing off the walls," Willa adds. "I mean, seriously, are your teeth vibrating?"

I shrug. "Because my heart is too heavy to be affected."

Shoving another large spoonful into my mouth, I fight back the tears that have suddenly sprung to life, threatening to spill. Back to life I should say. Because these bad boys have been off and on all day, and I'm losing the battle.

I still don't know who I'm more upset with—Dustin for all his nonsense or me for falling for it. Probably the latter. I knew better than to get back involved with him. Yet, I believed I was strong enough to be able to walk away. At least until he told me he loved me and that our relationship mattered to him. Then I was all ready to slide my chips across the table, leaving nothing to fall back on.

"We should have kept Operation: Avoid Dustin in place," I say softly, the regret in my voice palpable. "If I'd continued to avoid him, then none of this would have happened. I'd be okay right now."

"Would you really?" Sylvie asks.

"Yes! My heart wouldn't feel like Matty ran his toy truck over it nonstop for hours, with all those sharp plastic edges stabbing me with each new pass. I wouldn't be on my second ice cream of the day. I wouldn't have lost sleep last night as my brain replayed him telling me he loves me and that I'm his priority and that we can have our life together, over and over again for hours!" I ramble. My emotions are out of control; I can feel them flying everywhere, but I can't even begin to wrangle them. Not when I'm this broken. "I wouldn't have to feel the pain of him not choosing me all over again."

My voice cracks, choking out a small sob. Deep inside me, I want to be mad. To scream. To raise holy hell over all this. But I can't. Because deep down, right next to that desire to be mad, is something even bigger. My love for Dustin Wilder.

There is no denying how much I love him. How much I still want what I've always wanted—to spend my life with him, in his effortlessly strong arms, on the receiving end of that panty-melting smile, listening to that smooth as whiskey voice. I wanted that when I thought he was going to remain my small-town guy, taking over Dad's garage. I want it now that he's a freaking star. I'm pretty sure I'd want it if he were living in a cardboard box out by Rocky Pond. He, it seems, isn't on the same page though. No matter how much I thought he was.

"Can I say something?" Willa asks, a sass to her voice I wasn't expecting. "Because I really need to say something."

I turn to face my best friend, who is still standing, milkshake in one hand, the other planted on her hip. I nod, unsure about the look that is on her face.

"MacKenzie Noble, you're an idiot."

"What?!"

"Girl, I love you. We've been friends since we were five and nothing will ever change that. Which is why I can stand here right now and tell you that you are out of your damn mind."

"I'm...I'm out my mind?" I repeat back to her. Is she insane?

"Yes, you." She points at me, eyes wide, like this isn't tough to follow. Except it is. Because what I thought was a pity party, has turned into something else entirely. "You need to deal with your feelings."

"Ummm, hello?" I hold up my pineapple split, waving it in her direction. "I am dealing. I'm eating them."

"That is not what I mean. Do you love Dustin?"

The question catches me off guard. I thought the answer was obvious—hence the pity party.

"Yes, I love him. But—"

"But nothing. If you love him, then you love all of him. Even his faults. Such as being a dumb boy and not telling you things when he should."

"She makes a good point," Sylvie chimes in.

"She does not." I push up from the rocker, setting my ice cream down on the seat. "Yes, I love him. I've always loved him. But he doesn't love me the same way."

"Pretty sure he does," Willa says.

I shake my head, defeat taking over. "He'll never make me a priority. Despite what he says. He's proved that. Twice now."

"You didn't exactly give him a chance, did you?"

"What's that supposed to mean?" I shake my head, trying to make this all make sense. How did we go from eating our feelings to arguing? And why is Willa, of all people, defending Dustin?

"Kenz, I know he hurt you when he left the last time. And it was a shitty thing for him to do. But I also know he regrets that. *You* know he regrets that. He's apologized, profusely. And as far as making you a priority, from what I've seen, he's done nothing but that over this last week." Willa sighs, her shoulders drooping, her face softening. There's care and concern reflecting back at me as her gaze locks with mine. I swallow, her message starting to sink in. "I understand the hesitancy, after last time. But…you have to let him love you. You can't just automatically default to hurt."

"You weren't there, Willa; you didn't see his reaction. Or rather, his lack of one. He didn't say anything. Didn't even bother to try and defend himself."

"Because he still feels guilty," Sylvie injects. My head whips to look at her. She lifts one shoulder, a gesture that tells me she knows she's right. "He feels like he doesn't have the right to defend himself because he hurt you before. Willa's right—the trust thing goes both ways. You have to trust that he's not going to do it again, and that you really are his first concern. And there is no way, Kenzie, that you aren't."

"I am proud of you for standing up for yourself and letting him know that you were not happy with his lack of sharing. But telling him to get the fuck out was maybe a bit much."

"I didn't tell him to get the fuck out. I suggested he leave."

"Which is Southern for get the fuck out."

I close my eyes, sucking in the evening air. My heart still hurts. But now it's heavy with the additional burden that I might also be at fault. Because, fuck, my friends are right.

Dustin did apologize. A lot. And up until hearing about the show from Mrs. Chamberlain, there was nothing that led me to believe that he wasn't going to deliver on everything he promised. I was the one who got in my own way about that. Because of my own insecurity about the past.

And if I want a future with him, I have to trust him. The same trust I accused him of not having yesterday. I exhale long and hard. Time to decide if I want to be the pot or the kettle.

"Fuck."

Willa nods, Sylvie looking up at me, both of them waiting on me to continue.

"I did exactly what I accused him of doing, didn't I?"

"Not exactly, but pretty close," Sylvie answers.

"Think I can fix it? Is he going to be willing to give me a second…errrrr…third chance?"

"If you show him your tits, I'm sure he'll forgive you."

"Willa!" Sylvie scolds.

"Always works for me."

"And just who are you apologizing to?" I ask. I narrow my eyes, staring at her, trying to will the answer from her. I'm also enjoying the brief respite from my own interrogation. But Willa isn't having it.

"I mean in general. And this is about you."

"You just show people your tits in general?" Sylvie questions.

"That's not of concern right now."

"I rather think it would always be a concern if you're just showing them off."

"This is about Kenzie!"

Glancing at Sylvie, I give her a "we tried" look. "So, what now?"

Aimlessly, I turn back to my rocker, lowering myself into it. Too late, though, I remember I put my ice cream on the seat, my butt making direct contact with the frozen delight. I squeak as the cold permeates my leggings, my cheeks clenching. I can't bring myself to move, though, the embarrassment already creeping up my skin, my two best friends not wasting any time with their laughter.

"I probably deserved that, huh?" I surmise. "The universe's way of getting back at me for my little hissy fit yesterday."

A new set of emotions surrounds me. My heart still aches, squeezing as I remember the pain on Dustin's face as I ranted at him in the living room. Ranted, instead of asking or trying to understand. God, I really did do him dirty. He didn't deserve that. Not after all he's done this week for Dad. For me. Not after being the man I've always dreamed of him being.

I need to rectify this. Now.

"Well, maybe start by changing pants?" Sylvie suggests between bursts of laughter. "And then decide if he's what you want. And if he is, figure out what to say."

He is what I want. That part doesn't take any figuring out. The what to say portion, however—that's a much steeper hill.

My phone dings from my purse, making me suddenly grateful I'm not wearing pants that have back pockets. Tapping it to life, I see a text from my dad.

DAD

Late night at the garage. Up for a chat?

Leave it to him to know exactly what I need and when I need it. I shoot back a quick message, letting him know I'll be there in five. I need to clean up first.

"That was Dad. I'm gonna head over there, see if he has any idea on how I can…"

"Win back the love of your life?" Sylvie offers.

"Yeah, that."

Win back the love of my life. My inner romantic immediately rushes to grand ideas—flowers, sky writing, song and dance, literal on-my-knees groveling. The kind of thing you'd see in a movie. I know better though—none of those things would mean much to Dustin. To him, the right words will mean more than any gift. I just have to figure out what those are.

There is just one thing I have to do first.

Pushing to my feet, I look at Willa, as serious as can be. "Please tell me you grabbed napkins."

CHAPTER THIRTY

KENZIE

Bright light shines through the open garage bay spilling into the street. It's a welcome sight, warming my insides, giving me the psychological hug that I need. I can't quite make out what station is on the radio, but I know it's on, most likely turned up too loud. Some things never change.

"Hey!" I call out, wandering inside. The clang of a tool hitting the concrete floor is quickly followed by a muffled curse. Only that doesn't sound like my dad.

I stop in my tracks, and my heart skips a beat. Easing his way to his feet, back to me and pliers in hand, is the last person I expected to find here. And I know it's him—even from behind—because I know every inch of that body.

Dustin.

Frozen, I watch him spin around, just as surprised to see me as I am him. My heart can't decide if it's happy to see him or not, my brain firing commands to both turn and run away and run to him all at the same time. Either way, it can't make sense of him here.

"What…errr, you're…" I stammer, my mouth and brain working against each other. "Hi."

"Hi," he returns, clearing his throat. Something he only does when he doesn't know how else to react. Glad to know he's feeling just as awkward as I am.

"I'm just here to meet Dad."

"He's not here. He has a…he's meeting someone."

"Yeah, me."

"No, he said it was AnnaGrace Davis, over at the Kountry Kitchen."

AnnaGrace Davis, at Kountry Kitchen? That can't be. Didn't his text say the garage? I know it did. For a split second I consider reaching into my purse and pulling out my phone to read it again. Then it dawns on me.

This is a setup.

Orchestrated by my own dad.

He had help—probably from the two women who were just giving me the where-tos and what-fors regarding my own stupidity. But he one hundred percent set me up. For a man who has always taken a sense of pride in not involving himself in his daughters' personal lives, he certainly involved himself here.

And I owe him one.

"Dusty," I say, trying to figure out where to start. There is so much I need to get out, yet all of it seems like I'm starting in the middle.

"Kenzie." He takes a couple of steps closer, letting the pliers fall to the ground again. The clank echoes through the silence surrounding us, like the gun going off at the start of a race, prompting us to both speak.

"I'm sorry," we blurt out, our voices melding together to form a chorus of apology.

My heart sings, relief washing over me. Dustin's megawatt smile takes over, lighting me up inside. The urge to rush to him is still there, the few feet of space between us feeling like the Grand Canyon. But I don't give in. He might be smiling, but I don't know if that means he still wants me.

"Ladies first," he insists.

"Dustin, I'm sorry. I…I was a brat. I shouldn't have ambushed you the way I did. I should have trusted you. For all my insistence that you didn't trust me, it was me who was failing. I should have asked what was going on, why you didn't share—if you even could share—before jumping all over you and accusing you. I'm so sorry."

"I should have told you."

"Yes…I mean…I would have liked that. But I also have to accept there will probably be things in your career that you can't share with me right away. And I promise I will. It might take some adjusting on my end, but I'll get there. I was just so afraid of what happened before happening again, I over-reacted."

"There is nothing, not a single part of my life or career, that I can't share with you, Kenzie. Not all of it is for public consumption, but with you, baby, I have no secrets." Three long strides and he's directly in front of me. The Grand Canyon is now reduced to a few inches. A few inches that still seem like miles. "And I can't blame you for being afraid. I'm afraid too. I finally have you back, and I don't want to lose you again, especially over me being a dumbass. Which, ironically, is why I didn't mention the show. I wasn't going to do it unless I could make it work with me being here. Because you matter more than adding that to my plate. You are the most important thing in my life."

Heat races up my skin, making it hard to breathe. Dustin has sucked all of the oxygen out of the room, all by telling me the same thing he's been saying for the last week. Only now, I hear him. Really hear him. My insides melt, my heart soars, and every emotion I've ever felt bubbles up, taking the form of tears. Gah, why am I such a crier?

"Please believe me," he whispers, reaching out and placing a hand on my hip. "I love you."

Stick a fork in me, I'm done.

"I believe you, Dusty. I trust you. And I love you. Never stopped actually. Then, now. All of the long moments in between."

"We have that in common, you and me."

His grip tightens on my hip, the other hand joining in, pulling me into him. Our bodies are flush, his uniquely Dustin scent filling my nostrils, making me dizzy. I want to get lost in him, in the feel of his body against mine, just like this, for the rest of time. When his mouth lands on mine, softly at first, I give in, not wanting to hold anything back. Dustin groans, deepening the kiss. My thoughts exactly. Because this is heaven.

"But," I say, breaking away from the kiss, my eyes flying open, worry suddenly coursing through me. My lips tingle from the power of his, yelling at me for stopping. "It can't be that easy, can it?"

"What?"

"This. Us." A tear slips down my cheek, my body giving in to the overwhelming moment. I tug Dustin closer, which should be impossible, but the fear of losing him is starting to nibble away at me again. "We…"

"We had a fight. We're making up. It happens." His voice is calm and soothing. The soft kiss he places on my forehead makes warmth radiate through me, pushing away the worry once more. "Dare I say, we'll probably do it again. Maybe next time we just skip the whole 'get out' part and replace it with 'I'm taking a walk' or something?"

I sputter out a laugh. We probably will—however, in some weird way, I'm looking forward to it. Because that means he's mine to fight with. And make up with—which, let's not lie here, will be the fun part.

"Can I show you something?"

"Is that code?" I ask, wondering if Dustin's mind went to the same place mine did.

He shakes his head, a knowing grin and a naughty look in his eye taking over. "It's not. But now that you mention it, I've always had this fantasy of the dirty things I could do to you on the hood of a car." He waggles his eyebrows, pulling me closer and stealing another kiss.

"We have that in common, you and me," I answer, using his phrase from earlier.

Dustin groans, the noise very clearly a lament over trying to behave himself, then reaches into his pocket and pulls out his phone. I make a mental note that sneaking into the garage for a little fun definitely needs to be added to our to-do list. Right along with all the dirty things I want to do to him. And at home. And on his tour bus. If I'm not careful this list if going to be long. Actually, fuck careful, we have the rest of our life to make it happen.

"I, um...I'm shit at art, but I was playing around with ideas, and just thought..." he trails off, shrugging.

I look down at the screen, my eyes going wide. Dustin's right, he's a horrible artist—at least where normal drawing is concerned—but I know exactly what this is. The lines are a little rough, not a single one straight. The vision of it is perfectly clear, however.

A small, two-story cottage with a wraparound porch, gables over the two second-story windows, and a porch swing.

I gasp, hand flying up to cover my face, more tears joining the one from earlier. Dustin flicks his finger across the screen, flipping to a second photo, this one more of a floor plan style, except it doesn't match the size of the house.

"I wasn't quite sure how many bedrooms you'd want. At least two, I'm sure, but we could put as many as needed. Even just leave it to be added on to over time," Dustin says. I can hear the smile in his voice, but can't tear my eyes away from the phone. "So, main house would go here, and then this thing over here, would be the studio. Far enough away and totally soundproofed so I won't wake up whoever is in the house."

"Studio?"

"Yeah, if I'm moving to Hickory Hills full-time, I'll need a place to record."

Moving to Hickory Hills…

"This…this is here?"

I look up at him, hope filling my chest. He'd said he was going to, but seeing the plans makes it real amazing all over again.

"I was thinking, unless you hate the idea, that we could call it Falling Star Farms."

"I love that. But, but where are we going to find the land?"

"Already taken care of. Well, it's not officially official—the transaction isn't one hundred percent done yet. But…" Slipping his phone back into his pocket, he takes my hand, squeezing it. "That buyer that your dad has lined up for the land that Hideaway Hill is on, is me. That's where I was thinking we could put the cottage."

My jaw goes slack, falling open a tad as I process it all. Dustin is the one buying the land. Holy hell.

"Dusty…" I whisper, still trying to find my words.

"Before you say it, he gave me a damn good deal. Nothing more than the promise to love you for the rest of my life, and to keep you happy and smiling. Plus a dollar. I have the dollar, the other part…"

Throwing my arms around his neck, I fling myself at him, kissing him so hard he stumbles backward. Lucky for me, Dustin doesn't lose his balance, tightening his grip around me, kissing me just as hard in return. The whole world falls away, nothing but happiness radiating out of me. It almost seems too good to be true, but if my books have taught me anything over the years, sometimes fairy tales come true.

"You have the other part too," I answer, coming up for air as Dustin sets me down a long moment later. "Or, well, you know…"

"I do. And I'm sorry for not telling you about this either. We were planning a surprise; your dad had this whole idea, and who was I to tell him no?"

"I love you."

"I love you." Dustin leans in for another kiss, his hands finding my ass, then freezing. Mouth hovering just over mine, he says "Kenz, your ass is…sticky?"

Fuuuuuuck…

"OMG! I'm so embarrassed. Yes, I…I sat on my pineapple split."

"You sat on your pineapple split?" The guffaw that comes out of Dustin's mouth is loud and overpowering, the kind that would make you want to laugh right along with him. If it wasn't me he was laughing at.

"Not on purpose! Willa was letting me have it for how I acted and I was flustered and I put it down and then forgot and then sat and…"

"It's okay, baby." Giving my ice cream-soiled backside a pat, he kisses my forehead, soothing the embarrassment. "Willa yelled at me too. And I hope she knows that someday, when it's her turn, payback is a bitch."

I snicker, knowing that he means it. Maybe not the yelling part, but the meddling. I plan on joining him in that effort, and the day can't come soon enough.

"In the meantime, how about we get you home and cleaned up, so I can get you a different kind of dirty?"

"Lead the way, cowboy."

EPILOGUE

DUSTIN

Seven months later

"Truth or dare!" Nash announces, the fire crackling behind him. "No double dare or promise to repeat. If you don't want to answer your truth, then you have to do your dare. If you don't want to do your dare, you have to answer your truth. Heads is alphabetical and tails is birthday."

He winks at Willa, who rolls her eyes, already annoyed with him and we haven't even started. The rules haven't changed since we started this in high school, and I can't help but laugh to myself that he still feels the need to spell them out every time.

The crisp evening wind nips at us, making Kenzie snuggle in closer to me. She's already all but in my lap, but I don't say anything, tightening the blanket around us. Between the warmth of the fire and all the heat she's putting out, I'm going to be a roasted marshmallow myself in no time, but I'll take it. Because this is one of the most perfect moments I can imagine.

A bonfire. My best friends. The woman I love.

It doesn't get better than this.

"Tails!"

"Let me see that!" Willa exclaims, jumping up from her camp chair, her own blanket falling to the ground.

"Read it and weep, Princess," Nash taunts, earning him a scowl and the middle finger.

"Those two…" Kenzie mutters.

"One day you're going to have to explain to me what exactly happened while I was away, and how it all went south," I tell her.

"It went south before you left. They just stopped hiding it after college."

I nod, making a mental note to pry more about it later. This isn't the time.

"Truth or dare, Willa?"

"Truth."

"Best sex you ever had."

The scowl on her face is quickly replaced by an evil grin. Kenzie's fingers grip my thigh, her breath catching, almost like she knows the answer and is waiting to see if Willa actually admits to it.

"What do you know that I don't?" I ask her.

"Nothing. Just that the look on her face means she's up to no good."

"Just some guy," Willa answers pointedly. "We were backstage at a pageant. He told me that I didn't quite have the glow I needed before I went on stage, so he dropped to his knees right there and made me see stars. Pretty sure I won all because of that tongue. Wish I could remember his name, but it just wasn't that important."

"Errr, TMI," Sylvie comments, not looking up from her phone, her fingers tapping away furiously.

"Who are you texting?" Willa shoots back. "If you wanted

to talk to Camden all night that badly, you could have just invited him."

"It's not Camden. And I did invite him," Sylvie says, her voice going small as she admits that last part. I wondered why he wasn't here, dismissing the question just as quickly, assuming that I was making too much out of all the time Kenzie said they were spending together. "Doc Addison called, needing his help with the Russells' mare going into labor. She's pregnant with twins, which is super dangerous in horses, so Doc wanted some extra help."

"It's Mr. T, isn't it?" Kenzie asks, her voice conspiratorial.

I shoot her a look, trying to make sure I follow. Between breaking ground on the house, working on moving my home base from Nashville to Hickory Hills, driving to Atlanta at least once a week for *Small Town, Big Star*—which was thankfully picked up by CMT and not the Adored Network—and prepping for my summer tour, life has been crazier than normal. Add in Ken's treatment—which is going better than any doctors could have projected—and Moira's new baby, it's enough for anyone to be dizzy. I wouldn't change a single thing about it though.

Knowing that I get to come home to Kenzie is the best feeling in the world. Even when I'm on the road, I look forward to our end of the day calls, where she catches me up on everything I've missed so that I'm less out of the loop when I get back. Her voice is the melody that inspires every part of my day.

The mention of Mr. T, however, throws me. Because I know these two women, and they are not referring to a vintage TV show.

"I invited him to the competition next weekend, and he was just replying," Sylvie says. "He's single-handedly funded the entire season. I just think he should be there."

"What about Camden?" Noel asks, chiming in for the first time all night. "Don't be doing the good vet dirty."

"I'm not doing him dirty!" she defends. "We're…he's been a really big help this season. And I really value his friendship. But he doesn't want more. I don't think."

Those last three words were said so quietly I almost thought I imagined them. That is, until Kenzie whispers and asks if I heard them too. I nod, giving her my own conspiratorial smile. There's a spark in her eye, one I want to keep there permanently.

I know just the way to do it too. If Willa would hurry up.

"Willa, back to the game," Noel scolds.

"Oh, yeah. Hmmmm…" She pretends to think, tapping her finger on her chin, making a show out of it. Like we haven't had this planned for weeks.

The whole group is in on it. Well, everyone but one person. The most important person here.

From the two-tailed coin that we had to special order off the Internet, to the order of events, our secondary group chat has been filled with nothing but plans and excitement leading up to this. I just hope it goes as perfectly in real life as it has in my mind.

"Dustin," she continues. "I dare you to ask Kenzie a question."

"What kind of dare is that?" Kenzie laughs. "You're not even going to tell him what question?"

"She doesn't have to," I say.

Pushing to my feet, I spin and immediately drop down to one knee, a move I've been rehearsing, wanting to make sure I didn't fall on my ass in the process. Thankfully, I have it down, and am in position in time to see it all register on Kenzie's face. Hands fly up to cover her mouth as she gasps, eyes already filled with tears.

"MacKenzie Rose Noble, I love you. You are every song I

sing, and the muse that keeps me inspired beyond measure. No life is perfect, but with you by my side, it's about as close as it can possibly be. And I don't want to go another second without knowing that you are mine, all mine. So, what do you say, beautiful? Will you marry me?"

"Yes!" Kenzie screams, launching herself at me without hesitation. Her arms are around my neck, her body crashing into mine, sending us both to the ground before I can prepare. Shouts and laughter from our friends fill the air around us, background noise for the passionate kiss Kenzie lays on me.

"If you let me up, I can put the ring on your finger," I tell her as we come up for air.

She nods furiously, scrambling off me and to her feet. I brush us both off before sliding the custom-designed ring onto her finger. It sparkles in the glow of the firelight, matching the sparkle radiating off my beautiful bride-to-be.

"Time for bubbly!" Noel announces, the pop of a cork closely following.

He pours the drinks as the girls gush over Kenzie's ring, the three of us guys sitting back and enjoying the moment and their squeals. I'd thought of more than a dozen ways to do this, but none of them felt right without having our friends around us. The friends who have our backs and have been by our sides since day one. Someday Kenzie and I will get to return the favor, and I hope this occasion is as sweet for them as it is for us.

Kenzie turns back to me, slipping her hands into my back pockets and kissing me again. My heart swells, happiness overflowing as I hold her in my arms, knowing that I get to spend forever with her.

"What's that smile for?" she asks, her own giddiness radiating off her.

"Nothing." I laugh, knowing that my mile-wide grin is

going to be a permanent fixture for a while after a night like tonight.

"No, seriously. I know you, Dustin Wilder; that's your 'I'm up to something' smile. Tell me."

"Same thing it always is, Kenz. I'm just thinking 'bout you."

Want more Dustin and Kenzie? A sneak peek into what their future holds? Scan below for an extra scene!

<u>**Stand Alone Novellas**</u>

A Novel Seduction

I Think We're Alone Now

Hot Mess Christmas Express

Son of a Peach

ACKNOWLEDGMENTS

This story lived in my head - rent free - for over a year before my fingers ever hit the keys. It's no secret the song that inspired it- but really, there's lot of inspiration from Dustin Lynch throughout. To the point where it might be a little weird lol

Dustin - if you ever read this book, please be flattered…I promise that's how it's intended :)

Amy - for being my right hand, my Girl Friday, and the better half of my brain.

Kelly - for jumping on #teamclaire and not backing down.

KKSB - S is for sisters…and salty bitches. And you four are the best of the best.

Em & SM - for believing in this series and insisting there was more to it, even when I didn't want to listen.

The Anns and KatieRae - for being the best mental health support out there.

Lisa - thank you for always answering the phone, even when you know crazy is on the other end. Love you.

As always, Drew, for your unending, unwavering, unequivocal support in *everything*. Thank you for loving my particular brand of crazy. *Ik hou van jou*

ABOUT THE AUTHOR

USA TODAY Best Selling Author Claire Hastings is a walking, talking awkward moment. She loves Diet Coke, gummi bears, the beach, and books (obvs). When not reading she can usually be found hanging with friends at a soccer match or grabbing food (although she probably still has a book in her purse). She and her husband live in Atlanta.

She can be found here:

Instagram | Facebook | GoodReads | BookBub

You can sign up for her newsletter here.

9 798987 866115